WARRIORS

INTO THE
WILD

WARRIORS

INTO THE
WILD

ERIN
HUNTER

HARPERCOLLINS*PUBLISHERS*

For Billy—who left our Twoleg home to become a Warrior.
We still miss him very much.
And for Benjamin, his brother,
who is with him now in StarClan.

Special thanks to Kate Cary

ALLEGIANCES

THUNDERCLAN

LEADER

BLUESTAR—blue-gray she-cat, tinged with silver around her muzzle.

DEPUTY

REDTAIL—small tortoiseshell tom with a distinctive ginger tail.
APPRENTICE, DUSTPAW

MEDICINE CAT

SPOTTEDLEAF—beautiful dark tortoiseshell she-cat with a distinctive dappled coat.

WARRIORS

(toms, and she-cats without kits)

LIONHEART—magnificent golden tabby tom with thick fur like a lion's mane.
APPRENTICE, GRAYPAW

TIGERCLAW—big dark brown tabby tom with unusually long front claws.
APPRENTICE, RAVENPAW

WHITESTORM—big white tom.
APPRENTICE, SANDPAW

DARKSTRIPE—sleek black-and-gray tabby tom.

LONGTAIL—pale tabby tom with dark black stripes.

RUNNINGWIND—swift tabby tom.

WILLOWPELT—very pale gray she-cat with unusual blue eyes.

MOUSEFUR—small dusky brown she-cat.

APPRENTICES

(more than six moons old, in training to become warriors)

DUSTPAW—dark brown tabby tom.

GRAYPAW—long-haired solid gray tom.

RAVENPAW—small, skinny black tom with a tiny white dash on his chest, and white-tipped tail

SANDPAW—pale ginger she-cat.

FIREPAW—handsome ginger tom.

QUEENS
(she-cats expecting or nursing kits)

FROSTFUR—beautiful white coat and blue eyes.

BRINDLEFACE—pretty tabby.

GOLDENFLOWER—pale ginger coat.

SPECKLETAIL—pale tabby, and the oldest nursery queen.

ELDERS
(former warriors and queens, now retired)

HALFTAIL—big dark brown tabby tom with part of his tail missing.

SMALLEAR—gray tom with very small ears. The oldest tom in ThunderClan.

PATCHPELT—small black-and-white tom.

ONE-EYE—pale gray she-cat, the oldest cat in ThunderClan. Virtually blind and deaf.

DAPPLETAIL—once-pretty tortoiseshell she-cat with a lovely dappled coat.

SHADOWCLAN

LEADER
BROKENSTAR—long-haired dark brown tabby.

DEPUTY
BLACKFOOT—large white tom with huge jet-black paws.

MEDICINE CAT RUNNINGNOSE—small gray-and-white tom.

WARRIORS STUMPYTAIL—brown tabby tom.
  APPRENTICE, BROWNPAW

  BOULDER—silver tabby tom.
  APPRENTICE, WETPAW

  CLAWFACE—battle-scarred brown tom.
  APPRENTICE, LITTLEPAW

  NIGHTPELT—black tom.

QUEENS DAWNCLOUD—small tabby.

  BRIGHTFLOWER—black-and-white she-cat.

ELDERS ASHFUR—thin gray tom.

WINDCLAN

LEADER TALLSTAR—a black-and-white tom with a very long tail.

RIVERCLAN

LEADER CROOKEDSTAR—a huge light-colored tabby with a twisted jaw.

DEPUTY OAKHEART—a reddish brown tom.

CATS OUTSIDE CLANS

YELLOWFANG—old dark gray she-cat with a broad, flattened face.

SMUDGE—plump, friendly black-and-white kitten who lives in a house at the edge of the forest.

BARLEY—black-and-white tom who lives on a farm close to the forest.

HIGHSTONES

BARLEY'S FARM

WINDCLAN CAMP

FOURTREES

FALLS

OWL-TREE

RIVER

SUNNING-ROCKS

RIVERCLAN CAMP

THUNDERCLAN

RIVERCLAN

SHADOWCLAN

WINDCLAN

STARCLAN

CARRIONPLACE

SHADOWCLAN
CAMP

THUNDERPATH

THUNDERCLAN
CAMP

GREAT
SYCAMORE

SANDY
HOLLOW

SNAKEROCKS

TALLPINES

TREECUT PLACE

TWOLEGPLACE

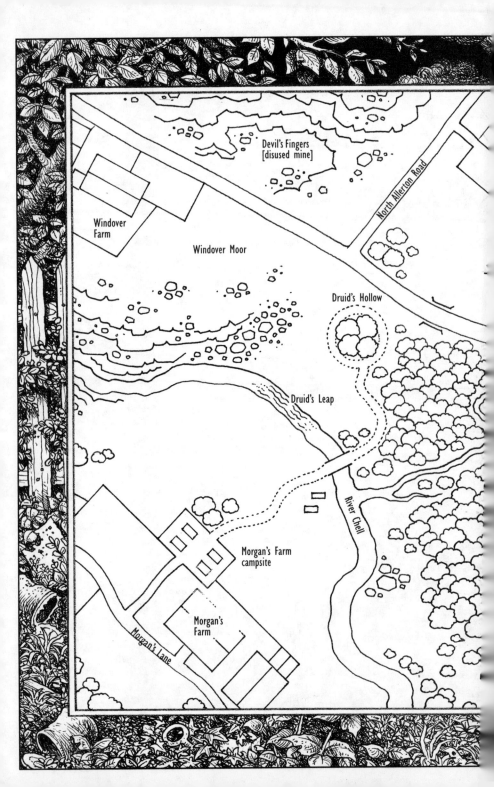

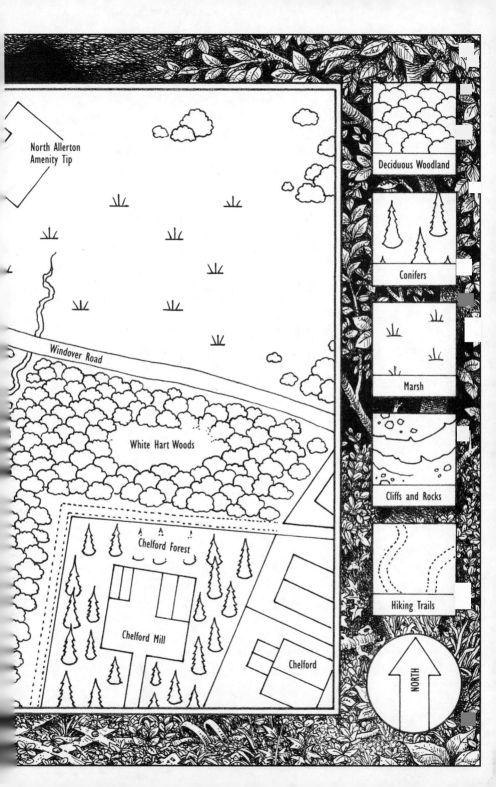

North Allerton
Amenity Tip

Windover Road

White Hart Woods

Chelford Forest

Chelford Mill

Chelford

Deciduous Woodland

Conifers

Marsh

Cliffs and Rocks

Hiking Trails

NORTH

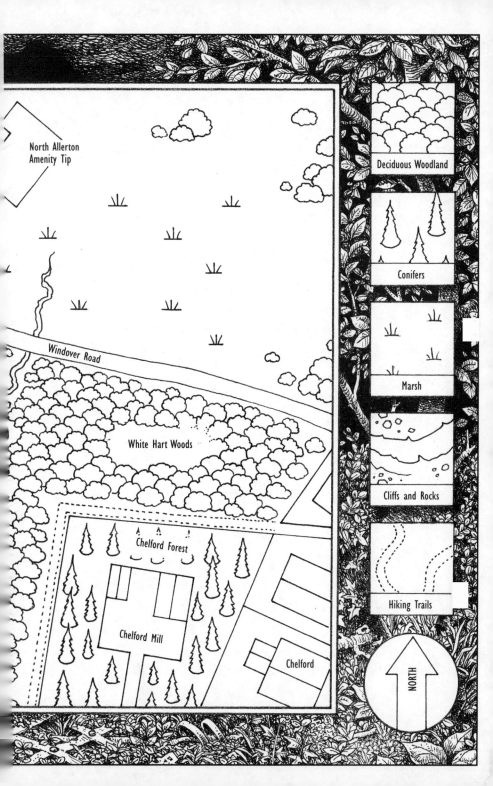

North Allerton
Amenity Tip

Windover Road

White Hart Woods

Chelford Forest

Chelford Mill

Chelford

Deciduous Woodland

Conifers

Marsh

Cliffs and Rocks

Hiking Trails

NORTH

PROLOGUE

A half-moon glowed on smooth granite boulders, turning them silver. The silence was broken only by the ripple of water from the swift black river and the whisper of trees in the forest beyond.

There was a stirring in the shadows, and from all around lithe dark shapes crept stealthily over the rocks. Unsheathed claws glinted in the moonlight. Wary eyes flashed like amber. And then, as if on a silent signal, the creatures leaped at each other, and suddenly the rocks were alive with wrestling, screeching cats.

At the center of the frenzy of fur and claws, a massive dark tabby pinned a bracken-colored tom to the ground and drew up his head triumphantly. "Oakheart!" the tabby growled. "How dare you hunt in our territory? The Sunningrocks belong to ThunderClan!"

"After tonight, Tigerclaw, this will be just another RiverClan hunting ground!" the bracken-colored tom spat back.

A warning yowl came from the shore, shrill and anxious. "Look out! More RiverClan warriors are coming!"

Tigerclaw turned to see sleek wet bodies sliding out of the

water below the rocks. The drenched RiverClan warriors bounded silently up the shore and hurled themselves into battle without even stopping to shake the water from their fur.

The dark tabby glared down at Oakheart. "You may swim like otters, but you and your warriors do not belong in this forest!" He drew back his lips and showed his teeth as the cat struggled beneath him.

The desperate scream of a ThunderClan she-cat rose above the clamor. A wiry RiverClan tom had pinned the brown warrior flat on her belly. Now he lunged toward her neck with jaws still dripping from his swim across the river.

Tigerclaw heard the cry and let go of Oakheart. With a mighty leap, he knocked the enemy warrior away from the she-cat. "Quick, Mousefur, run!" he ordered, before turning on the RiverClan tom who had threatened her. Mousefur scrambled to her paws, wincing from a deep gash on her shoulder, and raced away.

Behind her, Tigerclaw spat with rage as the RiverClan tom sliced open his nose. Blood blinded him for an instant, but he lunged forward regardless and sank his teeth into the hind leg of his enemy. The RiverClan cat squealed and struggled free.

"Tigerclaw!" The yowl came from a warrior with a tail as red as fox fur. "This is useless! There are too many RiverClan warriors!"

"No, Redtail. ThunderClan will never be beaten!" Tigerclaw yowled back, leaping to Redtail's side. "This is our territory!" Blood was welling around his broad black muzzle, and he shook his head impatiently, scattering scarlet drops onto the rocks.

"ThunderClan will honor your courage, Tigerclaw, but we cannot afford to lose any more of our warriors," Redtail urged. "Bluestar would never expect her warriors to fight against these impossible odds. We will have another chance to avenge this defeat." He met Tigerclaw's amber-eyed gaze steadily, then reared away and sprang onto a boulder at the edge of the trees.

"Retreat, ThunderClan! Retreat!" he yowled. At once his warriors squirmed and struggled away from their opponents. Spitting and snarling, they backed toward Redtail. For a heartbeat, the RiverClan cats looked confused. Was this battle so easily won? Then Oakheart yowled a jubilant cry. As soon as they heard him, the RiverClan warriors raised their voices and joined their deputy in caterwauling their victory.

Redtail looked down at his warriors. With a flick of his tail, he gave the signal and the ThunderClan cats dived down the far side of the Sunningrocks, then disappeared into the trees.

Tigerclaw followed last. He hesitated at the edge of the forest and glanced back at the bloodstained battlefield. His face was grim, his eyes furious slits. Then he leaped after his Clan into the silent forest.

In a deserted clearing, an old gray she-cat sat alone, staring up at the clear night sky. All around her in the shadows she could hear the breathing and stirrings of sleeping cats.

A small tortoiseshell she-cat emerged from a dark corner, her pawsteps quick and soundless.

The gray cat dipped her head in greeting. "How is

Mousefur?" she meowed.

"Her wounds are deep, Bluestar," answered the tortoiseshell, settling herself on the night-cool grass. "But she is young and strong; she will heal quickly."

"And the others?"

"They will all recover, too."

Bluestar sighed. "We are lucky not to have lost any of our warriors this time. You are a gifted medicine cat, Spottedleaf." She tilted her head again and studied the stars. "I am deeply troubled by tonight's defeat. ThunderClan has not been beaten in its own territory since I became leader," she murmured. "These are difficult times for our Clan. The season of newleaf is late, and there have been fewer kits. ThunderClan needs more warriors if it is to survive."

"But the year is only just beginning," Spottedleaf pointed out calmly. "There will be more kits when greenleaf comes."

The gray cat twitched her broad shoulders. "Perhaps. But training our young to become warriors takes time. If ThunderClan is to defend its territory, it must have new warriors as soon as possible."

"Are you asking StarClan for answers?" meowed Spottedleaf gently, following Bluestar's gaze and staring up at the swath of stars glittering in the dark sky.

"It is at times like this we need the words of ancient warriors to help us. Has StarClan spoken to you?" Bluestar asked.

"Not for some moons, Bluestar."

Suddenly a shooting star blazed over the treetops. Spottedleaf's tail twitched and the fur along her spine bristled.

Bluestar's ears pricked but she remained silent as Spottedleaf continued to gaze upward.

After a few moments, Spottedleaf lowered her head and turned to Bluestar. "It was a message from StarClan," she murmured. A distant look came into her eyes. "Fire alone can save our Clan."

"Fire?" Bluestar echoed. "But fire is feared by all the Clans! How can it save us?"

Spottedleaf shook her head. "I do not know," she admitted. "But this is the message StarClan has chosen to share with me."

The ThunderClan leader fixed her clear blue eyes on the medicine cat. "You have never been wrong before, Spottedleaf," she meowed. "If StarClan has spoken, then it must be so. Fire will save our Clan."

CHAPTER 1

It was very dark. Rusty could sense something was near. The young tomcat's eyes opened wide as he scanned the dense undergrowth. This place was unfamiliar, but the strange scents drew him onward, deeper into the shadows. His stomach growled, reminding him of his hunger. He opened his jaws slightly to let the warm smells of the forest reach the scent glands on the roof of his mouth. Musty odors of leaf mold mingled with the tempting aroma of a small furry creature.

Suddenly a flash of gray raced past him. Rusty stopped still, listening. It was hiding in the leaves less than two tail-lengths away. Rusty knew it was a mouse—he could feel the rapid pulsing of a tiny heart deep within his ear fur. He swallowed, stifling his rumbling stomach. Soon his hunger would be satisfied.

Slowly he lowered his body into position, crouching for the attack. He was downwind of the mouse. He knew it was not aware of him. With one final check on his prey's position, Rusty pushed back hard on his haunches and sprang, kicking up leaves on the forest floor as he rose.

The mouse dived for cover, heading toward a hole in the

ground. But Rusty was already on top of it. He scooped it into the air, hooking the helpless creature with his thorn-sharp claws, flinging it up in a high arc onto the leaf-covered ground. The mouse landed dazed, but alive. It tried to run, but Rusty snatched it up again. He tossed the mouse once more, this time a little farther away. The mouse managed to scramble a few paces before Rusty caught up with it.

Suddenly a noise roared nearby. Rusty looked around, and as he did so, the mouse was able to pull away from his claws. When Rusty turned back he saw it dart into the darkness among the tangled roots of a tree.

Angry, Rusty gave up the hunt. He spun around, his green eyes glaring, intent on searching out the noise that had cost him his kill. The sound rattled on, becoming more familiar. Rusty blinked open his eyes.

The forest had disappeared. He was inside a hot and airless kitchen, curled in his bed. Moonlight filtered through the window, casting shadows on the smooth, hard floor. The noise had been the rattle of hard, dried pellets of food as they were tipped into his dish. Rusty had been dreaming.

Lifting his head, he rested his chin on the side of his bed. His collar rubbed uncomfortably around his neck. In his dream he had felt fresh air ruffling the soft fur where the collar usually pinched. Rusty rolled onto his back, savoring the dream for a few more moments. He could still smell mouse. It was the third time since full moon that he'd had the dream, and every time the mouse had escaped his grasp.

He licked his lips. From his bed he could smell the bland

odor of his food. His owners always refilled his dish before they went to bed. The dusty smell chased away the warm scents of his dream. But the hunger rumbled on in his stomach, so Rusty stretched the sleep out of his limbs and padded across the kitchen floor to his dinner. The food felt dry and tasteless on his tongue. Rusty reluctantly swallowed one more mouthful. Then he turned away from the food dish and pushed his way out through the cat flap, hoping that the smell of the garden would bring back the feelings from his dream.

Outside, the moon was bright. It was raining lightly. Rusty stalked down the tidy garden, following the starlit gravel path, feeling the stones cold and sharp beneath his paws. He made his dirt beneath a large bush with glossy green leaves and heavy purple flowers. Their sickly sweet scent cloyed the damp air around him, and he curled his lip to drive the smell out of his nostrils.

Afterward, Rusty settled down on top of one of the posts in the fence that marked the limits of his garden. It was a favorite spot of his, as he could see right into the neighboring gardens as well as into the dense green forest on the other side of the garden fence.

The rain had stopped. Behind him, the close-cropped lawn was bathed in moonlight, but beyond his fence the woods were full of shadows. Rusty stretched his head forward to take a sniff of the damp air. His skin was warm and dry under his thick coat, but he could feel the weight of the raindrops that sparkled on his ginger fur.

He heard his owners giving him one last call from the back

door. If he went to them now, they would greet him with gentle words and caresses and welcome him onto their bed, where he would curl, purring, warm in the crook of a bent knee.

But this time Rusty ignored his owners' voices and turned his gaze back to the forest. The crisp smell of the woods had grown fresher after the rain.

Suddenly the fur on his spine prickled. Was something moving out there? Was something watching him? Rusty stared ahead, but it was impossible to see or smell anything in the dark, tree-scented air. He lifted his chin boldly, stood up, and stretched, one paw gripping each corner of the fencepost as he straightened his legs and arched his back. He closed his eyes and breathed in the smell of the woods once more. It seemed to promise him something, tempting him onward into the whispering shadows. Tensing his muscles, he crouched for a moment. Then he leaped lightly down into the rough grass on the other side of the garden fence. As he landed, the bell on his collar rang out through the still night air.

"Where are you off to, Rusty?" meowed a familiar voice behind him.

Rusty looked up. A young black-and-white cat was balancing ungracefully on the fence.

"Hello, Smudge," Rusty replied.

"You're not going to go into the woods, are you?" Smudge's amber eyes were huge.

"Just for a look," Rusty promised, shifting uncomfortably.

"You wouldn't get me in there. It's dangerous!" Smudge wrinkled his black nose with distaste. "Henry said he went into the woods once." The cat lifted his head and gestured with his nose over the rows of fences toward the garden where Henry lived.

"That fat old tabby never went into the woods!" Rusty scoffed. "He's hardly been beyond his own garden since his trip to the vet. All he wants to do is eat and sleep."

"No, really. He caught a robin there!" Smudge insisted.

"Well, if he did, then it was before the vet. Now he *complains* about birds because they disturb his dozing."

"Well, anyway," Smudge went on, ignoring the scorn in Rusty's mew, "Henry told me there are all sorts of dangerous animals out there. Huge wildcats who eat live rabbits for breakfast and sharpen their claws on old bones!"

"I'm only going for a look around," Rusty meowed. "I won't stay long."

"Well, don't say I didn't warn you!" purred Smudge. The black-and-white cat turned and plunged off the fence back down into his own garden.

Rusty sat down in the coarse grass beyond the garden fence. He gave his shoulder a nervous lick and wondered how much of Smudge's gossip was true.

Suddenly the movement of a tiny creature caught his eye. He watched it scuttle under some brambles.

Instinct made him drop into a low crouch. With one slow paw after another he drew his body forward through the undergrowth. Ears pricked, nostrils flared, eyes unblinking, he moved toward the animal. He could see it clearly now, sitting up among the barbed branches, nibbling on a large seed held between its paws. It was a mouse.

Rusty rocked his haunches from side to side, preparing to leap. He held his breath in case his bell rang again. Excitement coursed through him, making his heart pound. This was even better than his dreams! Then a sudden noise of cracking twigs and crunching leaves made him jump. His bell jangled treacherously, and the mouse darted away into the thickest tangle of the bramble bush.

Rusty stood very still and looked around. He could see the white tip of a red bushy tail trailing through a clump of tall ferns up ahead. He smelled a strong, strange scent, definitely a meat-eater, but neither cat nor dog. Distracted, Rusty forgot about the mouse and watched the red tail curiously. He wanted a better look.

All of Rusty's senses strained ahead as he prowled forward. Then he detected another noise. It came from behind, but sounded muted and distant. He swiveled his ears backward to hear it better. *Pawsteps?* he wondered, but he kept his eyes fixed on the strange red fur up ahead, and continued to creep onward. It was only when the faint rustling behind him became a loud and fast-approaching leaf-crackle that Rusty realized he was in danger.

The creature hit him like an explosion and Rusty was thrown sideways into a clump of nettles. Twisting and yowling, he tried to throw off the attacker that had fastened itself to his back. It was gripping him with incredibly sharp claws. Rusty could feel spiked teeth pricking at his neck. He writhed and squirmed from whisker to tail, but he couldn't free himself. For a second he felt helpless; then he froze. Thinking fast, he flipped over onto his back. He knew instinctively how dangerous it was to expose his soft belly, but it was his only chance.

He was lucky—the ploy seemed to work. He heard a "hhuuffff" beneath him as the breath was knocked out of his attacker. Thrashing fiercely, Rusty managed to wriggle free. Without looking back he sprinted toward his home.

Behind him, a rush of pawsteps told Rusty his attacker was giving chase. Even though the pain from his scratches stung beneath his fur, Rusty decided he would rather turn and fight than let himself be jumped on again.

He skidded to a stop, spun around, and faced his pursuer.

It was another kitten, with a thick coat of shaggy gray fur, strong legs, and a broad face. In a heartbeat, Rusty smelled that it was a tom, and sensed the power in the sturdy shoulders underneath the soft coat. Then the kitten crashed into Rusty at full pelt. Taken by surprise by Rusty's turnabout, it fell back into a dazed heap.

The impact knocked the breath out of Rusty, and he staggered. He quickly found his footing and arched his back, puffing out his orange fur, ready to spring onto the other kitten. But his attacker simply sat up and began to lick a forepaw, all signs of aggression gone.

Rusty felt strangely disappointed. Every part of him was tense, ready for battle.

"Hi there, kittypet!" meowed the gray tom cheerily. "You put up quite a fight for a tame kitty!"

Rusty remained on tiptoe for a second, wondering whether to attack anyway. Then he remembered the strength he had felt in this kitten's paws when he had pinned him to the ground. He dropped onto his pads, loosened his muscles, and let his spine unbend. "And I'll fight you again if I have to," he growled.

"I'm Graypaw, by the way," the gray kitten went on, ignoring Rusty's threat. "I'm training to be a ThunderClan warrior."

Rusty remained silent. He didn't understand what this Graywhatsit was meowing about, but he sensed the threat had passed. He hid his confusion by leaning down to lick his ruffled chest.

"What's a kittypet like you doing out in the woods? Don't you know it's dangerous?" asked Graypaw.

"If *you're* the most dangerous thing the woods has to offer, then I think I can handle it," Rusty bluffed.

Graypaw looked up at him for a moment, narrowing his big yellow eyes. "Oh, I'm far from the most dangerous. If I were even half a warrior, I'd have given an intruder like you some real wounds to think about."

Rusty felt a thrill of fear at these ominous words. What did this cat mean by "intruder"?

"Anyway," meowed Graypaw, using his sharp teeth to tug a clump of grass from between his claws, "I didn't think it was worth hurting you. You're obviously not from one of the other Clans."

"Other Clans?" Rusty echoed, confused.

Graypaw let out an impatient hiss. "You must have heard

of the four warrior Clans that hunt around here! I belong to ThunderClan. The other Clans are always trying to steal prey from our territory, especially ShadowClan. *They're* so fierce they would have ripped you to shreds, no questions asked."

Graypaw paused to spit angrily and continued: "They come to take prey that is rightfully ours. It's the job of the ThunderClan warriors to keep them out of our territory. When I've finished my training, I'll be so dangerous, I'll have the other Clans shaking in their flea-bitten skins. They won't dare come near us then!"

Rusty narrowed his eyes. This must be one of the wildcats Smudge had warned him about! Living rough in the woods, hunting and fighting each other for every last scrap of food. Yet Rusty didn't feel scared. In fact, it was hard not to admire this confident kitten. "So you're not a warrior yet?" he asked.

"Why? Did you think I was?" Graypaw purred proudly; then he shook his wide, furry head. "I won't be a real warrior for ages. I have to go through the training first. Kits have to be six moons old before they even *begin* training. Tonight is my first night out as an apprentice."

"Why don't you find yourself an owner with a nice cozy house instead? Your life would be much easier," Rusty meowed. "There are plenty of housefolk who'd take in a kitten like you. All you have to do is sit where they can see you and look hungry for a couple of days—"

"And they'd feed me pellets that look like rabbit droppings and soft slop!" Graypaw interrupted. "No way! I can't think of anything worse than being a *kittypet*! They're nothing but

Twoleg toys! Eating stuff that doesn't look like food, making dirt in a box of gravel, sticking their noses outside only when the Twolegs allow them? That's no life! Out here it's wild, and it's free. We come and go as we please." He finished his speech with a proud spit, then meowed mischievously, "Until you've tasted a fresh-killed mouse, you haven't lived. Have you ever tasted mouse?"

"No," Rusty admitted, a little defensively. "Not yet."

"I guess you'll never understand." Graypaw sighed. "You weren't born wild. It makes a big difference. You need to be born with warrior blood in your veins, or the feel of the wind in your whiskers. Kitties born into Twoleg nests could never feel the same way."

Rusty remembered the way he had felt in his dream. "That's not true!" he mewed indignantly.

Graypaw did not reply. He suddenly stiffened midlick, one paw still raised, and sniffed the air. "I smell cats from my Clan," he hissed. "You should go. They won't be pleased to find you hunting in our territory!"

Rusty looked around, wondering how Graypaw knew any cat was approaching. He couldn't smell anything different on the leaf-scented breeze. But his fur stood on end at the note of urgency in Graypaw's voice.

"Quick!" hissed Graypaw again. "Run!"

Rusty prepared to spring into the bushes, not knowing which way was safe to jump.

He was too late. A voice meowed behind him, firm and menacing. "What's going on here?"

Rusty turned to see a large gray she-cat strolling majestically out from the undergrowth. She was magnificent. White hairs streaked her muzzle, and an ugly scar parted the fur across her shoulders, but her smooth gray coat shone like silver in the moonlight.

"Bluestar!" Beside Rusty, Graypaw crouched down and narrowed his eyes. He crouched even lower when a second cat—a handsome, golden tabby—followed the gray cat into the clearing.

"You shouldn't be so near Twolegplace, Graypaw!" growled the golden tabby angrily, narrowing his green eyes.

"I know, Lionheart, I'm sorry." Graypaw looked down at his paws.

Rusty copied Graypaw and crouched low to the forest floor, his ears twitching nervously. These cats had an air of strength he had never seen in any of his garden friends. Maybe what Smudge had warned him about was true.

"Who is this?" asked the she-cat.

Rusty flinched as she turned her gaze on him. Her piercing blue eyes made him feel even more vulnerable.

"He's no threat," mewed Graypaw quickly. "He's not another Clan warrior, just a Twoleg pet from beyond our territories."

Just a Twoleg pet! The words inflamed Rusty, but he held his tongue. The warning look in Bluestar's stare told him that she had observed the anger in his eyes, and he looked away.

"This is Bluestar; she's *leader* of my Clan!" Graypaw hissed to Rusty under his breath. "And Lionheart. He's my mentor, which means he's training me to be a warrior."

"Thank you for the introduction, Graypaw," meowed Lionheart coolly.

Bluestar was still staring at Rusty. "You fight well for a Twoleg pet," she meowed.

Rusty and Graypaw exchanged confused glances. How could she know?

"We have been watching you both," Bluestar went on, as if she had read their thoughts. "We wondered how you would deal with an intruder, Graypaw. You attacked him bravely."

Graypaw looked pleased at Bluestar's praise.

"Sit up now, both of you!" Bluestar looked at Rusty. "You too, kittypet." He sat up immediately and held Bluestar's gaze evenly as she addressed him.

"You reacted well to the attack, kittypet. Graypaw is stronger than you, but you used your wits to defend yourself. And you turned to face him when he chased you. I've not seen a kittypet do that before."

Rusty managed to nod his thanks, taken aback by such unexpected praise. Her next words surprised him even more.

"I have been wondering how you would perform out here, beyond the Twolegplace. We patrol this border frequently, so I have often seen you sitting on your boundary, staring out into the forest. And now, at last, you have dared to place your paws here." Bluestar stared at Rusty thoughtfully. "You do seem to have a natural hunting ability. Sharp eyes. You would have caught that mouse if you had not hesitated so long."

"R-really?" Rusty stammered.

Lionheart spoke now. His deep meow was respectful but insistent. "Bluestar, this is a *kittypet*. He should not be hunting in ThunderClan territory. Send him home to his Twolegs!"

Rusty prickled at Lionheart's dismissive words. "Send me home?" he mewed impatiently. Bluestar's words had made him glow with pride. She had noticed him; she had been impressed by him. "But I've only come here to hunt for a mouse or two. I'm sure there's enough to go around."

Bluestar had turned her head to acknowledge Lionheart's words. Now her gaze snapped back to Rusty. Her blue eyes were blazing with anger. "There's never enough to go around," she spat. "If you didn't live such a soft, overfed life, you would know that!"

Rusty was confused by Bluestar's sudden rage, but one glance at the horrified look on Graypaw's face was enough to tell him he had spoken too freely. Lionheart stepped to his leader's side. Both warriors loomed over him now. Rusty looked into Bluestar's threatening stare and his pride dissolved. These were not cozy fireside cats he was dealing with—they were mean, hungry cats who were probably going to finish what Graypaw had started.

CHAPTER 2

"Well?" hissed Bluestar, her face only a mouse-length from his now. Lionheart remained silent as he towered over Rusty.

He flattened his ears and crouched under the golden warrior's cold stare. His fur prickled uncomfortably. "I am no threat to your Clan," he mewed, looking down at his trembling paws.

"You threaten our Clan when you take our food," yowled Bluestar. "You have plenty of food in your Twoleg nest already. You come here only to hunt for sport. But we hunt to survive."

The truth of the warrior queen's words pierced Rusty like a blackthorn, and suddenly he understood her anger. He stopped trembling, sat up, and straightened his ears. He raised his eyes to meet hers. "I had not thought of it that way before. I am sorry," he meowed solemnly. "I will not hunt here again."

Bluestar let her hackles fall and signaled to Lionheart to step back. "You are an unusual kittypet, Rusty," she meowed.

Graypaw's sigh of relief made Rusty's ears twitch. He heard the approval in Bluestar's voice and noticed as she swapped a meaningful glance with Lionheart. The look made him curious. What flashed between the two warriors?

Quietly he asked, "Is survival here really so hard?"

"Our territory covers only part of the forest," answered Bluestar. "We compete with other Clans for what we have. And this year, late newleaf means prey is scarce."

"Is your Clan very big?" Rusty meowed, his eyes wide.

"Big enough," replied Bluestar. "Our territory can support us, but there is no prey left over."

"Are you all warriors, then?" Rusty mewed. Bluestar's guarded answers were just making him more and more curious.

Lionheart answered him. "Some are warriors. Some are too young or too old or too busy caring for kits to hunt."

"And you all live and share prey together?" Rusty murmured in awe, thinking a little guiltily of his own easy, selfish life.

Bluestar looked again at Lionheart. The golden tabby stared back at her steadily. At last she returned her gaze to Rusty and meowed, "Perhaps you should find out these things for yourself. Would you like to join ThunderClan?"

Rusty was so surprised, he couldn't speak.

Bluestar went on: "If you did, you would train with Graypaw to become a Clan warrior."

"But kittypets can't be warriors!" Graypaw blurted out. "They don't have warrior blood!"

A sad look clouded Bluestar's eyes. "Warrior blood," she echoed with a sigh. "Too much of that has been spilled lately."

Bluestar fell silent and Lionheart meowed, "Bluestar is only offering you training, young kit. There is no guarantee you would become a full warrior. It might prove too difficult for you. After all, you are used to a comfortable life."

Rusty was stung by Lionheart's words. He swung his head around to face the golden tabby. "Why offer me the chance, then?"

But it was Bluestar who answered. "You are right to question our motives, young one. The fact is, ThunderClan needs more warriors."

"Understand that Bluestar does not make this offer lightly," warned Lionheart. "If you wish to train with us, we will have to take you into our Clan. You must either live with us and respect our ways, or return to your Twolegplace and never come back. You cannot live with a paw in each world."

A cool breeze stirred the undergrowth, ruffling Rusty's fur. He shivered, not with the cold, but with excitement at the incredible possibilities opening up in front of him.

"Are you wondering if it's worth giving up your comfortable kittypet life?" asked Bluestar gently. "But do you realize the price you will pay for your warmth and food?"

Rusty looked at her, puzzled. Surely his encounter with these cats had proved to him just how easy and luxurious his life was.

"I can tell that you are still a tom," Bluestar added, "despite the Twoleg stench that clings to your fur."

"What do you mean—*still* a tom?"

"You haven't yet been taken by the Twolegs to see the Cutter," meowed Bluestar gravely. "You would be very different then. Not quite so keen to fight a Clan cat, I suspect!"

Rusty was confused. He suddenly thought of Henry, who

had become fat and lazy since his visit to the vet. Was that what Bluestar meant by the Cutter?

"The Clan may not be able to offer you such easy food or warmth," continued Bluestar. "In the season of leaf-bare, nights in the forest can be cruel. The Clan will demand great loyalty and hard work. You will be expected to protect the Clan with your life if necessary. And there are many mouths to feed. But the rewards are great. You will remain a tom. You will be trained in the ways of the wild. You will learn what it is to be a real cat. The strength and the fellowship of the Clan will always be with you, even when you hunt alone."

Rusty's head reeled. Bluestar seemed to be offering him the life he had lived so many times, and so tantalizingly, in his dreams, but could he live like that for real?

Lionheart interrupted his thoughts. "Come, Bluestar, let's not waste any more time here. We must be ready to join the other patrol at moonhigh. Tigerclaw will wonder what has become of us." He stood up and flicked his tail expectantly.

"Wait," Rusty meowed. "Can I think about your offer?"

Bluestar looked at him for a long moment and nodded. "Lionheart will be here tomorrow at sunhigh," she told him. "Give him your answer then."

Bluestar murmured a low signal, and in a single movement the three cats turned and disappeared into the undergrowth.

Rusty blinked. He stared—excited, uncertain—up past the ferns that encircled him, through the canopy of leaves, to the stars that glittered in the clear sky. The scent of the Clan cats still hung heavy in the evening air. And as Rusty turned and headed for home, he felt a strange sensation inside him, tugging him back into the depths of the forest. His fur prickled deliciously in the light wind, and the rustling leaves seemed to whisper his name into the shadows.

CHAPTER 3

That morning, as Rusty slept off his night's wanderings, the mouse dream came again, even more vivid than before. Free of his collar, beneath the moon, he stalked the timid creature. But this time he was aware of being watched. Shining from the shadows of the forest he saw dozens of yellow eyes. The Clan cats had entered his dream world.

Rusty woke, blinking in the bright sunshine that was streaming across the kitchen floor. His fur felt heavy and thick with warmth. His food bowl had been topped up, and his water bowl rinsed out and filled with bitter-tasting Twoleg water. Rusty preferred drinking from puddles outside, but when it was hot, or he was very thirsty, he had to admit it was easier to lap up the water indoors. Could he really abandon this comfortable life?

He ate, then pushed his way out of the cat flap into the garden. The day promised to be warm, and the garden was heavy with the smell of early blossoms.

"Hello, Rusty!" mewed a voice from the fence. It was Smudge. "You should have been awake an hour ago. The baby sparrows were out stretching their wings."

"Did you catch any?" Rusty asked.

Smudge yawned and licked his nose. "Couldn't be bothered. I'd already eaten enough at home. Anyway, why weren't *you* out earlier? Yesterday you were complaining about Henry sleeping his time away, and today you're not much better yourself."

Rusty sat down on the cool earth beside the fence and curled his tail neatly over his front paws. "I was in the woods last night," he reminded his friend. At once he felt the blood stir in his veins and his fur stiffen.

Smudge looked down at him, his eyes wide. "Oh, yes, I forgot! How was it? Did you catch anything? Or did anything catch you?"

Rusty paused, not sure how to tell his old friend what had happened. "I met some wild cats," he began.

"What!" Smudge was clearly shocked. "Did you get into a fight?"

"Sort of." Rusty could feel the energy surging through his body again as he recalled the strength and power of the Clan cats.

"Were you hurt? What happened?" Smudge prompted him eagerly.

"There were three of them. Bigger and stronger than any of us."

"And you fought all three of them!" Smudge interrupted, his tail twitching with excitement.

"No!" Rusty mewed hastily. "Just the youngest one; the other two came later."

"How come they didn't shred you to pieces?"

"They just warned me to leave their territory. But then . . ." Rusty hesitated.

"What!" mewed Smudge impatiently.

"They asked me to join their Clan."

Smudge's whiskers quivered disbelievingly.

"They did!" Rusty insisted.

"Why would they do that?"

"I don't know," Rusty admitted. "I think they need extra paws in their Clan."

"Sounds a bit odd to me," Smudge mewed doubtfully. "I wouldn't trust them if I were you."

Rusty looked at Smudge. His black-and-white friend had never shown any interest in venturing into the woods. He was perfectly content living with his housefolk. He would never understand the restless longing that Rusty's dreams stirred in him night after night.

"But I do trust them," Rusty purred softly. "And I've made up my mind. I'm going to join them."

Smudge scrambled down from the fence and stood in front of Rusty. "Please don't go, Rusty," he mewed in alarm. "I might never see you again."

Rusty nudged him affectionately with his head. "Don't worry. My housefolk will get another cat. You'll get on with him fine. You get along with everyone!"

"But it won't be the same!" Smudge wailed.

Rusty twitched his tail impatiently. "That's just the point. If I stay around here till they take me to the Cutter, I won't be the same either."

Smudge looked puzzled. "The Cutter?" he echoed.

"The vet," Rusty explained. "To be altered, like Henry was."

Smudge shrugged and stared down at his paws. "But Henry's all right," he mumbled. "I mean, I know he's a bit lazier now, but he's not unhappy. We could still have fun."

Rusty felt his heart fill with sadness at the thought of leaving his friend. "I'm sorry, Smudge. I'll miss you, but I have to go."

Smudge didn't reply, but stepped forward and gently touched Rusty's nose with his own. "Fair enough. I can see I can't stop you, but at least let's spend one more morning together."

Rusty found himself enjoying the morning even more than usual, visiting his old haunts with Smudge, sharing words with the cats he had grown up with. Every one of his senses felt supercharged, as if he were poised before a huge jump. As sunhigh approached, Rusty grew more and more impatient to see if Lionheart would really be waiting for him. The idle buzz of meows from his old friends seemed to fade into the background as all his senses strained toward the woods.

Rusty jumped down from his garden fence for the last time and crept into the woods. He had said his good-byes to Smudge. Now all his thoughts were focused on the forest and the cats who lived in it.

As he approached the spot where he had met with the Clan cats the night before, he sat down and tasted the air. Tall trees shielded the ground from the midday sunshine, making it comfortably cool. Here and there a patch of sunlight shone through a gap in the leaves and lit up the forest floor. Rusty could smell the same cat-scent as last night, but he had no idea whether it was old or new. He lifted his head and sniffed uncertainly.

"You have a lot to learn," meowed a deep voice. "Even the tiniest Clan kit knows when another cat is nearby."

Rusty saw a pair of green eyes glinting from beneath a bramble bush. Now he recognized the scent: it was Lionheart.

"Can you tell if I am alone?" asked the golden tabby, stepping into the light.

Hastily, Rusty sniffed again. The scents of Bluestar and Graypaw were still there, but not as strong as the previous night. Hesitantly, he mewed, "Bluestar and Graypaw aren't with you this time."

"That's right," meowed Lionheart. "But someone else is."

Rusty stiffened as a second Clan cat strode into the clearing.

"This is Whitestorm," purred Lionheart. "One of ThunderClan's senior warriors."

Rusty looked at the tom and felt his spine tingle with cold fear. Was this a trap? Long-bodied and muscular, Whitestorm stood in front of Rusty and gazed down at him. His white coat was thick and unmarked and his eyes were the yellow of sunbaked sand. Rusty flattened his ears warily, and tensed his muscles in preparation for a fight.

"Relax, before your fear-scent brings unwanted attention," growled Lionheart. "We are here only to take you to our camp."

Rusty sat very still, hardly daring to breathe, as Whitestorm stretched his nose forward and gave him a curious sniff.

"Hello, young one," murmured the white cat. "I've heard a lot about you."

Rusty dipped his head in greeting.

"Come, we can speak more once we are in the camp," ordered Lionheart, and, without pausing, he and Whitestorm leaped away into the undergrowth. Rusty jumped to his paws and followed as quickly as he could.

The two warriors made no allowances for Rusty as they sped through the forest, and before long he was struggling to keep up. Their pace barely slowed as they led him over fallen trees that they cleared in a single leap, but which Rusty had to scramble over paw by paw. They passed through sharply fragrant pine trees, where they had to jump across deep gullies churned up by a Twoleg tree-eater. From the safety of his garden fence, Rusty had often heard it roaring and snarling in the distance. One gully was too wide to jump, half-filled with slimy, foul-smelling water. The Clan cats waded through without hesitating.

Rusty had never put a paw in water before. But he was determined not to show any signs of weakness, so he narrowed his eyes and followed, trying to ignore the uncomfortable wetness that soaked his belly fur.

At last Lionheart and Whitestorm paused. Rusty skidded to a halt behind them and stood panting while the two warriors stepped onto a rock that rested on the edge of a small ravine.

"We are very close to our camp now," meowed Lionheart.

Rusty strained to see any signs of life—moving leaves, a glimpse of fur among the bushes below, but his eyes saw nothing except the same undergrowth that covered the rest of the forest floor.

"Use your nose. You must be able to scent it," hissed Whitestorm impatiently.

Rusty closed his eyes and sniffed. Whitestorm was right. The scents here were very different from the cat-scent he was used to. The air smelled stronger, speaking of many, many different cats.

He nodded thoughtfully and announced, "I can smell cats."

Lionheart and Whitestorm exchanged amused looks.

"There will come a time, if you are accepted into the Clan, when you will know each cat-scent by name," Lionheart meowed. "Follow me!" He led the way nimbly down the boulders to the bottom of the ravine, and pushed his way through a thick patch of gorse. Rusty followed, and Whitestorm took up the rear. As his sides scraped against the prickly gorse, Rusty looked down and noticed that the grass beneath his paws was flattened into a broad, strong-smelling track. This must be the main entrance into the camp, he thought.

Beyond the gorse, a clearing opened up. The ground at the center was bare, hard earth, shaped by many generations of pawsteps. This camp had been here a long time. The clearing was dappled by sunshine, and the air felt warm and still.

Rusty looked around, his eyes wide. There were cats everywhere, sitting alone or in groups, sharing food or purring quietly as they groomed one another.

"Just after sunhigh, when the day is hottest, is a time for sharing tongues," Lionheart explained.

"Sharing tongues?" Rusty echoed.

"Clan cats always spend time grooming each other and sharing the news of the day," Whitestorm told him. "We call it sharing tongues. It is a custom that binds the members of the Clan together."

The cats had obviously smelled Rusty's foreign scent, for heads began to turn and stare curiously in his direction.

Suddenly shy of meeting any cat's gaze directly, Rusty looked around the clearing. It was edged with thick grass, dotted with treestumps and a fallen tree. A thick curtain of ferns and gorse shielded the camp from the rest of the woods.

"Over there," meowed Lionheart, flicking his tail toward an impenetrable-looking tangle of brambles, "is the nursery, where the kits are cared for."

Rusty swiveled his ears toward the bushes. He couldn't see through the knot of prickly branches, but he could hear the mewling of several kittens from somewhere inside. As he watched, a ginger she-cat squirmed out through a small gap in the front. *That must be one of the queens*, Rusty thought.

A tabby queen with distinctive black markings appeared around the bramble bush. The two she-cats exchanged a friendly lick between the ears before the tabby slipped inside the nursery, murmuring to the squealing kits.

"The care of our kits is shared by all of the queens," meowed Lionheart. "All cats serve the Clan. Loyalty to the Clan is the first law in our warrior code, a lesson you must learn quickly if you wish to stay with us."

"Here comes Bluestar," meowed Whitestorm, sniffing the air.

Rusty sniffed the air too, and was pleased that he was able to recognize the scent of the gray she-cat a moment before she appeared from the shadow of a large boulder that lay beside them at the head of the clearing.

"He came," Bluestar purred, addressing the warriors.

Whitestorm replied, "Lionheart was convinced he would not."

Rusty noticed the tip of Bluestar's tail twitch impatiently. "Well, what do you think of him?" she asked.

"He kept up well on the return journey, despite his puny size," Whitestorm admitted. "He certainly seems strong for a kittypet."

"So it is agreed?" Bluestar looked at Lionheart and Whitestorm.

Both cats nodded.

"Then I shall announce his arrival to the Clan." Bluestar leaped up onto the boulder and yowled, "Let all those cats old enough to catch their own prey join here beneath the Highrock for a Clan meeting."

Her clear call brought all the cats trotting toward her, emerging like liquid shadows from the edges of the clearing. Rusty stayed where he was, flanked by Lionheart and Whitestorm. The other cats settled themselves below the Highrock and looked expectantly up at their leader.

Rusty felt a rush of relief as he recognized Graypaw's thick gray fur among the cats. Beside him sat a young tortoiseshell queen, her black-tipped tail tucked neatly over small white paws. A large dark gray tabby crouched behind them, the black stripes on his fur looking like shadows on a moonlit forest floor.

When the cats were still, Bluestar spoke. "ThunderClan needs more warriors," she began. "Never before have we had so few apprentices in training. It has been decided that ThunderClan will take in an outsider to train as a warrior. . . ."

Rusty heard indignant mutterings erupt among the Clan cats, but Bluestar silenced them with a firm yowl. "I have found a cat who is willing to become an apprentice of ThunderClan."

"*Lucky* to become an apprentice," caterwauled a loud voice above the ripple of shock that spread through the cats.

Rusty craned his neck and saw a pale tabby cat standing up and glaring defiantly at the leader.

Bluestar ignored the tabby and addressed all of her Clan. "Lionheart and Whitestorm have met this young cat, and they agree with me that we should train him with the other apprentices."

Rusty looked up at Lionheart, then back at the Clan, to find all eyes were on him now. His fur prickled and he swallowed nervously. There was silence for a moment. Rusty was sure they must all be able to hear his heart pulsing and smell his fear-scent.

Now a deafening crescendo of caterwauling rose from the crowd.

"Where does he come from?"

"Which Clan does he belong to?"

"What a strange scent he carries! That's not the scent of any Clan *I* know!"

Then one yowl in particular sounded out above the rest.

"Look at his collar! He's a kittypet!" It was the pale tabby again. "Once a kittypet, always a kittypet. This Clan needs wildborn warriors to defend it, not another soft mouth to feed."

Lionheart bent down and hissed into Rusty's ear, "That tabby is Longtail. He smells your fear. They all do. You must prove to him and the other cats that your fear won't hold you back."

But Rusty couldn't move. How could he ever prove to these fierce cats that he wasn't just a kittypet?

The tabby continued to jeer at him. "Your collar is a mark of the Twolegs, and that noisy jingling will make you a poor hunter at best. At worst, it will bring the Twolegs into our territory, looking for the poor lost kittypet who fills the woods with his pitiful tinkling."

All the cats howled in agreement.

Longtail went on, well aware that he had the support of his audience. "The noise of your treacherous bell will alert our enemies, even if your Twoleg *stench* doesn't!"

Lionheart hissed into Rusty's ear once more: "Do you back down from a challenge?"

Rusty still did not move. But this time he was trying to pinpoint Longtail's position. There he was, just behind a dusky brown queen. Rusty flattened his ears, narrowed his eyes and, hissing, leaped through the startled cats to fling himself onto his tormentor.

Longtail was completely unprepared for Rusty's attack. He staggered sideways, losing his footing on the hard-baked earth. Filled with rage and desperate to prove himself, Rusty dug his claws deep into the tabby cat's fur and sank in his teeth. No subtle rituals of swiping and boxing preceded this fight. The two cats were locked in a screaming, writhing tussle that flipped and somersaulted around the clearing at the heart of the camp. The other cats had to spring out of the way to avoid the screeching whirlwind of fur.

As Rusty scratched and struggled, he was suddenly aware that he felt no fear, only exhilaration. Through the roaring of the blood in his ears, he could hear the cats around them wailing with excitement.

Then Rusty felt his collar tighten around his neck. Longtail had gripped it between his teeth and was tugging, and tugging hard. Rusty felt a terrible pressure at his throat. Unable to breathe, he started to panic. He writhed and twisted, but each movement only made the pressure worse. Retching and gulping for air, he summoned up all his strength and tried to pull away from Longtail's grip. And suddenly, with a loud snap, he was free.

Longtail tumbled away from him. Rusty scrambled to his paws and looked around. Longtail was crouching three tail-lengths away. And, dangling from Longtail's mouth, Rusty saw his collar, mangled and broken.

At once, Bluestar leaped down from the Highrock and silenced the noisy crowd with a thunderous caterwaul. Rusty and Longtail remained fixed to the spot, gasping for breath. Clumps of fur hung from their ruffled coats. Rusty could feel a cut stinging above his eye. Longtail's left ear was badly torn, and blood dripped down his lean shoulders onto the dusty ground.

They stared at each other, their hostility not yet spent.

Bluestar stepped forward and took the collar from Longtail. She placed it on the ground in front of her and meowed, "The newcomer has lost his Twoleg collar in a battle for his honor. StarClan has spoken its approval—this cat has been released from the hold of his Twoleg owners, and is free to join ThunderClan as an apprentice."

Rusty looked at Bluestar and solemnly nodded his acceptance. He stood up and stepped forward into a shaft of sunshine, welcoming the warmth on his sore muscles. The pool of light blazed bright on his orange pelt, making his fur glow. Rusty lifted his head proudly and looked at the cats that surrounded him. This time no cat argued or jeered. He had shown himself to be a worthy opponent in battle.

Bluestar approached Rusty and placed the shredded collar on the ground in front of him. She touched his ear gently with her nose. "You look like a brand of fire in this sunlight," she murmured. Her eyes flashed briefly, as if her words had more meaning for her than Rusty knew. "You have fought well." Then she turned to the Clan and announced, "From this day forward, until he has earned his warrior name, this apprentice will be called Firepaw, in honor of his flame-colored coat."

She stepped back and, with the other cats, waited silently for his next move. Without hesitating, Rusty turned and kicked dust and grass over his collar as though burying his dirt.

Longtail growled and limped out of the clearing toward a fern-shaded corner. The cats split into groups, murmuring to each other excitedly.

"Hey, Firepaw!"

Rusty heard Graypaw's friendly voice behind him. *Firepaw!* A thrill of pride surged through him at the sound of his new name. He turned to greet the gray apprentice with a welcoming sniff.

"Great fight, Firepaw!" mewed Graypaw. "Especially for a kittypet! Longtail is a warrior, although he only finished his training two moons ago. That scar you left on his ear won't let him forget you in a hurry. You've spoiled his good looks, that's for sure."

"Thanks, Graypaw," Firepaw replied. "He put up quite a fight, though!" He licked his front paw and began to wipe clean the deep scratch that stung above his eye. As he washed he heard his new name again, echoing among the meows of the cats.

"Firepaw!"

"Hey, Firepaw!"

"Welcome, young Firepaw!"

Firepaw closed his eyes for a moment and let the voices wash over him.

"Good name, too!" Graypaw mewed approvingly, jolting him awake.

Firepaw looked around. "Where did Longtail creep off to?"

"I think he was heading toward Spottedleaf's den." Graypaw tipped his head toward the fern-enclosed corner Longtail had disappeared into. "She's our medicine cat. Not bad-looking either. Younger and a lot prettier than most—"

A low yowl next to the two cats stopped Graypaw midspeech.

They both turned, and Firepaw recognized the powerful gray tabby cat who had sat behind Graypaw earlier.

"Darkstripe," mewed Graypaw, dipping his head respectfully.

The sleek tom looked at Firepaw for a moment. "Lucky your collar snapped when it did. Longtail is a young warrior, but I can't imagine him being beaten by a kittypet!" He spat the word *kittypet* scornfully, then turned and stalked off.

"Now Darkstripe," Graypaw hissed to Firepaw under his breath, "is neither young, nor pretty. . . ."

Firepaw was about to agree with his new friend when he was interrupted by a warning yowl from an old gray cat sitting at the edge of the clearing.

"Smallear smells trouble!" Graypaw meowed, immediately alert.

Firepaw barely had time to look around before a young cat crashed through the bushes and into the camp. He was skinny and—apart from the white tip of his long, thin tail—jet black from head to toe.

Graypaw gasped. "That's Ravenpaw! Why is he alone? Where's Tigerclaw?"

Firepaw looked at Ravenpaw staggering across the floor of the clearing. He was panting heavily. His coat was ruffled and dusty, and his eyes were wild with fear.

"Who are Ravenpaw and Tigerclaw?" Firepaw whispered to Graypaw, as several other cats raced past him to greet the new arrival.

"Ravenpaw's an apprentice. Tigerclaw's his mentor,"

Graypaw explained quickly. "Ravenpaw went out with Tigerclaw and Redtail at sunrise on a mission against RiverClan, the lucky furball!"

"Redtail?" Firepaw echoed, thoroughly confused by all these names.

"Bluestar's deputy," hissed Graypaw. "But why on earth has Ravenpaw come back alone?" he added to himself. He lifted his head to listen as Bluestar stepped forward.

"Ravenpaw?" The she-cat spoke calmly, but a look of worry clouded her blue eyes. The other cats drew back, curling their lips with anxiety.

"What has happened?" Bluestar jumped onto the Highrock and looked down at the trembling cat. "Speak, Ravenpaw!"

Ravenpaw was still struggling for breath, and his sides heaved fitfully while the dust around him turned red with blood, but still he managed to scramble up onto the Highrock and stand beside Bluestar. He turned to the crowd of eager faces that surrounded him, and summoned enough breath to declare, "Redtail is dead!"

CHAPTER 4

❧

Shocked yowls rose from the Clan cats and echoed through the forest.

Ravenpaw staggered slightly. His right foreleg glistened, wet with blood that flowed from the deep gash on his shoulder. "We m-met five RiverClan warriors beside the stream, not far from the Sunningrocks," he went on shakily. "Oakheart was among them."

"Oakheart!" Graypaw gasped beside Firepaw. "He is the deputy of RiverClan. He's one of the greatest warriors in the forest. Lucky Ravenpaw! Wish it could have been me. I'd have really—" Graypaw was silenced by a fierce glance from the old gray tom who had first sensed Ravenpaw's return.

Firepaw turned his attention back to Ravenpaw.

"Redtail warned Oakheart to keep his hunting parties out of ThunderClan territory. He said the next RiverClan warrior to be caught in ThunderClan territory would be killed, but Oak . . . Oakheart would not back down. He said his Cl-Clan had to be fed, whatever we threatened." Ravenpaw paused to wheeze for breath. His wound was still bleeding heavily, and he stood awkwardly to keep the weight off his shoulder.

"That's when the RiverClan cats attacked. It was hard to see what was happening. The fighting was vicious. I saw Oakheart had Redtail pinned to the ground, but then Redtail . . ." Suddenly Ravenpaw's eyes rolled in his head and he lurched sideways. Half scrambling, half falling, he slithered off the Highrock and collapsed on the ground below.

A ginger queen bounded toward him and crouched at his side. She licked his cheek briefly and called out, "Spottedleaf!"

Out of the fern-shaded corner trotted the pretty tortoise-shell Firepaw had noticed sitting beside Graypaw earlier. She hurried over to Ravenpaw and mewed for the queen to stand back. Then she used her small pink nose to roll the apprentice over so that she could take a good look at the wound. She glanced up and meowed, "It's all right, Goldenflower, his wounds aren't fatal. But I'll need to fetch some cobwebs to stop the bleeding."

As Spottedleaf sprinted back to her den, the hushed silence in the clearing was broken by a mournful howl. All eyes turned to the direction it had come from.

A massive dark brown tabby staggered through the gorse tunnel. Between his sharp teeth the warrior held not prey, but the lifeless body of another cat. He dragged the tattered creature into the center of the clearing.

Firepaw craned his neck and glimpsed a flash of bright ginger tail hanging limply in the dust.

Shock rippled through the Clan like a chill breeze. Beside Firepaw, Graypaw dropped into a crouch as grief swept over him. "Redtail!"

"How did this happen, Tigerclaw?" demanded Bluestar from her position on the Highrock.

Tigerclaw let the scruff of Redtail's neck fall from his mouth. He looked steadily back at Bluestar. "He died with honor, struck down by Oakheart. I couldn't save him, but I managed to take Oakheart's life while he was still gloating over his victory." Tigerclaw's voice was strong and deep. "Redtail's death was not in vain, for I doubt we'll see RiverClan hunters in our territory again."

Firepaw glanced at Graypaw. The apprentice's eyes were dark with sadness.

After a moment's pause, several of the cats moved forward to lick Redtail's bedraggled fur. As they groomed they purred hushed phrases to the dead warrior.

Firepaw whispered into Graypaw's ear, "What are they doing?"

Graypaw didn't take his eyes off the dead cat as he replied. "His spirit may have left to join StarClan, but the Clan will share tongues with Redtail one last time."

"StarClan?" Firepaw echoed.

"It's the tribe of heavenly warriors that watches over all Clan cats. You can see them in Silverpelt."

Firepaw looked confused, so Graypaw explained. "Silverpelt is that thick band of stars you see each night stretching across the sky. Each star is a StarClan warrior. Redtail will be among them tonight."

Firepaw nodded, and Graypaw stepped forward to share tongues with his dead deputy.

Bluestar had remained silent while the first cats came to pay their respects to Redtail. Now she leaped down from the Highrock and walked slowly toward Redtail's body. The other cats retreated and watched as their leader crouched down to share tongues with her old comrade one last time.

When she had finished she raised her head and spoke. Her voice was low and thick with grief, and the Clan listened in silence. "Redtail was a brave warrior. His loyalty to ThunderClan could never be doubted. I always relied on his judgment, for it bore witness to the needs of the Clan, and was never swayed by self-interest or pride. He would have made a fine leader."

Then she lowered herself onto her belly, her head bowed, her paws stretched neatly before her, and silently she grieved for her lost friend. Several other cats came and lay down beside her, their bowed heads and hunched backs echoing her mournful pose.

Firepaw watched. He had not known Redtail, but he couldn't help feeling moved as he witnessed the Clan mourn.

Graypaw came and stood beside him again. "Dustpaw will be sad," he remarked.

"Dustpaw?"

"Redtail's apprentice. That brown-striped tabby over there. I wonder who his new mentor will be?"

Firepaw glanced over at the small tom who squatted near Redtail's body, staring unseeing at the ground. Firepaw looked past him to the Clan leader. "How long will Blusetar sit with him?" he asked.

"Probably the whole night," replied Graypaw. "Redtail was her deputy for many, many moons. She won't want to let him go too quickly. He was one of the best warriors. Not as big and powerful as Tigerclaw or Lionheart, but quick and clever."

Firepaw looked at Tigerclaw, admiring the strength that swelled in his powerful muscles and broad head. His massive body showed signs of his warrior life. One of his ears was split into a deep vee shape, and a thick scar sliced the bridge of his nose.

Suddenly Tigerclaw stood up and stalked over to Ravenpaw. Spottedleaf was crouching beside Tigerclaw's wounded apprentice, using her teeth and front paws to press wads of cobweb onto his shoulder wound.

Firepaw leaned toward Graypaw and asked, "What's Spottedleaf doing?"

"Stopping the bleeding. It looked like a nasty cut. And Ravenpaw seemed really shaken up. He's always been a bit jumpy, but I've never seen him this bad before. Let's go and see if he's woken up yet."

They made their way through the grieving cats toward the spot where Ravenpaw lay and settled themselves a respectful distance away to wait until Tigerclaw had finished speaking.

"So, Spottedleaf." Tigerclaw addressed the tortoiseshell with a confident meow. "How is he? Do you think you can save him? I've spent a lot of time training him up, and I don't want my efforts to be wasted at the first battle."

Spottedleaf didn't look up from her patient as she replied. "Yes, a pity if, after all your valuable training, he dies in his first fight, eh?" Firepaw could hear a teasing purr in her soft mew.

"Will he live?" Tigerclaw demanded.

"Of course. He just needs to rest."

Tigerclaw snorted and looked down at the motionless black shape. He jabbed Ravenpaw with one of his front claws. "Come on, then! Get up!"

Ravenpaw didn't move.

"Look at the length of that claw!" Firepaw hissed.

"Too right!" replied Graypaw with feeling. "I know *I* wouldn't want to get into a fight with him!"

"Not so fast, Tigerclaw!" Spottedleaf placed her paw over Tigerclaw's sharp talon and gently moved it away. "This apprentice needs to keep as still as possible until the cut has healed. We don't want him opening his wound by jumping about trying to please you. Leave him alone."

Firepaw found himself holding his breath as he waited for Tigerclaw's reaction. He guessed that few cats dared to give orders to the warrior like that. The big tabby stiffened, and seemed about to speak when Spottedleaf mewed teasingly, "Even *you* know better than to argue with a medicine cat, Tigerclaw."

Tigerclaw's eyes flashed at the little tortoiseshell's words. "I wouldn't dare argue with *you*, dear Spottedleaf," he purred. He turned to leave and caught sight of Graypaw and Firepaw. "Who's this?" he asked Graypaw, towering above them.

"He's the new apprentice," Graypaw mewed.

"He smells like a kittypet!" snorted the warrior.

"I *was* a house cat," Firepaw meowed boldly, "but I am going to train to be a warrior."

Tigerclaw looked at him with sudden interest. "Ah, yes. Now I remember. Bluestar mentioned that she had stumbled across some stray kittypet. So she's actually going to try you out, is she?"

Firepaw sat up very straight, anxious to impress this distinguished Clan warrior. "That's right," he mewed respectfully.

Tigerclaw eyed him thoughtfully. "Then I shall watch your progress with interest."

Firepaw puffed his chest out proudly as Tigerclaw stalked away. "Do you think he liked me?"

"I don't think Tigerclaw *likes* any apprentices!" whispered Graypaw.

Just then Ravenpaw stirred and twitched his ears. "Has he gone?" he mumbled.

"Who? Tigerclaw?" replied Graypaw, trotting toward him. "Yep, he's gone."

"Hi, there," Firepaw began, about to introduce himself.

"Go away, both of you!" Spottedleaf protested. "How am I meant to help this cat with all these interruptions!" She impatiently flicked her tail at Graypaw and Firepaw and pushed her way between them and her patient.

Firepaw realized she was serious, despite the lively glimmer in her warm amber eyes.

"Come on then, Firepaw," mewed Graypaw. "I'll show you around. See you later, Ravenpaw."

The two cats left Spottedleaf with Ravenpaw and walked across the clearing.

Graypaw looked thoughtful. He was clearly taking his duties as a guide very seriously. "You know the Highrock already," he began, flicking his tail toward the big, smooth rock. "Bluestar always addresses the Clan from there. Her den is down there." He lifted his nose toward a hollow in the side of the Highrock. "Her den was carved out many moons ago by an ancient stream." Hanging lichen draped the entrance, sheltering the leader's nest from wind and rain.

"The warriors sleep over here," Graypaw went on.

Firepaw followed him to a large bush a few paces away from the Highrock. There was a clear view from here right down to the gorse entrance into the camp. The branches of the bush hung low, but Firepaw could see a sheltered space inside where the warriors made their nests.

"The senior warriors sleep nearest the center, where it's warmest," explained Graypaw. "They usually share their fresh-kill together over by that clump of nettles. The younger warriors eat nearby. Sometimes they are invited to join the senior warriors for eating, which is a big honor."

"What about the other Clan cats?" Firepaw asked, fascinated but feeling rather overwhelmed by all the traditions and rituals of Clan life.

"Well, the queens share warrior quarters when they work as warriors, but when they are expecting kits, or nursing them, they stay in a nest near the nursery. The elders have their own place on the other side of the clearing. Come on, I'll show you."

Firepaw trotted after Graypaw, across the clearing, and past the shadowy corner where Spottedleaf had her den.

They stopped beside a fallen tree that sheltered a patch of lush grass. Crouched among the soft greenery were four elderly cats tucking into a plump young rabbit.

"Dustpaw and Sandpaw would have brought them that," whispered Graypaw. "One of the apprentices' duties is catching fresh-kill for the elders."

"Hello, youngster," one of the elders greeted Graypaw.

"Hello, Smallear," mewed Graypaw, nodding respectfully.

"This must be our new apprentice. Firepaw, isn't it?" meowed a second tom. His patchy fur was dark brown, and there was only a stump where his tail should have been.

"That's right," Firepaw replied, copying Graypaw's polite nod.

"I'm Halftail," purred the brown tom. "Welcome to the Clan."

"Have you two eaten?" meowed Smallear.

Firepaw and Graypaw both shook their heads.

"Well, there's enough here. Dustpaw and Sandpaw are turning into fine hunters. Would you mind if these youngsters shared a mouse, One-eye?"

The pale gray queen who lay beside him shook her head. Firepaw noticed one of her eyes was clouded and sightless.

"What about you, Dappletail?"

The other elder, a tortoiseshell she-cat with a gray muzzle, meowed in a voice cracked with age, "Of course not."

"Thank you," mewed Graypaw eagerly. He stepped forward and took a large mouse from the pile of prey, then dropped it at Firepaw's feet. "You still not tasted mouse?" he asked.

"No," Firepaw admitted. He suddenly felt excited by the warm smells that were rising from this piece of fresh-kill. His whole body quivered at the thought of sharing his first real food as a Clan member.

"In that case, you can have first bite. Just save me some!" Graypaw dipped his head and stood back to give Firepaw room.

Firepaw crouched down and took a large bite from the mouse. It was juicy and tender, and sang with the flavors of the forest.

"What do you think?" asked Graypaw.

"Fantastic!" mumbled Firepaw, his mouth still full.

"Move over then," mewed Graypaw, stepping forward and bending his head to take a bite.

As the two apprentices shared the mouse, they listened to the elders talk among themselves.

"How long before Bluestar appoints a new deputy?" asked Smallear.

"What did you say, Smallear?" mewed One-eye.

"I think your hearing has become as poor as your eyesight!" snapped Smallear impatiently. "I said, how long before Bluestar appoints a new deputy?"

One-eye ignored Smallear's irritated reply and spoke instead to the tortoiseshell queen. "Dappletail, do you remember the day many moons ago when Bluestar herself was appointed deputy?"

Dappletail mewed earnestly, "Oh, yes! It was not long after she lost her kits."

"She'll not be happy to be appointing a new deputy,"

Smallear observed. "Redtail served her long and well. But she'll need to make up her mind quickly. According to Clan custom, the choice has to be made before moonhigh after the death of the old deputy."

"At least this time the choice is obvious," meowed Halftail.

Firepaw raised his head and looked around the clearing. Who could Halftail mean? To Firepaw, all the warriors looked worthy of becoming deputy. Perhaps he meant Tigerclaw; after all, he had avenged Redtail's death.

Tigerclaw was sitting not far off, his ears angled toward the elders' conversation.

As Firepaw stretched with his tongue to lick the last traces of mouse from his whiskers, Bluestar's voice called from the Highrock. Redtail's body still lay in the clearing below, pale gray in the fading light. "A new deputy must be appointed," she meowed. "But first, let us give thanks to StarClan for the life of Redtail. Tonight he sits with his fellow warriors among the stars."

Silence fell as all the cats looked up into the sky, which was beginning to darken as evening crept over the forest.

"And now I shall name ThunderClan's new deputy," Bluestar continued. "I say these words before the body of Redtail, so that his spirit may hear and approve my choice."

Firepaw looked at Tigerclaw. He couldn't help noticing the hunger in the big warrior's amber eyes as he stared up at the Highrock.

"Lionheart," meowed Bluestar, "will be the new deputy of ThunderClan."

Firepaw was curious to see Tigerclaw's reaction. But the dark warrior's face revealed nothing as he moved to congratulate Lionheart with a nudge so hearty that it almost pushed the golden tabby off balance.

"Why didn't she make Tigerclaw deputy?" Firepaw whispered to Graypaw.

"Probably because Lionheart has been a warrior longer, so he has a lot more experience," Graypaw murmured back, still looking up at Bluestar.

Bluestar spoke again. "Redtail was also mentor to young Dustpaw. Since there must be no delay in the training of our apprentices, I shall appoint Dustpaw's new mentor immediately. Darkstripe, you are ready for your first apprentice, so you will continue Dustpaw's training. You had a fine mentor in Tigerclaw, and I expect you to pass on some of the excellent skills you were taught."

The tabby warrior swelled with pride as he showed his acceptance with a solemn nod. He strode over to Dustpaw, bent his head, and rather awkwardly touched noses with his new apprentice. Dustpaw flicked his tail respectfully, but his eyes were still dull with grief for his lost mentor.

Bluestar raised her voice. "I shall keep a vigil with Redtail's body tonight, before we bury him at sunrise." She jumped down from the Highrock and walked over to lie beside Redtail's body once more. Many of the other cats joined her, Dustpaw and Smallear among them.

"Should we sit with them too?" Firepaw suggested. He had to admit the idea didn't appeal to him much. It had been a busy day and he was beginning to feel tired. All he wanted to do was find somewhere warm and dry to curl up and sleep.

Graypaw shook his head. "No, only those who were closest to Redtail will share his final night. I'll show you where we sleep. The apprentices' den is over here."

Firepaw followed Graypaw to a thick bush of ferns that lay behind a mossy tree stump.

"All the apprentices share their fresh-kill by this stump," Graypaw told him.

"How many apprentices are there?" Firepaw asked.

"Not as many as usual—just me, you, Ravenpaw, Dustpaw, and Sandpaw."

As Graypaw and Firepaw settled themselves beside the tree stump, a young she-cat crawled out from beneath the ferns. Her coat was ginger, like Firepaw's, but much paler, with barely visible stripes of darker fur.

"So here comes the new apprentice!" she meowed, narrowing her eyes.

"Hello," Firepaw mewed.

The young cat sniffed rudely. "He smells like a kittypet! Don't tell me I'm going to have to share my nest with that revolting stench!"

Firepaw felt rather taken aback. Since his fight with Longtail, all the cats had been quite friendly. Maybe they had just been distracted by Ravenpaw's news, he thought.

"You'll have to excuse Sandpaw," apologized Graypaw. "I think she must have a furball stuck somewhere. She's not usually this bad-tempered."

"Psst!" spat Sandpaw crossly.

"Hold on, youngsters." The deep voice of Whitestorm sounded behind the apprentices. "Sandpaw! As my apprentice, I expected you to be a little more welcoming to this newcomer."

Sandpaw held up her head and looked defiant. "I'm sorry, Whitestorm," she purred, not sounding sorry at all. "I just didn't expect to be training with a *kittypet*, that's all!"

"I'm sure you'll get used to it, Sandpaw," meowed Whitestorm calmly. "Now, it's getting late, and training starts early tomorrow. You three should get some sleep." He gave Sandpaw a stern look, and she nodded obediently. As he walked off, she spun around and vanished into the clump of ferns, sniffing once more as she brushed past Firepaw.

With a flick of his tail, Graypaw invited Firepaw to follow him, and led the way after Sandpaw. Inside the sleeping area, the ground was lined with soft moss, and the pale moonlight turned everything a delicate shade of green. The air was fragrant with fern scent, and warmer than outside.

"Where do I sleep?" Firepaw asked.

"Anywhere, just so long as it's not near me!" snarled Sandpaw, who was prodding some moss with her paw.

Graypaw and Firepaw exchanged glances, but said nothing. Firepaw raked together a pile of moss with his claws. When he had gathered his bed into a cozy nest, he circled until it was comfortable and settled down. His whole body felt drowsy with contentment. This was his home now. He was a member of ThunderClan.

CHAPTER 5

❧

"Hey, Firepaw, wake up!" Graypaw's meow broke into Firepaw's dream. He had been chasing a squirrel, up and up, into the topmost branches of a tall oak.

"Training begins at sunrise. Dustpaw and Sandpaw are already up," Graypaw added urgently.

Firepaw stretched sleepily, then remembered: today was his first day of training. He leaped to his paws. His drowsiness evaporated as excitement surged through his veins.

Graypaw was giving himself a hasty wash. Between licks, he meowed, "I've just spoken to Lionheart. Ravenpaw won't be training with us till his wound is better. He'll probably stay at Spottedleaf's den for another day or two. Dustpaw and Sandpaw are on hunting duty. So Lionheart thought you and I could train with him and Tigerclaw this morning. We'd better hurry, though," he added. "They'll be waiting!"

Graypaw led Firepaw quickly through the gorse entrance of the camp and up the side of the rock-strewn valley. As they climbed over the crest of the ravine, a cool breeze ruffled their fur. Fat, white clouds raced across the blue sky overhead. Firepaw felt fierce joy well up inside him as he followed

Graypaw down a tree-shaded slope and into a sandy hollow.

Tigerclaw and Lionheart were indeed waiting, sitting a few tail-lengths apart on the sun-warmed sand.

"In future, I expect you both to be punctual," growled Tigerclaw.

"Don't be too severe, Tigerclaw; it was a busy night last night. I expect they were tired," meowed Lionheart gently. "You have not yet been assigned a mentor, Firepaw," he went on. "For now, Tigerclaw and I will share your training."

Firepaw nodded enthusiastically, his tail held high, unable to disguise his delight at having two such great warriors as his mentors.

"Come," meowed Tigerclaw impatiently. "Today we are going to show you the edges of our territory, so that you know where you will be hunting and what boundaries you need to protect. Graypaw, it won't do you any harm to remind yourself of the Clan's outer limits."

Without another word, Tigerclaw leaped up and bounded out of the sandy hollow. Lionheart nodded to Graypaw and they took off with equal speed. Firepaw scrambled after them, his paws slipping on the soft sand.

The trees were thick in this part of the forest, birch and ash trees overshadowed by mighty oaks. The ground was carpeted with crisp dead leaves that rustled beneath their paws. Tigerclaw paused to spray his scent on a thick clump of ferns. The other cats stopped beside him.

"There is a Twoleg path here," murmured Lionheart. "Use your nose, Firepaw. Can you smell anything?"

Firepaw sniffed. There was the faint scent of a Twoleg, and the stronger smell of a dog, familiar to him from his old home. "A Twoleg has walked his dog along here, but they are gone now," he mewed.

"Good," meowed Lionheart. "Do you think it is safe to cross?"

Firepaw sniffed again. The odors were weak and seemed overlaid with fresher forest smells. "Yes," he replied.

Tigerclaw nodded, and the four cats stalked out from beneath the ferns and crossed the sharp stones of the narrow Twoleg path.

The trees beyond were pine. They grew tall and straight, row after row. It was easy to walk silently here. The ground was thick with layers of dead needles, which prickled against Firepaw's pads but felt spongy underneath. There was no undergrowth here to hide in, and Firepaw sensed tension in the other cats as they stalked unprotected between the tree trunks.

"Twolegs put these trees here," meowed Tigerclaw. "They cut them down with foul-smelling creatures, which spew enough fumes to make a kit go blind. Then they take the fallen trees to the Treecut place that lies near here."

Firepaw stopped and listened for the roar of the tree-eater, which he had heard before.

"The Treecut place will be silent for a few moons more, until the time of greenleaf," explained Graypaw, noticing his pause.

The cats padded on through the pine forest.

"Twolegplace lies in that direction," meowed Tigerclaw, flicking his thick tail to one side. "No doubt you can smell it, Firepaw. Today, however, we will head the other way."

Eventually they reached another Twoleg path that marked the far edge of the pine forest. They quickly crossed over into the safe bushes of the oak woods beyond. But Firepaw still sensed anxiety in the other cats.

"We're approaching RiverClan territory," whispered Graypaw. "The Sunningrocks are over there." He pointed with his soft muzzle to a treeless mound of boulders.

Firepaw felt his fur stand on end. This was where Redtail had been slain.

Lionheart stopped by a flat gray rock. "This is the boundary between ThunderClan and RiverClan territory. RiverClan rules the hunting grounds beside the great river," he meowed. "Breathe deeply, Firepaw."

The pungent smell of unfamiliar cats hit the roof of Firepaw's mouth. He was surprised how different it smelled from the warm cat scents of the ThunderClan camp. And he was also surprised to realize just how familiar and comforting the ThunderClan scents seemed to him already.

"That is the smell of RiverClan," Tigerclaw growled beside him. "Remember it well. It will be strongest at the boundary, because their warriors will have scent-marked the trees along here." With these words, the dark tabby lifted his tail and sprayed his own mark on the flat rock.

"We'll follow this boundary line, as it leads straight to Fourtrees," Lionheart meowed.

He set off quickly, away from the Sunningrocks, followed by Tigerclaw. Graypaw and Firepaw trotted after them.

"What is Fourtrees?" Firepaw panted.

"It is where the territories of all four Clans meet," replied Graypaw. "There are four great oaks there, as old as the Clans—"

"Be quiet!" ordered Tigerclaw. "Don't forget how close we are to enemy territory!"

The two apprentices fell silent and Firepaw concentrated on walking silently. They crossed a shallow stream, keeping their paws dry by leaping from boulder to boulder across the pebbly riverbed.

By the time they reached Fourtrees, Firepaw was feeling completely out of breath and his paws ached. He wasn't used to traveling so far and so fast. He was quite relieved when Lionheart and Tigerclaw led them out of the thick woods and stopped at the brow of a bush-covered slope.

It was sunhigh now. The clouds had cleared, and the wind had dropped. Below, in the dazzling sunlight, stood four enormous oaks, their dark green crowns reaching almost to the top of the steep slope.

"As Graypaw told you," meowed Lionheart to Firepaw, "this is Fourtrees, where the territories of all four Clans meet. WindClan governs the high ground ahead of us, where the sun sets. You won't be able to catch their scent today—the wind is blowing toward them. But you'll learn it soon enough."

"And ShadowClan holds power over there, in the darkest part of the forest," added Graypaw, flicking his head sideways. "The elders say that the cold winds from the north blow over the ShadowClan cats and chill their hearts."

"So many Clans!" Firepaw exclaimed. *And so well organized,* he added to himself, remembering Smudge's lurid tales of wildcats wreaking terror in the forest.

"You see now why prey is so precious," meowed Lionheart. "Why we must fight to protect what little we have."

"But that seems foolish! Why can't the Clans work together and share their hunting grounds, instead of fighting each other?" Firepaw suggested boldly.

A shocked silence greeted his words.

Tigerclaw was the first to reply. "That is treacherous thinking, kittypet," he snapped.

"Don't be too fierce, Tigerclaw," warned Lionheart. "The ways of the Clans are new to this apprentice." He looked at Firepaw. "You speak from your heart, young Firepaw. This will make you a stronger warrior one day."

Tigerclaw growled. "Or it might make him give in to kittypet weakness right at the moment of attack."

Lionheart glanced briefly at Tigerclaw before he continued. "The four Clans do come together peacefully, in a Gathering each moon. Here"—he bent his head toward the four mighty oaks below—"is where they meet. The truce lasts for as long as the moon is at its fullest."

"Then there must be a meeting very soon?" Firepaw suggested, remembering how bright the moonlight had been the night before.

"Indeed there is!" answered Lionheart, sounding impressed.

"Tonight, in fact. The Gatherings are very important because they allow the Clans to come together in peace for one night. But you must understand that longer alliances bring more trouble than they're worth."

"It is our Clan loyalty that makes us strong," Tigerclaw meowed in agreement. "If you weaken that loyalty, you weaken our chances of survival."

Firepaw nodded. "I understand," he mewed.

"Come on," meowed Lionheart, standing up. "Let's keep moving."

They paced along the ridge of the valley where Fourtrees stood. Now they were heading away from the sun as it began to sink in the afternoon sky. They crossed the stream at a place where it was narrow enough to leap over in one jump.

Firepaw sniffed the air. A new cat-scent touched his mouth glands, strong and sour. "Which Clan is that?" he asked.

"ShadowClan," answered Tigerclaw grimly. "We are traveling along their border. Keep your wits about you, Firepaw. Fresher scents mean that a ShadowClan patrol is in the area."

As Firepaw nodded, he heard a new noise. He stiffened, but the other cats kept up their pace, heading straight for the ominous rumbling.

"What's that?" he called, trotting to catch up with them.

"You'll see in a moment," replied Lionheart.

Firepaw peered through the trees ahead. They seemed to be getting thinner, letting in a broad band of sunlight. "Are we at the edge of the woods?" he asked. Then he stopped and took a deep breath. The green forest scents were overlaid with other strange, dark smells. This time it was not cat-scent, but an odor that reminded him of his old Twoleg home. And the rumbling was getting louder, a ceaseless roar that made the ground tremble and ached in Firepaw's ears.

"This is the Thunderpath," meowed Tigerclaw.

Firepaw followed as Lionheart led them toward the edge of the forest. Then he sat down and all four cats looked out.

Firepaw could see a gray path like a river, cutting its way through the forest. The hard gray stone stretched ahead of him so far that the trees on the other side seemed blurred and tiny. Firepaw shuddered at the bitter smell that rose from the path.

Next moment he leaped back, his fur bristling, as a gigantic monster roared past. The branches of the trees on either side flapped madly in the wind that chased the speeding monster. Firepaw stared around at the other cats, his eyes wide, unable to speak. He had seen paths like this before near his old Twoleg home, but never this wide, nor with monsters so swift and fierce.

"Scared me too the first time," remarked Graypaw. "But at least it helps to keep ShadowClan warriors from crossing into our territory. The Thunderpath runs for many pawsteps along our boundary line. And don't worry; those monsters never seem to leave the Thunderpath. You'll be fine as long as you don't go too near."

"It's time we returned to camp," meowed Lionheart. "You have seen all our boundaries now. But we'll avoid Snakerocks, even though the way around is longer. An untrained apprentice would be easy prey for an adder, and I expect you are getting tired, Firepaw."

Firepaw couldn't help feeling relieved at the thought of returning to the camp. His head was spinnning with all the new smells and sights, and Lionheart was right: he was tired, and hungry. He fell in behind Graypaw as the cats turned away from the Thunderpath and headed back into the forest.

The dewy scents of evening filled the air as Firepaw made his way through the gorse entrance into the ThunderClan camp. Fresh-kill was waiting for them. Firepaw and Graypaw took their share from the pile that lay in a shady part of the clearing and carried it to the tree stump outside their quarters.

Dustpaw and Sandpaw were already there, munching hungrily.

"Hi, there, kittypet," mewed Dustpaw, narrowing his eyes scornfully at Firepaw. "Enjoy the food *we* caught for you."

"Who knows, you might even learn to catch your own one day!" sneered Sandpaw.

"Are you two still on hunting duty?" asked Graypaw innocently. "Never mind. We've been patrolling our territory borders. You'll be glad to know all is safe."

"I'm sure the other Clans were terrified when they smelled you two coming!" yowled Dustpaw.

"They didn't even dare show their faces," retorted Graypaw, unable to hide his anger.

"Well, we'll ask them tonight when we see them at the

Clan Gathering," mewed Sandpaw.

"Are you going?" Firepaw blurted out, impressed in spite of the apprentices' hostility.

"Of course," replied Dustpaw loftily. "It's a great honor, you know. But don't worry; we'll tell you all about it in the morning."

Graypaw ignored Dustpaw's gloating and started eating his fresh-kill. Firepaw was hungry too, and crouched down to eat. He couldn't help feeling a twinge of envy that Dustpaw and Sandpaw were actually going to meet the other Clans tonight.

A loud call from Bluestar made Firepaw look up. He watched several of the Clan warriors and elders gather in the clearing. It was time for the Clan party to leave for the Gathering. Dustpaw and Sandpaw leaped to their feet and trotted off to join the other cats.

"'Bye, you two," called Sandpaw over her shoulder. "Have a nice, quiet evening!"

The assembled cats stalked out of the camp entrance in single file, with Bluestar at the head. Her fur glowed like silver in the moonlight, and she looked calm and confident as she led her Clan to the brief truce between old enemies.

"Have you ever been to a Gathering?" Firepaw asked Graypaw wistfully.

"Not yet," replied Graypaw, crunching loudly on a mouse bone. "But it won't be long now; just you wait. All the apprentices get to go sometime."

The two apprentices ate the rest of their meal in silence.

When they had finished, Graypaw wandered over to Firepaw and began to groom his head. Together they washed, sharing tongues as Firepaw had seen the other cats do when he first arrived. Then, tired after the long trek, they pushed their way into their den. They settled down in their nests and quickly fell asleep.

The following morning, Graypaw and Firepaw arrived early at the sandy hollow. They had crept out before Sandpaw and Dustpaw woke. Firepaw had been eager to hear about the Gathering, but Graypaw had dragged him away. "You'll hear all about it later, if I know those two," he had mewed.

It promised to be another warm day. And this time Ravenpaw came to join them. Thanks to Spottedleaf, his wound was healing well.

Graypaw played around, scooping leaves into the air and leaping after them. Firepaw watched, his tail twitching with amusement. Ravenpaw sat quietly at one side of the hollow, looking tense and unhappy.

"Cheer up, Ravenpaw!" called Graypaw. "I know you don't like training, but you're not usually this miserable!"

The scents of Lionheart and Tigerclaw warned the apprentices of their approach, and Ravenpaw mewed hastily, "I suppose I'm just worried about my shoulder getting hurt again."

At that moment, Tigerclaw emerged from the bushes, closely followed by Lionheart.

"Warriors should suffer their pain silently," growled

Tigerclaw. He looked Ravenpaw straight in the eye. "You need to learn to hold your tongue."

Ravenpaw flinched and dropped his eyes to the ground.

"Tigerclaw's a bit grumpy today," Graypaw whispered into Firepaw's ear.

Lionheart glanced at his apprentice sternly and announced, "Today we are going to practice stalking. Now, there is a big difference between creeping up on a rabbit and creeping up on a mouse. Can any of you tell me why?"

Firepaw had no idea, and Ravenpaw seemed to have taken Tigerclaw's comment to heart and was holding his tongue.

"Come on!" snorted Tigerclaw impatiently.

It was Graypaw who answered: "Because a rabbit will smell you before he sees you, but a mouse will feel your pawsteps through the ground before he even smells you."

"Exactly, Graypaw! So what must you bear in mind when hunting mice?"

"Step lightly?" Firepaw suggested.

Lionheart looked approvingly at him. "Quite right, Firepaw. You must take all your weight into your haunches, so that your paws make no impact on the forest floor. Let's try it!"

Firepaw watched as Graypaw and Ravenpaw immediately dropped into a stalking crouch.

"Nicely done, Graypaw!" meowed Lionheart as the two apprentices began to move forward stealthily.

"Keep your rear down, Ravenpaw, you look like a duck!" spat Tigerclaw. "Now you try it, Firepaw."

Firepaw crouched down and began to creep across the

forest floor. He felt himself fall instinctively into the right position, and as he stepped forward, as silently and lightly as he could, he felt a glow of pride that his muscles responded so smoothly.

"Well, it's obvious you've known nothing but softness!" growled Tigerclaw. "You stalk like a lumbering kittypet! Do you think dinner is going to come and lie down in your food dish and wait to be eaten?"

Firepaw sat up quickly as Tigerclaw spoke, a little taken aback by his harsh words. He listened carefully to the warrior, determined to get everything right.

"His pace and forward movement will come later, but his crouch is perfectly balanced," Lionheart pointed out mildly.

"Which is better than Ravenpaw, I suppose," complained Tigerclaw. He cast a scornful look at the black cat. "Even after two moons of training, you're still putting all your weight on your left side."

Ravenpaw looked even more dejected, and Firepaw couldn't stop himself from blurting out, "His injury is bothering him, that's all!"

Tigerclaw whipped his head around and glared at Firepaw. "Injuries are a fact of life. He should be able to adapt. Even you, Firepaw, have learned something this morning. If Ravenpaw picked up things as quickly as you, he'd be a credit to me instead of an embarrassment. Imagine being shown up by a kittypet!" he spat angrily at his apprentice.

Firepaw felt his fur prickle with discomfort. He couldn't meet Ravenpaw's eyes, so he looked down at his paws.

"Well, *I'm* more lopsided than a one-legged badger," mewed Graypaw, breaking off from his careful stalking to stagger comically across the clearing. "I think I'll have to settle for hunting stupid mice. They won't stand a chance. I shall just wander up to them and sit on them till they surrender."

"Concentrate, young Graypaw. This is no time for your jokes!" meowed Lionheart sternly. "Perhaps you might focus your mind better if you try out your stalking for real."

All three apprentices looked up brightly.

"I want each one of you to try catching real prey," meowed Lionheart. "Ravenpaw, you look beside the Owltree. Graypaw, there might be something in that big bramble patch over there. And you, Firepaw, follow the rabbit track over that rise; you'll find the dry bed of a winter stream. You may find something there."

The three apprentices bounded away, even Ravenpaw finding some extra energy for this challenge.

With the blood pounding in his ears, Firepaw crept slowly up over the rise. Sure enough, a streambed cut through the trees ahead of him. In leaf-fall, he guessed it would carry the rainwater away from the forest and into the great river that cut through RiverClan territory. Now it was dry.

Firepaw crept quietly down the bank and crouched on its sandy floor. Every sense felt on fire with tension. Silently he scanned the empty stream for signs of life. He watched for any tiny movement, his mouth open so he could pick up the smallest scent, his ears twisted forward.

Then he smelled mouse. He recognized the odor instantly,

remembering his first taste the night before. Wild energy surged through him, but he remained motionless, trying desperately to pinpoint the prey.

He strained his ears forward until he picked up the rapid pulsing of a tiny mouse heart. Then a flash of brown caught his eye. The creature was scrambling through the long grass that draped the edges of the stream. Firepaw shifted closer, remembering to keep his weight on his haunches until he was within striking distance. Then he pushed back hard on his hindpaws and sprang, kicking up sand as he rose.

The mouse raced away. But Firepaw was quicker. He scooped it into the air with one paw, threw it onto the sandy streambed, and lunged on top of it. He killed it quickly with one sharp bite.

Firepaw carefully lifted the warm body between his teeth and returned with his tail held high to the hollow where Tigerclaw and Lionheart waited. He had made his first kill. He was a true ThunderClan apprentice now.

CHAPTER 6

Early-morning sunlight streamed down onto the forest floor as Firepaw roamed in search of prey. Two moons had passed since he had begun his training. He felt at ease in this environment now. His senses had been awoken and educated in the ways of the woods.

Firepaw paused to sniff the earth and the cold blind things that moved within it. He caught the scent of a Twoleg that had wandered the forest recently. Now that greenleaf was fully here, leaves were thick on the branches and tiny creatures were busy beneath the carpet of leaf mold.

Firepaw made a lean, strong shape as he moved silently through the trees, all his senses alert for the scent trail that would end in a swift kill. Today he had been set his first solo task. He was determined to do well, even if his task was only to bring back fresh-kill for the Clan.

He headed for the stream that he had crossed on that first trek through the ThunderClan hunting grounds. It gurgled and spattered as it ran downhill over the smooth, round pebbles. Firepaw paused briefly to lap at the cold, clear water, then lifted his head and tested the air again for any scent of prey.

The stench of a fox lay heavy in the air here. The smell was stale, so the fox must have drunk here earlier in the day. Firepaw recognized the odor; he had smelled it on his first visit to the forest. Since then, Lionheart had taught him it was fox-scent, but, apart from the glimpse of the fox's brush he had caught on that first outing, Firepaw had still never seen one properly.

He struggled to screen out the fox-stench and concentrate on prey-scent. Suddenly his whiskers prickled as he homed in on the warm blood-beat of prey—a water vole busy about its nest.

A moment later he saw the vole. The fat brown body was darting back and forth along the bank as it gathered grass stalks. Firepaw's mouth watered in anticipation. His last meal had been many hours ago, but he dared not hunt for himself until the Clan had been fed. He remembered the words repeated by Lionheart and Tigerclaw time and time again: "The Clan must be fed first."

Dropping into a crouch, Firepaw began to stalk the little creature. His orange belly fur brushed against the damp grass. He crept closer, his eyes never leaving his prey. Almost there. Another moment and he would be near enough to spring. . . .

Suddenly there was a loud rustle in the ferns behind him. The water vole's ears twitched and it disappeared down a hole in the bank.

Firepaw felt the hackles rising along his spine. Whatever had ruined his first good chance of catching prey would have to pay.

He sniffed the air. He could tell it was a cat, but he realized with a jolt that he couldn't identify which Clan it belonged to—the stale stench of fox still confused his smell-sense.

A growl rose in his throat as he began doubling back in a wide circle. He pricked up his ears and opened his eyes wide, seeking out any movement. He heard the undergrowth rustle again. It was louder now, off to one side. Firepaw edged closer. He could see the ferns moving, but the fronds still hid the enemy from view. A twig snapped with a sharp cracking noise. *From the noise it's making, it must be big,* Firepaw thought, preparing himself for a fierce battle.

He leaped for the trunk of an ash and climbed swiftly and silently up to an overhanging branch. Below him the invisible warrior came closer, and closer still. Firepaw held his breath, judging his moment as the ferns were pushed aside and a large grayish shape emerged.

"Gr-aaar!" The battle cry rumbled in Firepaw's throat. Claws unsheathed, he launched himself at the enemy and landed squarely on a set of furry, muscular shoulders. He dug in hard, gripping with thorn-sharp claws, ready to deal out a powerful warning bite.

"Wa-ah! What'sat?" The body below him shot straight up in the air, carrying him with it.

"Uh! Graypaw?" Firepaw recognized the astonished voice and caught his friend's familiar smell, but he was too fired up to loosen his grip.

"Ambush! Murr-oww!" spat Graypaw, not realizing that the cat gripping onto his back was Firepaw. He rolled over and over in an attempt to dislodge his attacker.

"Uufff-ff!" Firepaw rolled with him, squashed and flattened beneath the heavy body. "It's me—Firepaw!" he yowled as he struggled to pull free and sheath his claws. Rolling away, he sprang to his feet and gave himself a shake, which rippled all the way along his body to the end of his tail. "Graypaw! It's me," he repeated. "I thought you were an enemy warrior!"

Graypaw rose to his feet. He winced and shook himself. "It felt like it!" he grumbled, twisting his head around to lick his sore shoulders. "You've raked me to shreds!"

"Sorry," Firepaw mumbled. "But what was I supposed to think, with you creeping up on me like that?"

"Creeping up!" Graypaw's eyes were round with indignation. "That was my best stealth crouch."

"Stealth! You still stalk like a lopsided badger!" Firepaw teased. He flattened his ears playfully.

Graypaw gave a hiss of delight. "I'll show you lopsided!"

The two cats leaped at each other and began rolling over and over in a play-fight. Graypaw swiped at Firepaw with a hefty paw and the young apprentice's head buzzed with stars.

"Uufff-ff!" Firepaw shook his head to clear it and then launched a counterattack.

He managed to get in a couple of paw strikes before Graypaw overpowered him and held him down. Firepaw let his body go limp.

"You give up too easily!" mewed Graypaw, loosening his grip. As he did so, Firepaw sprang to his feet, firing Graypaw off his back and into the undergrowth.

Firepaw leaped after him and pinned him to the ground. "'Surprise is the warrior's greatest weapon,'" he crowed, quoting one of Lionheart's favorite phrases. He jumped nimbly off Graypaw and began to squirm around in the leaf litter, enjoying his easy victory and the warmth of the earth against his back.

Graypaw seemed unbothered by his second defeat of the morning. It was too fine a day for bad temper. "So how're you getting on with your task?" he asked.

Firepaw sat up. "I was doing just fine till you came along! I was about to catch a vole when your noisy trampling frightened it off."

"Oh, sorry," mewed Graypaw.

Firepaw looked at his crestfallen friend. "That's okay. You didn't know," he purred. "Anyway," he continued, "shouldn't you be heading to meet the patrol on the WindClan border? I thought you had to give them a message from Bluestar."

"Yeah, but there's plenty of time. I was going to do a little hunting first. I'm starving!"

"Me too. But I've got to hunt for the Clan before I can hunt for myself."

"I bet Dustpaw and Sandpaw used to swallow a shrew or two when they were on hunting duty," snorted Graypaw.

"I wouldn't be surprised if they did, but this is my first solo assignment. . . ."

"And you want to do it right; I know." Graypaw sighed.

"What is the message from Bluestar, anyway?" Firepaw asked, changing the subject.

"She wants the patrol to wait at the Great Sycamore until she joins them at sunhigh. Seems that some ShadowClan cats have been prowling around. Bluestar wants to check things out."

"You'd best get going then," Firepaw reminded him.

"The WindClan hunting grounds aren't too far from here. There's plenty of time," answered Graypaw confidently. "And I suppose I should help out after losing you that vole."

"It doesn't matter," Firepaw mewed. "I'll find another. It's such a warm day, there should be quite a few out and about."

"True. But you still have to catch them." Graypaw nibbled at a front claw, stripping off a piece of the outer sheath thoughtfully. "You know, that could take you until way past sunhigh, maybe even until sunset."

Firepaw nodded without enthusiasm as his belly gave a rumble. He would probably have to make three or four hunting trips before he had caught enough prey. Silverpelt would be in the sky before he got a chance to eat.

Graypaw stroked his whiskers. "Come on; I'll help you get started. I owe you that, at least. We should be able to catch a couple of voles before I have to get going."

Firepaw followed Graypaw upstream, glad of the company and the help. The fox-stench was still in the air, but suddenly it smelled stronger.

Firepaw paused. "Can you smell that?" he asked.

Graypaw stopped and sniffed the air too. "Fox. Yeah, I smelled it earlier."

"Doesn't it smell fresher to you now, though?" Firepaw asked.

Graypaw sniffed again, opening his mouth slightly. "You're right," he murmured, lowering his voice. He swiveled his head to look across the stream at the bushes in the woods beyond. "Look!" he whispered.

Firepaw looked. He saw something red and thick-haired moving among the bushes. It stepped into a clearing in the undergrowth and Firepaw saw a low body, glinting red in the dappled sunlight. Its tail was heavily furred and it had a long, narrow snout.

"So that's a fox?" Firepaw whispered. "What an ugly muzzle!"

"You can say that again!" agreed Graypaw.

"I was following one of those when we first . . . met," whispered Firepaw.

"More likely it was following you, you idiot!" hissed Graypaw. "Never trust a fox. Looks like a dog, behaves like a cat. We must warn the queens that one has strayed into our territory. Foxes are as bad as badgers when it comes to killing young kits. I'm just glad you didn't catch up with the one you saw last time. He'd have made mousemeat out of a tiny scrap like you." Firepaw looked a little put out, and Graypaw added, "You'd stand a better chance these days, though. Anyway, Bluestar will probably send a warrior patrol to scare it off. Put the queens' minds at rest."

The fox had not noticed them, so the two apprentices continued along the stream.

"So what does a badger look like?" Firepaw asked as they prowled along, sniffing to either side.

"Black and white, short legs. You'll know one when you meet

one. They're bad-tempered, lumbering animals. They're less likely to raid the nursery than a fox, but they have a vicious bite. How do you think old Halftail earned his name? He hasn't been able to climb a tree since a badger bit his tail off!"

"Why not?"

"Scared of falling. A cat needs his tail if he wants to land on his feet. It helps him spin in midair."

Firepaw nodded in understanding.

As Firepaw had predicted, hunting was good that day. Before long, Graypaw had pounced on a small mouse and Firepaw had caught a thrush. He quickly took its life. No time to practice killing techniques today; there were too many hungry mouths waiting back at camp. Firepaw kicked earth over the prey, so that it would be safe from predators until he came back for it.

Suddenly a squirrel broke cover.

Firepaw burst into action. "After it!" he called, pelting at full stretch over the springy woodland floor with Graypaw at his heels.

They slid to a halt as the squirrel scampered upward into a birch.

"Lost it!" Graypaw growled in disappointment.

Panting, the two cats stopped to catch their breath. The acrid stench that hit their mouths and noses surprised them.

"The Thunderpath," Firepaw mewed. "I didn't realize we'd come so far."

The two cats edged forward to peer out of the forest at the great, dark path. It was the first time they had been here alone. A trail of noisy creatures growled along the hard surface, their dead eyes staring straight ahead.

"Yuck!" Graypaw snorted. "Those monsters really stink!"

Firepaw twitched his ears in agreement. The choking smells made his throat sting. "Have you ever been across the Thunderpath?" he mewed.

Graypaw shook his head.

Firepaw took a step out of the cover of the forest. A border of oily grass lay between the trees and the Thunderpath. He crept slowly out onto it, and then shrank back as a stinking monster hurtled past.

"Hey! Where are you going?" Graypaw mewed.

Firepaw didn't reply. He waited till there were no monsters in sight. Then he edged forward again, across the grass, right to the edge of the path. Cautiously, he reached out a paw to touch it. It felt warm, almost sticky, heated by the sun. He looked up, staring across the Thunderpath. Was that a pair of eyes glinting out of the forest on the other side? He sniffed the air, but smelled nothing except the stench of the great gray path. The eyes on the other side were still shining in the shadows. Then they blinked, slowly.

Firepaw was sure now. It was a ShadowClan warrior, and it was staring straight at him.

"Firepaw!" Graypaw's voice made Firepaw jump, just as a huge monster, taller than a tree, roared past his nose. The wind from it almost toppled him over. Firepaw turned and ran as fast as he could back into the safety of the forest.

"You mouse-brained fool!" spat Graypaw. His whiskers

trembled with fear and anger. "What were you doing?"

"I just wondered what the Thunderpath felt like," Firepaw muttered. His whiskers were trembling too.

"Come on," hissed Graypaw edgily. "Let's get out of here!"

Firepaw followed Graypaw as he leaped away back into the forest. Once they were a safe distance from the Thunderpath, Graypaw stopped to catch his breath.

Firepaw sat down and began to lick his ruffled fur. "I think I saw a ShadowClan warrior," he mewed between licks. "In the forest on the other side of the Thunderpath."

"A ShadowClan warrior!" echoed Graypaw, his eyes wide. "Really?"

"I'm pretty sure."

"Well, it's a good thing that monster came past when it did," retorted Graypaw. "Where there's one ShadowClan warrior, there's more, and we're no match for them yet. We'd better get out of here." He looked up at the sun, which was almost directly overhead. "I'd better get a move on if I want to meet that patrol on time," he mewed. "See you later." He sprang away into the undergrowth, calling as he went, "You never know; Lionheart might let me come and help you with the hunting once I've delivered this message."

Firepaw watched him go. He envied Graypaw, wishing he were off to join a warrior patrol. But at least he'd have something to tell Dustpaw and Sandpaw when he returned to camp. Today he had seen his first ShadowClan warrior.

CHAPTER 7

Firepaw retraced his steps and headed back toward the stream. He thought of those eyes burning from the darkness of the ShadowClan territory.

Suddenly he caught a faint smell on the breeze.

A stranger! Perhaps that ShadowClan warrior . . .

Instantly a growl rumbled in Firepaw's throat. The scent message told him many things. The stranger was a she-cat, not young and definitely not from ThunderClan. She carried no distinct scent from any of the Clans, but Firepaw could tell she was tired, hungry, and sick, and she was in an ugly mood.

Dropping low, Firepaw moved forward, heading toward the scent. Then he paused in puzzlement. The warrior scent was fainter now. He sniffed again.

Suddenly, with a lightning movement, a snarling ball of fur burst from the bushes behind him.

Firepaw screeched in shock as the she-cat slammed into him, knocking him sideways. Two heavy paws clamped down onto his shoulders, and iron jaws closed around the back of his neck. "Murr-oww!" he grunted, already thinking fast. If

the other cat were to sink its fangs too deep, it would all be over.

He forced himself to go limp, relaxing his muscles as if in submission, and let out a pretend howl of alarm.

The she-cat opened her mouth to give a triumphant yowl. "Ah, a puny apprentice. Easy prey for Yellowfang," she hissed.

At the insult, Firepaw felt a surge of fury. *Just wait.* He'd show this coughed-up furball what kind of warrior he was! *But not yet,* he told himself. *Wait until you feel her teeth again.*

Yellowfang bit down. Firepaw surged upward with all the strength in his powerful young body. The she-cat gave a snarl of surprise as she was thrown clear. She tumbled backward into a gorse bush.

Firepaw shook himself. "Not such easy prey, huh?"

Yellowfang hissed defiance as she tore herself free from the clinging branches. "Not bad, young apprentice," she spat back. "But you'll need to do a lot better!"

Firepaw blinked when he saw his opponent clearly for the first time. The she-cat had a broad, almost flat face, and round orange eyes. Her dark gray fur was long and matted into smelly clumps. Her ears were torn and ragged, and her muzzle was traced with the scars of many old battles.

Firepaw stood his ground. He puffed out his chest and glared a challenge into the intruder's face. "You're in ThunderClan's hunting ground. Move on!"

"Who's going to make me?" Yellowfang drew back her lip defiantly, exposing stained and broken teeth. "I will hunt. *Then* I will leave. Or maybe I'll just stay awhile. . . ."

"Enough talk," Firepaw spat, feeling the stir of ancient cat spirits deep inside him. There was no trace of the house cat in him now. His warrior blood was up. He was itching to fight, to defend his territory and protect his Clan.

Yellowfang seemed to sense the change in him. Her fierce orange eyes sparked with new respect. Dipping her head and breaking eye contact, she started to back off. "No need to be hasty, now," she purred in a silky tone.

Firepaw wasn't fooled by her trickery. Claws extended and fur on end, he leaped forward, his war cry ringing out: "Grr-aaar!"

With a hiss of rage the other cat responded. Snarling and spitting, young cat and old locked together. They rolled over and over, teeth and claws flashing. Ears pressed flat to his head, Firepaw fought to get a grip. But the she-cat's clumpy fur snagged in his claws, and he couldn't break through to skin.

Then Yellowfang reared up on her back legs. With her filthy tail bristling, she looked even bigger.

Firepaw sensed Yellowfang's huge jaws lunging toward him. He leaned backward, just in time. *Snap!* Bared teeth closed on the air next to his ear.

Instinctively Firepaw lashed out with a backswipe. His paw caught the side of Yellowfang's head. The force of it sent shock waves up his front leg.

"Yee-ow!" Stunned, Yellowfang dropped onto four paws. She shook her head to clear it.

In the single heartbeat before the she-cat recovered,

Firepaw saw his chance. He threw himself forward, crouching low, and clamped his jaws tight on Yellowfang's back leg. "Mur-ugh!" The taste of the matted fur was horrible, but he chomped down hard.

"Reow-ow-wow!" Yellowfang screamed in agony and whipped around to snap at Firepaw's tail.

Her teeth connected and pain lanced up Firepaw's spine, but it only made him angrier. He ripped his tail from his opponent's grip, and lashed it back and forth in rage.

Yellowfang crouched, ready for a fresh attack. Her breath seemed to wheeze up from her foul-smelling lungs. The scent blasted Firepaw's nose. Up close, the message of desperation and weakness, and the aching void of the she-cat's hunger, was almost painful.

Something stirred inside him, an unwarriorlike feeling he didn't want: pity. He tried not to dwell on this instinct—he knew his loyalty must be to his Clan—but he couldn't shake free of it. "You speak from your heart, young Firepaw." Lionheart's words echoed in his head once more. "This will make you a stronger warrior one day." Then Tigerclaw's warning rang in his ears: "Or it might make him give in to kitty-pet weakness right at the moment of attack."

Yellowfang lunged forward and Firepaw jerked instantly back into aggression. The bigger cat tried to reach up onto his shoulders and get a killing grip, but this time she was hampered by her wounded leg.

"Gar-off!" Firepaw arched his spine, but Yellowfang managed to dig in her claws and hung on tight. The bigger cat's weight forced him to the ground.

Firepaw tasted earth on his tongue and spat out a mouthful of grit. "Pah!"

He twisted nimbly to avoid Yellowfang's thrashing back legs and the thorn-sharp claws that were trying to rake at his soft underbelly. Over and over they rolled, biting and snapping.

Moments later they broke apart. Firepaw was gasping for breath now. But he sensed that Yellowfang was weakening. The she-cat was badly wounded, and her back legs could barely support her scrawny body.

"Had enough yet?" Firepaw growled. If the intruder gave way, he'd let her go with just a warning bite to remember him by.

"Never!" Yellowfang hissed back bravely. But her injured leg gave way and she slumped to the ground. She tried to get up and failed. Her eyes were dull as she hissed up at Firepaw, "If I weren't so hungry and tired, I'd have shredded you into mousedust." The she-cat's mouth twisted in pain and defiance. "Finish me off. I won't stop you."

Firepaw hesitated. He'd never killed another cat before. Perhaps, in the heat of battle, he would, but a mercy killing, in cold blood? This was something very different.

"What are you waiting for?" Yellowfang taunted. "You're dithering like a kittypet!"

Firepaw smarted at the she-cat's words. Could she smell the scent of Twolegs on him, even now, after all this time?

"I'm an apprentice warrior of ThunderClan!" he snapped.

Yellowfang narrowed her eyes. She'd seen Firepaw flinch at her words and she knew she'd hit a nerve. "Ha," she snorted. "Don't tell me ThunderClan is so desperate they have to recruit kittypets now?"

"ThunderClan is not desperate!" hissed Firepaw.

"Prove it then! Act like a warrior and finish me off. You'll be doing me a favor."

Firepaw stared at her. He would not be goaded into killing this miserable creature. He felt his muscles relax as curiosity pricked him. How had a Clan cat gotten in such a state? ThunderClan elders were looked after better than kits! "You seem in an awful hurry to die," he meowed.

"Yeah? Well, that's my business, mousefodder," Yellowfang snapped. "What's your problem, kitty? Are you trying to *talk* me to death?"

Her words were brave, but Firepaw could smell the hunger and sickness that were coming off the other cat in waves. She was going to die anyway if she didn't eat soon. And since she could hardly hunt for herself, perhaps he should kill her now. The two cats looked at each other, uncertainty in both their gazes.

"Wait here," Firepaw ordered at last.

Yellowfang seemed to deflate. Her hackles smoothed out and her tail lost its gorse-bush stiffness. "Are you kidding, kitty? I'm going nowhere." She grunted, limping painfully toward a patch of soft heather. She flopped down and began licking her leg wound.

Firepaw glanced briefly over his shoulder at her and hissed

quietly in exasperation before heading for the trees.

As he padded silently through the ferns, sun-warmed odors filled his nose, and he caught the sour reek of a long-dead rat. He heard the scratching of insects beneath bark, the rustle of furry things scurrying over leaves. His first thought had been to go and dig up the thrush he had killed earlier, but that would take too long.

Maybe he should go and scoop up the rat carcass. Easy meat, but a starving cat needed fresh-kill. Only when times were very hard would a warrior eat crow food.

Just then he paused, scenting a young rabbit ahead. A few more steps and he saw it. Flattening himself down, he stalked the creature. He was barely a mouse-length away before it detected him. By then it was too late. The white bobtail darting away sent the thrill of the chase surging through Firepaw's veins. A rush of speed, a flash of claws, and he had it.

He held the wriggling body fast and finished it off quickly.

Yellowfang looked up tiredly as Firepaw dropped the rabbit on the ground beside her. Her grizzled jaw dropped. "Well, hello again, kitty! I thought you'd gone to fetch your little warrior friends."

"Yeah? Well, I might still do that. And don't call me kitty." Firepaw growled, shoving the rabbit nearer with his nose. He felt embarrassed by his kindness. "Look, if you don't want this . . ."

"Ah—no," Yellowfang meowed hastily. "I do want it."

Firepaw watched the she-cat rip open the prey and start to swallow it down. His own hunger rose up and his mouth filled with water. He knew he shouldn't even be *thinking* about eating. He still had to take back enough prey for the Clan, but the fresh-kill smelled delicious.

"Mmm-mm." A few minutes later, Yellowfang gave a huge sigh and flopped onto her side. "First fresh-kill I've had for days." She licked her muzzle clean and settled down to give herself a thorough wash.

As if one wash is going to make much difference, Firepaw thought, his nose twitching. She was the arch-cat of stench.

He eyed the tattered remnants of the prey. There wasn't much left to line a growing cat's belly, but his fight with Yellowfang had sharpened his appetite even more; he gave in to his hunger and gulped down the scraps. It was delicious. He licked his lips, savoring every last taste, tingling from head to paw.

Yellowfang watched him closely, showing her stained teeth. "Better than the muck Twolegs feed some of our brothers, isn't it?" she mewed slyly. Knowing she had found his sore spot, she was trying to antagonize him.

Firepaw ignored her and began to wash.

"It's poison," Yellowfang went on. "Rat droppings! Only a spineless bag of fur would accept such disgusting frogspawn—" She broke off and tensed. "Shhh . . . warriors coming."

Firepaw was also aware of cats approaching. He could hear their soft paw-fall on the leaf litter and the sound of fur swishing through branches. He smelled the wind brushing against their coats. Familiar smells. These were ThunderClan warriors, confident enough in their own territory not to care about the noise they made.

Firepaw licked his lips guiltily, hoping to wash away any traces of the scraps he'd just swallowed. Then he looked at Yellowfang and the fresh pile of rabbit bones that lay beside her. "The Clan must be fed *first!*" Lionheart's voice rang though his head once more. But surely he would understand why Firepaw had fed this wretched creature. His mind reeled, suddenly fearful of what would happen to him. His first apprentice task, and he had ended up breaking the warrior code!

CHAPTER 8

Yellowfang growled in defiance at the approaching pawsteps, but Firepaw could sense her panic. The she-cat struggled to her feet. "So long. Thanks for the meal." She tried to limp away on three legs and then winced in pain. "Nuh! This leg's stiffened up while I've been resting."

Now it was too late for her to run. Silent shadows slipped out of the trees, and in a heartbeat the ThunderClan patrol had encircled Firepaw and Yellowfang. Firepaw recognized them: Tigerclaw, Darkstripe, Willowpelt, and Bluestar, all of them lean and hard-muscled. Firepaw smelled Yellowfang's fear at the sight of them.

Graypaw followed close behind. He bounded out of the bushes and stood beside the warrior patrol.

Firepaw mewed a hasty greeting to his Clan. But only Graypaw returned it. "Hi, Firepaw!" he called out.

"Silence!" Tigerclaw growled.

Firepaw glanced at Yellowfang and groaned inwardly; he could still smell the fear-scent on her, but instead of cowering in submission, the scruffy creature was glaring in defiance.

"Firepaw?" Bluestar's question was cool and measured. "What have we here? An enemy warrior—and recently fed, by the smell of you both." Her eyes burned into him, and Firepaw dropped his head.

"She was weak and hungry . . ." he began.

"And what about you? Was your hunger so bad that you had to feed yourself before you had gathered prey for your Clan?" Bluestar went on. "I assume that you have a *very* good reason for breaking the warrior code?"

Firepaw was not fooled by the leader's soft tone. Bluestar was furious—and rightly so. He crouched lower to the ground.

Before he could speak there was a loud hiss from Tigerclaw. "Once a kittypet, always a kittypet!"

Bluestar ignored Tigerclaw and looked instead at Yellowfang. Suddenly she looked surprised. "Well, well, Firepaw! It seems you have captured us a ShadowClan cat. And one I know well. You are ShadowClan's medicine cat, aren't you?" she meowed to Yellowfang. "What are you doing so far into ThunderClan territory?"

"I *was* the ShadowClan medicine cat. Now I choose to travel alone," hissed Yellowfang.

Firepaw listened, astonished. Had he heard right? Yellowfang was a ShadowClan warrior? Her filthy condition must have masked her territorial scent. He might have enjoyed tackling her more if he'd known.

"Yellowfang!" Tigerclaw meowed mockingly. "It looks like you have fallen on hard times if you can be beaten by an apprentice!"

Now Darkstripe spoke. "This old cat is no use to us. Let's kill her now. As for this *kittypet*, he has broken the warrior code by feeding an enemy warrior. He should be punished."

"Keep your claws in, Darkstripe," Bluestar purred calmly. "All the Clans speak of Yellowfang's bravery and wisdom. It may help us to hear what she has to say. Come; we'll take her back to camp. Then we'll decide what to do with her—and with Firepaw. Can you walk?" she asked Yellowfang. "Or do you need help?"

"I've still got three good legs," the grizzled she-cat snapped back, limping forward.

Firepaw saw that Yellowfang's eyes were glazed with pain, but she seemed determined not to show any weakness. He noticed a look of respect flicker across Bluestar's face before the ThunderClan leader turned and slowly led the way through the trees. The other warriors took up positions on either side of Yellowfang, and the patrol moved off, carefully keeping pace with their lame prisoner.

Firepaw and Graypaw fell in step together at the back of the group.

"Have *you* heard of Yellowfang?" Firepaw hissed to Graypaw.

"A bit. Apparently she was a warrior before she became a medicine cat, which is unusual. I can't imagine her as a *loner,* though. She has lived her whole life in ShadowClan."

"What's a loner?"

Graypaw glanced at him. "A loner is a cat that isn't part of a Clan or cared for by Twolegs. Tigerclaw says they are untrustworthy and selfish. They often live around Twoleg dwellings, but belong to no one and catch their own food."

"I might end up a loner once Bluestar has finished with me," Firepaw mewed.

"Bluestar is very fair," Graypaw reassured him. "She won't throw you out. She certainly seems pleased to have such an important ShadowClan cat as a prisoner. I'm sure she's not going to make a fuss about your feeding the poor old mange-bag."

"But they keep moaning about prey being scarce! Oh, why did I eat that rabbit?" Firepaw felt shame burn through his fur.

"Well, yeah." Graypaw nudged his friend. "That *was* mouse-brained. You really broke the warrior code there, but no cat is perfect!"

Firepaw didn't answer but trekked onward with a heavy heart. This was not the way he had hoped his first solo task would end.

As the patrol passed the sentries who guarded the camp entrance, the rest of ThunderClan came running to welcome their warriors home.

Queens, kits, and elders crowded on either side. They peered curiously at Yellowfang as she was led into the camp. Some of the elders recognized the old she-cat. Word spread quickly through the Clan that this was ShadowClan's medicine cat, and a steady jeering hum rose up around them.

Yellowfang seemed deaf to the taunts. Firepaw couldn't

help admiring the way she limped with dignity through the corridor of stares and insults. He knew she was in a great deal of pain, and hungry in spite of the rabbit he had caught for her.

When the patrol reached the Highrock, Bluestar nodded toward the dusty ground in front of it. Yellowfang followed the ThunderClan leader's silent command, sinking gratefully onto the earth. Still ignoring the hostile stares around her, she began licking her wounded leg.

Firepaw noticed Spottedleaf emerge from her corner. She must have scented the presence of an injured cat in the camp. He watched the crowd part to let the young tortoiseshell through.

Yellowfang glared at Spottedleaf and hissed, "I know how to take care of my own wounds. I don't need your help."

Spottedleaf said nothing but nodded respectfully and stepped back.

Some of the cats had been out hunting, and fresh-kill was brought for the returning warriors to eat. They each took some food and carried it away to the nettle patch to eat it. Then the other Clan cats crowded forward to take their own share.

Firepaw paced hungrily around the clearing and watched as the cats crouched in their usual groups, chewing and gulping. He longed for a morsel, but didn't dare to take anything from the pile. He had broken the warrior code. He guessed that this meant he was forbidden his share in the fresh-kill.

He paused beside the Highrock where Bluestar was sharing

words with Tigerclaw. Uncertain, Firepaw looked to his leader for a signal that he was allowed to eat. But the gray cat and her senior warrior were busy murmuring at one another in low tones. Firepaw wondered if they were talking about him. Desperate to know his fate, he strained his ears to hear what they were saying.

Tigerclaw's yowl sounded impatient. "It's just too dangerous to bring an enemy warrior into the heart of ThunderClan! Now that *she* knows the camp, even the youngest ShadowClan kit will hear of it. We will have to move."

"Calm down, Tigerclaw," Bluestar purred. "Why should we move? Yellowfang says that she is traveling alone now. There is no reason for ShadowClan to hear of it."

"Do you really believe that? What on earth was that foolish kittypet thinking of?" Tigerclaw spat.

"But think for a moment, Tigerclaw," mewed Bluestar. "Why would the ShadowClan medicine cat choose to leave her Clan? You seem to be afraid that Yellowfang will share our Clan secrets with ShadowClan, but have you thought about how many ShadowClan secrets she might share with *us*?"

Firepaw could see by the way Tigerclaw's fur began to flatten that Bluestar's words made sense. The warrior nodded briefly, and then stalked off to take his share of the fresh-kill.

Bluestar remained where she was. She looked out across the clearing, where some of the younger kits were fighting and tumbling playfully in the dust. Then she stood up and began to walk toward Firepaw. His heart lurched. What was she going to say to him?

But Bluestar walked straight past him. She did not even glance at him; her eyes were clouded with unknown distant thoughts. "Frostfur!" she called out as she approached the nursery.

A pure white cat with dark blue eyes slipped out of the brambles. Inside, the noise of mewling grew louder.

"Hush, kits," purred the white cat reassuringly. "I won't be long." Then she turned to her leader. "Yes, Bluestar? What is it?"

"One of our apprentices has seen a fox in the area. Warn the other queens to guard the nursery carefully. And make sure all kits less than six moons stay inside the camp until our warriors have driven it away."

Frostfur nodded. "I will pass on the warning, Bluestar. Thank you." Then she turned and squeezed back into the nursery to quiet the crying kits.

At last Bluestar strode over to the pile of fresh-kill and took her share. A plump wood pigeon had been left for her there. Firepaw looked on longingly as she carried it away to eat with the senior warriors.

Finally his hunger drove him forward. Graypaw was with Ravenpaw, wolfing down a small finch beside the tree stump. He saw Firepaw approach the pile and flicked his head encouragingly. Firepaw bent his neck, ready to take a small wood mouse in his teeth.

"Not for you," Tigerclaw growled, striding up behind him and pawing the mouse away. "You didn't bring back any prey. The elders will eat your share. Take it to them."

Firepaw looked over to Bluestar.

She nodded shortly. "Do as he says."

Obediently, Firepaw picked up the mouse and carried it across to Smallear. The delicious smell of it wafted up Firepaw's nose. He wanted nothing more than to crunch it up with his strong teeth. He could almost feel its life energy flooding his young body.

With great self-control, he laid the prey down in front of the gray tom and then backed away politely. He expected no thanks and was offered none.

Now he was glad that he had gobbled up the remains of the rabbit he had caught for Yellowfang. There would be nothing else for him to eat until he went out hunting again tomorrow.

Firepaw wandered over to Graypaw. His friend had eaten his fill and lay with Ravenpaw outside the apprentices' den. He was stretched out on his side, rhythmically washing a foreleg.

Graypaw saw Firepaw approach, and paused in his licking. "Has Bluestar mentioned your punishment yet?" he asked.

"Not yet," Firepaw replied gloomily.

Graypaw narrowed his eyes sympathetically and said nothing.

Bluestar's call sounded across the clearing. "Let all those cats old enough to catch their own prey join together for a meeting of our Clan."

Most of the warriors had finished eating and, like Graypaw, were busy grooming themselves. They lifted themselves gracefully to their paws and walked over to the Highrock, where Bluestar waited to speak.

"Come on," mewed Graypaw. He leaped up. Ravenpaw and Firepaw followed him as he scampered over and nudged his way forward into a good position.

"I'm sure you have all heard about the prisoner we brought back with us today," Bluestar began. "But there is something else you need to know." She glanced down at the raddled she-cat who lay very still beside the Highrock. "Can you hear me from there?" she asked.

"I may be old, but I'm not deaf yet!" Yellowfang spat in reply.

Bluestar ignored the prisoner's hostile tone and continued. "I'm afraid I have some very grave news. Today I traveled with a patrol into WindClan territory. The air was filled with the scent of ShadowClan. Almost every tree had been sprayed by ShadowClan warriors. And we met no WindClan cats even though we journeyed deep into their heartland."

Her words were met with silence. Firepaw saw confusion in the faces of the Clan cats.

"Do you mean ShadowClan has chased them out?" called Smallear hesitantly.

"We can't be sure," Bluestar meowed. "Certainly the scent of ShadowClan was everywhere. We found blood, too, and fur. There must have been a battle, though we found no bodies from either Clan."

A shocked yowl rose from the crowd in a single voice. Firepaw felt the cats around him stiffen with shock and fury.

Never before had one Clan driven another from its hunting grounds.

"How can WindClan have been driven out?" One-eye croaked hoarsely. "ShadowClan is fierce, but WindClan is many. They have lived in the uplands for generations. Why have they been chased out now?" She shook her head anxiously, her whiskers trembling.

"I don't know the answers to any of your questions," meowed Bluestar. "It is well known that ShadowClan has recently appointed a new leader, following the death of Raggedstar. Their new leader, Brokenstar, gave no hint of any threat when we met him at the last Gathering."

"Perhaps Yellowfang has answers?" snarled Darkstripe. "After all, she is of ShadowClan!"

"I am no traitor! Nothing would make me share the secrets of ShadowClan with a brute like you!" growled Yellowfang, glaring aggressively at Darkstripe. The ThunderClan warrior moved forward, ears flat, eyes closed to slits, ready for a fight.

"Stop!" yowled Bluestar.

Darkstripe immediately halted in his tracks, even though Yellowfang goaded him on with blazing eyes and a ferocious hiss.

"That's enough!" Bluestar growled. "This situation is too serious for us to be fighting among ourselves. ThunderClan must prepare itself. From this moonrise onward, warriors will travel in larger groups. Other Clan members will remain close to the camp. Patrols will travel the boundary edges more frequently, and all the kits must stay in the nursery."

The cats below her nodded in agreement.

Bluestar continued. "Our need for warriors is our greatest obstacle. We shall get around this by speeding up the training of our apprentices. They need to be ready even sooner to fight for our Clan."

Firepaw saw Dustpaw and Sandpaw exchange a thrilled glance. Graypaw was gazing up at Bluestar, his eyes wide with excitement. Ravenpaw just shuffled his paws anxiously. The black apprentice's wide eyes showed worry rather than excitement.

Bluestar went on. "One young cat has been sharing mentors with Graypaw and Ravenpaw. By teaching him, I shall speed up the training of all three apprentices." She paused and looked down at her Clan. "I shall take on Firepaw as my own apprentice."

Firepaw opened his eyes wide in amazement. Bluestar was to be his mentor?

Beside him, Graypaw gasped, unable to hide his surprise. "What an honor! It's been *moons* since Bluestar had an apprentice. Usually she trains only the kits of deputies!"

Then a familiar voice rose from the front of the crowd. It was Tigerclaw. "So Firepaw is to be rewarded, not punished, for feeding an enemy warrior when he should have been feeding his own Clan?"

"Firepaw is my apprentice now. I will deal with him," answered Bluestar. She stared into Tigerclaw's fierce eyes for a moment before lifting her head to address the whole Clan once more. "Yellowfang will be allowed to stay here until she has recovered her strength. We are warriors, not savages. She is to be treated with respect and courtesy."

"But the Clan cannot support Yellowfang," Darkstripe protested. "We have too many mouths to feed already."

"Yeah!" Graypaw whispered into Firepaw's ear. "And some of them are bigger than others!"

"I don't need anyone to care for me!" spat Yellowfang. "And I'll split open anyone who tries!"

"Friendly, isn't she?" Graypaw murmured.

Firepaw flicked the tip of his tail in silent agreement. There were muffled meows from the other warriors as they grudgingly recognized the enemy warrior's fighting spirit.

Bluestar ignored the murmuring. "We shall kill two prey with one blow, as it were. Firepaw, as punishment for breaking the warrior code, it will be your responsibility to care for Yellowfang. You will hunt for her and tend her wounds. You will fetch fresh bedding and clear away her dirt."

"Yes, Bluestar," mewed Firepaw, his head bowed in submission. *Clear away her dirt!* he thought to himself. *Ugh!*

Mocking yowls came from Dustpaw and Sandpaw. "Good idea!" hissed Dustpaw. "Firepaw had better be good at cracking fleas!"

"And hunting!" added Sandpaw. "That sack of bones is going to need feeding up!"

"Enough!" Bluestar interrupted them. "I hope Firepaw will find no shame in caring for Yellowfang. She is a healer, and she is his elder. For those reasons alone he should respect her!" She shot a sharp glance at Sandpaw and

Dustpaw. "And there is no humiliation in caring for another cat when it is unable to take care of itself. The meeting is over. I would like to speak to my senior warriors alone now." With that, she jumped down from the Highrock and marched toward her den.

Lionheart followed her. The other Clan cats began to move away from the Highrock. One or two congratulated Firepaw on being chosen as Bluestar's apprentice; others mockingly wished him luck looking after Yellowfang. Firepaw felt so dazed by Bluestar's announcement that he just nodded blankly.

Longtail padded up to him. The vee-shaped nick that Firepaw had cut into the tip of his ear still showed. The young warrior drew back his whiskers into an ugly snarl. "Well, I hope you'll think twice about bringing strays back into the camp next time," he sneered. "Like I said, outsiders *always* bring trouble."

CHAPTER 9

"I'd go and see to Yellowfang, if I were you," whispered Graypaw, as Longtail strode away. "She's doesn't look very happy."

Firepaw glanced over at the old she-cat. She was still lying beside the Highrock. Graypaw was right; she was glaring at him.

"Well, here goes," he mewed. "Wish me luck!"

"You'll need the whole of StarClan on your side for this one," answered Graypaw. "Call out if you need a hand. If she looks like she's going to have you, I'll sneak up behind her and whack her on the head with a stiff rabbit."

Firepaw purred with amusement and trotted off toward Yellowfang. His cheerfulness quickly evaporated as he neared the injured queen.

The old cat was clearly in a terrible mood. She hissed a warning and showed her teeth. "Stop right there, *kittypet!*"

Firepaw sighed. It seemed he was in for a fight. He was still hungry and beginning to feel tired. He longed to curl up in his nest for an afternoon nap. The last thing he wanted was to argue with this pitiful clump of fur and teeth. "You can call me what you like," he mewed wearily. "I'm just following Bluestar's orders."

"You *are* a kittypet, though, aren't you?" Yellowfang wheezed.

She's tired too, Firepaw thought. There was less fire in her voice, although her spite was as strong as ever.

"I used to live with Twolegs when I was a kitten," Firepaw replied calmly.

"Your mother a kittypet? Your father a kittypet?"

"Yes, they were." Firepaw looked down at the ground, feeling resentment burn inside him. It was bad enough that members of his own Clan still viewed him as an outsider. He certainly didn't have to answer to this foul-tempered prisoner.

Yellowfang seemed to take his silence as an invitation to go on. "Kittypet blood is not the same as warrior blood. Why don't you run home to your Twolegs now instead of looking after me? It's humiliating, being fussed over by a lowborn cat like *you*!"

Firepaw's patience ran out. He snarled, "You'd still feel humiliated if I *were* warrior-born. You'd feel ashamed whether I was a precious she-cat from your own Clan or a wretched Twoleg that had picked you off the ground." He lashed his tail from side to side. "It's the fact that you need to rely on *any* cat that you find so humiliating!"

Yellowfang stared at him, her orange eyes very wide.

Firepaw carried on fiercely: "You're just going to have to get used to being cared for until you are well enough to look after yourself, you spiteful old bone bag!"

He stopped as Yellowfang began to make a low, harsh, wheezing sound.

Alarmed, Firepaw took a step toward her. The she-cat was trembling all over and her eyes had narrowed into tiny slits. Was she having some kind of a fit?

"Look, I didn't mean . . ." he began, before he suddenly realized that she was *laughing*!

"Mr-ow, ow-ow," she mewled, a purr rumbling up from deep inside her chest.

Firepaw didn't know what to do.

"You have spirit, kittypet," Yellowfang croaked, stopping at last. "Now, I'm tired and my leg hurts. I need sleep and something to put on this wound. Go and find that pretty little medicine cat of yours and ask her for some herbs. I think you'll find a goldenrod poultice would help. And, while you're at it, I wouldn't mind a few poppy seeds to chew on. The pain is killing me!"

Stunned by her change of mood, Firepaw turned quickly and sprinted toward Spottedleaf's den.

He had never been in this part of the camp before. With his ears pricked, he padded through a cool green tunnel of ferns that led into a small grassy clearing. A tall rock stood at one side, split down the middle by a crack wide enough for a cat to make its den inside. Out of this opening trotted Spottedleaf. As usual, she looked bright-eyed and friendly, her dappled coat gleaming with a hundred shades of amber and brown.

Firepaw shyly mewed a greeting, and reeled off Yellowfang's list of herbs and seeds.

"I've got most of those in my den," replied Spottedleaf. "I'll fetch some marigold leaves too. If she dresses her wound with that, it'll keep off any infection. Wait here."

"Thanks," Firepaw mewed as the medicine cat disappeared back into her den. He strained his eyes, trying to catch a glimpse of her inside. But the den was too dark to see anything; he could only hear the sound of rustling and smell the heady scents of unfamiliar herbs.

Spottedleaf emerged from the gloom and dropped a bundle folded in leaves by Firepaw's feet. "Tell Yellowfang to go easy on the poppy seeds. I don't want her to deaden the pain entirely. A little pain can be useful, as it will help me judge how well she is healing."

Firepaw nodded and picked up the herbs with his teeth. "Thanks, Spottedleaf!" he mewed through the mouthful of leaves, then headed back through the fern tunnel into the main clearing.

Tigerclaw was sitting outside the warriors' den, watching him closely. As Firepaw trotted over to Yellowfang, carrying the herbs, he could feel the amber-eyed stare burning the fur on the back of his neck. He turned his head and looked at Tigerclaw curiously. The warrior narrowed his eyes and looked away.

Firepaw dropped the bundle beside Yellowfang.

"Good," she meowed. "Now, before you leave me in peace, find me something to eat. I'm starving!"

The sun had risen three times since Yellowfang had entered the camp. Firepaw woke early and nudged Graypaw, who was still asleep beside him, his nose tucked under his thick tail. "Wake up," Firepaw mewed. "Or you'll be late for training."

Graypaw lifted his head sleepily and growled in reluctant agreement.

Firepaw prodded Ravenpaw.

The black cat opened his eyes immediately and leaped to his feet. "What is it?" he mewed, looking around wildly.

"Calm down, Ravenpaw. It's time for training soon," Firepaw soothed.

Dustpaw and Sandpaw began to stir too, in their mossy nests on the far side of the den. Firepaw stood up and pushed his way out of the ferns.

The morning was warm. Firepaw could see a deep blue sky through the leaves and branches that overhung the camp. Today, however, a heavy dew glistened on the fern fronds and sparkled on the grass. Firepaw sniffed the air. Greenleaf was drawing to a close, and soon it would start to feel colder.

He lay down and rolled in the earth beside the tree stump, stretching his legs and tipping his head back to rub it on the cool ground. Then he flipped over onto his side, and looked across the clearing to see if Yellowfang was awake yet.

She had been given a resting place at the other end of the fallen tree where the elders gathered to eat. Her nest lay tucked against its mossy trunk, out of hearing of the elders, but in full view of the warriors' den across the clearing. Firepaw could just see a mound of pale gray fur, rising and falling in time to a gentle rumble of sleep.

Graypaw trotted out of the den behind him, followed by

Sandpaw and Dustpaw. Ravenpaw appeared last, with a nervous glance around the clearing before he emerged fully into the open.

"Another day looking after that mangy old fleabag, eh, Firepaw?" mewed Dustpaw. "I bet you wish you were out training with us."

Firepaw sat up and shook the dust from his fur. He wasn't going to let himself get annoyed by Dustpaw's taunts.

"Don't worry, Firepaw," murmured Graypaw. "Bluestar will have you back in training before long."

"Perhaps she thinks a kittypet is better off staying in camp, tending to the sick," mewed Sandpaw rudely, tossing her sleek ginger head and throwing him a scornful look.

Firepaw decided to ignore her barbed comments. "What is Whitestorm teaching you today, Sandpaw?" he mewed.

"We're doing battle training today. He's going to teach me how a real warrior fights," Sandpaw replied proudly.

"Lionheart's taking me to the Great Sycamore," mewed Graypaw, "to practice my climbing. I'd best go. He'll be waiting."

"I'll come with you to the top of the ravine," mewed Firepaw. "I have to catch breakfast for Yellowfang. Coming, Ravenpaw? Tigerclaw must have something planned for you."

Ravenpaw sighed and nodded, then followed Graypaw and Firepaw as they trotted out of the camp. Even though his injury was completely healed, he still seemed to have little enthusiasm for warrior training.

⚜   ⚜   ⚜

"Here," mewed Firepaw. He dropped a large mouse and a chaffinch onto the ground beside Yellowfang.

"About time," she growled. The she-cat had still been sleeping when Firepaw had entered the camp after his hunting trip. But the smell of fresh-kill must have woken her, for now she had pulled herself into a sitting position.

She dropped her head and hungrily gulped down Firepaw's offerings. She had developed a massive appetite as her strength returned. Her wound was healing well, but her temper remained as fierce and unpredictable as ever.

She finished her meal and complained, "The base of my tail itches like fury, but I can't reach it. Give it a wash, will you?"

With an inward shudder, Firepaw crouched down and set to work.

As he cracked the plump fleas between his teeth, he noticed a gang of small kits tumbling in the dusty earth nearby. They were mauling each other and play-fighting, sometimes quite viciously. Yellowfang, who had closed her eyes as Firepaw groomed her, half opened one eye to observe the kits as they played. To his surprise, Firepaw felt her spine stiffen beneath his teeth.

He listened for a moment to the tiny yelps and squeaks of the kits.

"Feel my teeth, Brokenstar!" mewed one small tabby. He leaped onto the back of a little gray-and-white kit, who was pretending to be the ShadowClan leader. The two kits bundled toward the Highrock. Suddenly the gray-and-white kit gave a mighty heave and flung the tabby from his back. With a startled squeak, the little tabby cannoned into Yellowfang's side.

Instantly the old she-cat leaped to her feet, fur on end, spitting violently. "Stay away from me, you scrap of fur!" she hissed.

The tabby kit took one look at the furious cat, turned tail, and ran. He hid himself behind a tabby queen, who was staring furiously across the clearing at Yellowfang.

The gray-and-white kit froze where he stood. Then, paw by paw, he cautiously backed away toward the safety of the nursery.

Yellowfang's reaction had shocked Firepaw. He thought he'd seen her at her most vicious when they fought after their first meeting, but her eyes burned with a new rage now. "I think the kits are finding it hard being confined to camp," he mewed cautiously. "They're getting restless."

"I don't care how restless they are," growled Yellowfang. "Just keep them away from me!"

"Don't you like kits?" Firepaw asked, curious in spite of himself. "Did you never have kits of your own?"

"Don't you know medicine cats don't have kits?" hissed Yellowfang furiously.

"But I heard you were a warrior before that," Firepaw ventured.

"I have no kits!" Yellowfang spat. She snatched her tail away from him and sat up. "Anyway"—her voice suddenly lowered, and she sounded almost wistful—"accidents seem to happen to kits when I'm around them."

Her orange eyes clouded with emotion. She laid her chin flat on her forepaws and stared ahead. Firepaw watched her shoulders sink as she released a long, silent sigh.

Firepaw looked at her curiously. What could she mean? Was the old she-cat being serious? It was hard to tell; Yellowfang seemed to swing from mood to mood so quickly. He shrugged to himself and went on with the grooming.

"There are a couple of ticks I couldn't pull out," he told her when he had finished.

"I should hope you didn't even try, you idiot!" snapped Yellowfang. "I don't want any tick heads embedded in my rear, thank you very much. Ask Spottedleaf for a little mouse bile to rub on them. A splash of that in their breathing holes and they'll soon loosen their grip."

"I'll get some now!" Firepaw offered. He was glad of a chance to get away from the grumpy cat for a while. And it was certainly no hardship to go and see Spottedleaf again.

He walked toward the fern tunnel. Cats crossed the clearing around him, carrying sticks and twigs in their teeth. While he had been grooming Yellowfang, the camp had grown active. It had been like this every day since Bluestar had announced WindClan's disappearance. The queens were weaving twigs and leaves into a dense green wall around the sides of the nursery, making sure that the narrow entrance was the only way in and out of the bramble patch. Other cats were working at the edges of the camp, filling in any spaces in the thick undergrowth.

Even the elders were busy, scraping out a hole in the ground. Warriors filed steadily past, piling pieces of fresh-kill beside them, ready to be stored inside the newly dug hole. There was an air of quiet concentration, a determination to make the Clan as secure and well supplied as possible.

If ShadowClan made a move on their territory, ThunderClan would shelter inside the camp. They would not let themselves be driven from their hunting grounds as easily as WindClan had been.

Darkstripe, Longtail, Willowpelt, and Dustpaw were waiting silently at the camp entrance. Their eyes were fixed on the opening to the gorse tunnel. A patrol was just returning, dusty and paw-sore. As soon as the warriors entered the camp, Darkstripe and his companions approached and exchanged words with them. Then they slipped quickly out of the camp. ThunderClan's borders were not being left unguarded for a moment.

Firepaw headed down the fern tunnel that led to Spottedleaf's den. As he entered the clearing, he could see Spottedleaf was preparing some sweet-smelling herbs.

"Can I have some mouse bile for Yellowfang's ticks?" Firepaw mewed.

"In a moment," replied Spottedleaf, pawing two piles of herbs together and mixing the fragrant heap with one delicately extended claw.

"Busy?" Firepaw asked, settling down on a warm patch of earth.

"I want to be prepared for any casualties," Spottedleaf

murmured, glancing up at him with her clear amber eyes. Firepaw met her gaze for a moment, then looked away, an uncomfortable feeling prickling his fur. Spottedleaf turned her attention back to the herbs.

Firepaw waited, happy to sit quietly and watch her at work.

"Right," she mewed at last. "What was it you wanted? Mouse bile?"

"Yes, please." Firepaw stood up and stretched each back leg in turn. The sun had warmed his fur and made him feel sleepy.

Spottedleaf bounded into her den and brought something out. She held it gingerly in her mouth. It was a small wad of moss dangling on the end of a thin strip of bark. She passed it to Firepaw. He tasted her warm, sweet breath as he took the bark strip between his teeth.

"The moss is soaked in bile," Spottedleaf explained. "Don't get any in your mouth, or you'll have a foul taste for days. Press it onto the ticks and then wash your paws—in a stream, not with your tongue!"

Firepaw nodded and trotted back to Yellowfang, feeling suddenly cheerful and tingling with energy.

"Hold still!" he mewed to the old she-cat. Carefully he used his forepaws to press the moss onto each tick.

"You may as well clear away my dirt now your paws are already foul!" she meowed when he had finished. "I'm going to take a nap." She yawned, revealing her blackened and broken teeth. The warmth of the day was making her sleepy, too.

"Then you can go and do whatever it is you apprentices do," she murmured.

When Firepaw had cleared away Yellowfang's dirt, he left her dozing and made his way to the gorse tunnel. He was keen to get to the stream and rinse his paws.

"Firepaw!" a voice called from the side of the clearing.

Firepaw turned. It was Halftail.

"Where are you off to?" meowed the old cat curiously. "You ought to be helping with the preparations."

"I've just been putting mouse bile on Yellowfang's ticks," replied Firepaw.

Amusement flickered through Halftail's whiskers. "So now you're off to the nearest stream! Well, don't come back without fresh-kill. We need as much as we can find."

"Yes, Halftail," Firepaw replied.

He made his way out of the camp and up the side of the ravine. He trotted down to the stream where he and Graypaw had hunted on the day he had found Yellowfang. Without hesitating he jumped down into the cold, clear water. It came up to his haunches, and wet his belly fur. The shock made him gasp, and he shivered.

A rustle in the bushes above him made him look up, although the familiar scent that reached his nose told him there was nothing to be alarmed about.

"What are you doing in there?" Graypaw and Ravenpaw were standing looking at him as if he were mad.

"Mouse bile." Firepaw grimaced. "Don't ask! Where are Lionheart and Tigerclaw?"

"They've gone to join the next patrol," answered Graypaw. "They ordered us to spend the rest of the afternoon hunting."

"Halftail told me the same thing," Firepaw mewed, flinching as a chilly current of water rushed around his paws. "Everyone's busy back at camp. You'd think we were about to be attacked at any moment." He climbed up onto the bank, dripping.

"Who says we won't be?" mewed Ravenpaw, his eyes flicking from side to side as if he expected an enemy patrol to leap out of the bushes at any time.

Firepaw looked at the heap of fresh-kill that was piled beside the two apprentices. "Looks like you've done all right today," he mewed.

"Yeah," mewed Graypaw proudly. "And we've still got the rest of the afternoon to hunt. Do you want to join us?"

"You bet!" Firepaw purred. He gave himself a final shake, then bounded into the undergrowth after his friends.

Firepaw could tell that the cats back at camp were impressed with the amount of prey the three apprentices had managed to catch during their afternoon hunt. They were welcomed back with high tails and friendly nuzzles. It took them four journeys to carry their bumper catch to the storage hole the elders had dug.

Lionheart and Tigerclaw had just returned with their patrol as Firepaw, Graypaw, and Ravenpaw carried their last load into the camp.

"Well done, you three," meowed Lionheart. "I hear you've

been busy. The store is almost full. You might as well add that last lot to the pile of fresh-kill for tonight. And take some of it back to your den with you. You deserve a feast!"

The three apprentices flicked their tails with delight.

"I hope you've not been neglecting Yellowfang with all this hunting, Firepaw," Tigerclaw growled warningly.

Firepaw shook his head impatiently, eager to get away. He was starving. He had obeyed the warrior code this time and not eaten a morsel while he was hunting for the Clan. Nor had Graypaw or Ravenpaw.

They trotted away and dropped the last of their catch on the fresh-kill that already lay at the center of the clearing. Then each of them took a piece and carried it back to their tree stump. The den was empty.

"Where are Dustpaw and Sandpaw?" asked Ravenpaw.

"They must still be out on patrol," Firepaw guessed.

"Good," meowed Graypaw. "Peace and quiet."

They ate their fill and lay back to wash. The cool evening air was welcome after the heat of the day.

"Hey! Guess what!" mewed Graypaw suddenly. "Ravenpaw managed to squeeze a compliment out of old Tigerclaw this morning!"

"Really?" Firepaw gasped. "What on earth did you do to please Tigerclaw—fly?"

"Well," Ravenpaw began shyly, looking at his paws, "I caught a crow."

"How'd you manage that?" Firepaw mewed, impressed.

"It was an old one," Ravenpaw admitted modestly.

"But it was huge," added Graypaw. "Even Tigerclaw couldn't find fault with that! He's been in such a bad mood since Bluestar took you on as her apprentice." He licked his paw thoughtfully for a moment. "Hang on, make that since Lionheart was made deputy."

"He's just worried about ShadowClan, and the extra patrols," mewed Ravenpaw, hastily. "You should try not to annoy him."

Their conversation was interrupted by a loud yowl from the other side of the clearing.

"Oh, no." Firepaw groaned, getting to his paws. "I forgot to take Yellowfang her share!"

"You wait here," mewed Graypaw, leaping up. "I'll take her something."

"No, I'd better go," Firepaw protested. "This is my punishment, not yours."

"No one will notice," argued Graypaw. "They're all busy eating. You know me: quiet as a mouse, quick as a fish. Wait here."

Firepaw sat down again, unable to hide his relief. He watched his friend trot away from the tree stump to the pile of fresh-kill.

As if he were carrying out orders, Graypaw confidently picked out two of the juiciest-looking mice. Quickly, he began to pad across the clearing toward Yellowfang.

"Stop, Graypaw!" A loud growl rumbled from the entrance to the warriors' den. Tigerclaw strode out and marched over to Graypaw. "Where are you taking those mice?" he demanded.

With a sinking feeling in his stomach, Firepaw watched, helpless, from the tree stump. Beside him, Ravenpaw froze midchew and crouched over his meal with his eyes wider than ever.

"Umm . . ." Graypaw dropped the mice and shuffled his paws uncomfortably.

"Not helping young Firepaw by feeding that greedy traitor over there, are you?"

Firepaw watched Graypaw study his paws for a moment. Finally he replied, "I, er, I was just feeling hungry. I was going to take them off and eat them by myself. If I let that pair get a look in"—he glanced at Firepaw and Ravenpaw—"they'll leave me with nothing but bones and fur."

"Oh, *really*?" mewed Tigerclaw. "Well, if you're so hungry, you might as well eat them here and now!"

"But—" Graypaw began, looking up at the senior warrior in alarm.

"Now!" growled Tigerclaw.

Graypaw bent his head quickly and began to eat the mice. He demolished the first one in a couple of bites and swallowed it quickly. The second mouse took longer for him to eat. Firepaw thought he'd never manage to swallow it, and his own stomach clenched in sympathy, but eventually Graypaw gave a final, difficult gulp and the last bit of mouse disappeared.

"Better now?" asked Tigerclaw, his voice smooth with mock sympathy.

"Much," replied Graypaw, stifling a burp.

"Good." Tigerclaw stalked off again, back to his den.

Graypaw slunk uncomfortably back to Firepaw and Ravenpaw.

"Thanks, Graypaw," Firepaw mewed gratefully, nudging his friend's soft fur. "That was quick thinking."

The noise of Yellowfang's yowl rose into the air once more. Firepaw sighed and got to his paws. He would make sure he took her enough to see her through the night. He wanted to turn in early. His stomach was full and his paws were tired.

"Are you okay, Graypaw?" he asked as he turned to leave.

"Mrr-ow-ow," moaned Graypaw. He was hunched into a low crouch, squinting with pain. "I've eaten too much!"

"Go and see Spottedleaf," Firepaw suggested. "I'm sure she'll find something to help."

"I hope so," mewed Graypaw, tottering slowly away.

Firepaw wanted to watch him go, until another angry yowl from Yellowfang sent him sprinting across the clearing.

CHAPTER 10

❧

By *the following morning,* a thin drizzle soaked the treetops and dripped down into the camp.

Firepaw woke up feeling damp. It had been an uncomfortable night. He stood up and shook himself vigorously, fluffing out his fur. Then he left the apprentices' den and trotted across the clearing to Yellowfang's nest.

Yellowfang was just stirring. She lifted her head and squinted at Firepaw as he approached. "My bones ache this morning. Has it been raining all night?"

"Since just after moonhigh," Firepaw replied. He reached out and prodded her mossy nest cautiously. "Your bedding is soaking wet. Why don't you move nearer to the nursery? It's more sheltered there."

"What? And be kept awake all night by those mewling kits! I'd rather get wet!" Yellowfang growled.

Firepaw watched her circle stiffly on her mossy bed. "Then at least let me fetch you some dry bedding," he offered, keen to drop the subject of kits if it upset the old she-cat so much.

"Thank you, Firepaw," replied Yellowfang quietly, settling down again.

Firepaw felt stunned. He wondered if Yellowfang was feeling all right. It was the first time she had thanked him for anything, and the first time she had not called him *kittypet*.

"Well, don't just stand there like a startled squirrel; go and fetch some moss!" she snapped.

Firepaw's whiskers twitched with amusement. This was more like the Yellowfang he was used to. He nodded and sprinted off.

He almost crashed into Speckletail in the middle of the clearing. This was the queen who had watched Yellowfang's angry outburst at the tabby kit the day before.

"Sorry, Speckletail," Firepaw mewed. "Are you on your way to see Yellowfang?"

"What would I want with *that* unnatural creature?" replied Speckletail crossly. "Actually it's you I was looking for. Bluestar wants to see you."

Firepaw hurried toward the Highrock and Bluestar's den.

Bluestar was sitting outside, her head bobbing rhythmically as she licked the gray fur below her throat. She paused when she noticed Firepaw. "How is Yellowfang today?" she meowed.

"Her bedding is wet, so I was going to fetch her more," Firepaw replied.

"I'll ask one of the queens to see to that." Bluestar gave her chest another lick, and then eyed Firepaw carefully. "Is she fit enough to hunt for herself yet?" she asked.

"I don't think so," Firepaw meowed, "but she can walk well enough now."

"I see," meowed Bluestar. She looked thoughtful for a

moment. "It is time for you to return to your training, Firepaw. But you'll need to work hard to make up for time you have lost."

"Great! I mean, thank you, Bluestar!" Firepaw stammered.

"You will go out with Tigerclaw, Graypaw, and Ravenpaw this morning," Bluestar continued. "I've asked Tigerclaw to assess the warrior skills of all our apprentices. Don't worry about Yellowfang; I'll make sure someone sees to her while you are gone."

Firepaw nodded.

"Now, join your companions," Bluestar ordered. "I expect they're waiting for you."

"Thank you, Bluestar," Firepaw mewed. He turned with a flick of his tail and darted toward his den.

Bluestar was right; Graypaw and Ravenpaw were both waiting for him by their favorite tree stump. Graypaw looked stiff and uncomfortable, his long fur clumped by the dampness of the air. Ravenpaw was pacing around the tree stump, lost in thought, the white tip of his tail twitching.

"So, you're joining us today!" Graypaw called as Firepaw approached. "Some day, huh?" He shook himself roughly to get rid of the clinging wetness.

"Yes. Bluestar told me that Tigerclaw is going to assess us today. Are Sandpaw and Dustpaw coming too?"

"Whitestorm and Darkstripe took them out on warrior patrol. I suppose Tigerclaw is going to look at them later," Graypaw answered.

"Come on! We should get going," urged Ravenpaw. He had stopped pacing and now hovered beside them anxiously.

"Fine by me," mewed Graypaw. "Hopefully some exercise will warm me up a bit!"

The three cats trotted through the gorse track and out of the camp. They hurried to the sandy hollow. Tigerclaw had not arrived, so they hung around in the shelter of a pine tree, their fur fluffed up against the chill.

"Are you worried about the assessment?" Firepaw asked Ravenpaw, as the young cat padded backward and forward with quick, nervous pawsteps. "There's no need to be. You're Tigerclaw's apprentice, after all. When he reports back to Bluestar, he's going to want to tell her how good you are."

"You can never tell with Tigerclaw," mewed Ravenpaw, still pacing.

"For goodness' sake, sit down," Graypaw grumbled. "At this rate you'll be worn out before we begin!"

By the time Tigerclaw arrived, the sky had changed. The clouds looked less like thick gray fur, and more like the soft white balls of down that queens used to line the nests of their newborns. Blue skies couldn't be far behind, but the breeze that brought the softer clouds carried a fresh chill.

Tigerclaw greeted them briskly and launched straight into the exercise details. "Lionheart and I have spent the last few weeks trying to teach you how to hunt decently," he meowed. "Today you'll have a chance to show me how much you have learned. Each of you will take a different route and hunt as much prey as possible. And whatever you catch will be added to the supplies in the camp."

The three apprentices looked at one another, nervous and excited. Firepaw felt his heart begin to beat faster at the prospect of a challenge.

"Ravenpaw, you will follow the trail beyond the Great Sycamore as far as the Snakerocks. That should be easy enough for your pitiful skills. You, Graypaw," Tigerclaw continued, "will take the route along the stream, as far as the Thunderpath."

"Great," mewed Graypaw. "Wet paws for me!" Tigerclaw's stare silenced him.

"And finally you, Firepaw. What a shame your great mentor couldn't be here today to witness your performance for herself. You shall take the route through the Tallpines, past the Treecut place, to the woods beyond."

Firepaw nodded, frantically tracing the route in his head.

"And remember," Tigerclaw finished, fixing them all with his pale-eyed stare, "I shall be watching all of you."

Ravenpaw was the first to sprint away toward the Snakerocks. Tigerclaw took a different track into the woods, leaving Graypaw and Firepaw alone in the hollow, trying to guess who Tigerclaw would follow first.

"I don't know why he thinks Snakerocks is an easy route!" mewed Graypaw. "The place is crawling with adders. Birds and mice stay away from there because there are so many snakes!"

"Ravenpaw'll have to spend his whole time trying not to get bitten," Firepaw agreed.

"Oh, he'll be okay," mewed Graypaw. "Not even an adder would be fast enough to catch Ravenpaw at the moment, he's so jumpy. I'd better get going. See you back here later on. Good luck!"

Graypaw raced off toward the stream. Firepaw paused to sniff the air, then bounded up the side of the hollow and began to head for the Tallpines.

It felt strange to be going in this direction, toward the Twoleg place he had been raised in. Cautiously Firepaw crossed the narrow path into the pine forest. He looked through the straight rows of trees, across the flat forest floor, alert for the sight and scent of prey.

A movement caught his eye. It was a mouse, scrabbling through the pine needles. Remembering his first lesson, Firepaw dropped into the stalking position, keeping his weight in his haunches, his paws light on the ground. The technique worked perfectly. The mouse didn't detect Firepaw until his final leap. He caught it with one paw and killed it swiftly. Then he buried it, so that he could pick it up on his return journey.

Firepaw traveled a little farther into the Tallpines. The ground here was deeply rutted by the tracks of the huge Twoleg monster that tore down the trees. Firepaw took a deep breath, his mouth open. The monster's acid breath had not touched the air here for a while.

Firepaw followed the deep tracks, jumping across the ruts. They were half-filled with rain, which made him feel thirsty. He was tempted to stop and take a few mouthfuls, but he hesitated. One lap of that muddy trench water and he'd taste the monster's foul-smelling tracks for days.

He decided to wait. Perhaps there would be a rainwater puddle beyond the Tallpines. He hurried onward through the trees and crossed the Twoleg path on the far boundary.

He was back amid the thick undergrowth of oak woods. He moved onward until he found a puddle and lapped up a few mouthfuls of the fresh water. Firepaw's fur began to prickle with some extra awareness. He recognized sounds and scents familiar from his old watching place on the fence post, and knew instantly where he was. These were the woods that bordered the Twolegplace. He must be very close to his old home now.

Ahead Firepaw could smell Twolegs and hear their voices, loud and raucous like crows. It was a group of young Twolegs, playing in the woods. Firepaw crouched and peered ahead through the ferns. The sounds were distant enough to be safe. He changed direction, skirting the noises, making sure he was not seen.

Firepaw stayed alert and watchful, but not just for Twolegs—Tigerclaw might be somewhere nearby. He thought he heard a twig snap in the bushes behind him. He sniffed the air, but smelled nothing new. Was he being watched now? he wondered.

Out of the corner of his eye, Firepaw sensed movement. At first he thought it was Tigerclaw's dark brown fur, but then he saw a flash of white. He stopped, crouched, and inhaled deeply. The smell was unfamiliar; it was a cat, but not a ThunderClan cat. Firepaw felt his fur bristle with the instincts of a Clan warrior. He would have to chase the intruder out of ThunderClan territory!

Firepaw watched the creature moving through the undergrowth. He could see its outline clearly as it skittered between the ferns. Firepaw waited for it to wander nearer. He crouched lower, his tail waving back and forth in slow rhythm. As the black-and-white cat neared, Firepaw rocked his haunches from side to side as he prepared to spring. One more heartbeat; then he leaped.

The black-and-white cat jumped into the air, terrified, and raced away through the trees. Firepaw gave chase.

It's a kittypet! he thought as he raced through the undergrowth, smelling its fear-scent. *In* my *territory!* He was closing in rapidly on the fleeing animal. It had slowed its headlong rush, preparing to scramble up the wide, mossy trunk of a fallen tree. With the blood roaring in his ears, Firepaw leaped onto its back in a single bound.

Firepaw could feel the cat struggling beneath him as he gripped on with all his claws. It let out a desperate and terrified yowl.

Firepaw released his grip and backed away. The black-and-white cat cringed at the foot of the fallen tree, trembling, and looked up at him. Firepaw lifted his nose, feeling a ripple of disgust at the intruder's easy surrender. This soft, plump house cat, with its round eyes and narrow face, looked very different from the lean, broad-headed cats Firepaw lived with now. And yet something about this cat seemed familiar.

Firepaw stared harder. He sniffed, drawing in the other cat's scent. *I don't recognize the smell,* he thought, searching his memory.

Then it came to him.

"Smudge!" he meowed out loud.

"H-ho-how d-d-do you know my n-name?" stammered Smudge, still crouching.

"It's me!" Firepaw meowed.

The house cat looked confused.

"We were kittens together. I lived in the garden next to you!" Firepaw insisted.

"Rusty?" mewled Smudge in disbelief. "Is that you? Did you find the wildcats again? Or are you living with new housefolk? You must be, if you're still alive!"

"I'm called Firepaw now," Firepaw meowed. He relaxed his shoulders and let his fur fall flat into a sleek orange pelt.

Smudge relaxed too. His ears pricked up. "*Firepaw?*" he echoed, amused. "Well, Firepaw, it looks like your new housefolk don't feed you enough! You certainly weren't this scrawny last time we met!"

"I don't need Twolegs to feed me," Firepaw replied. "I've got a whole forest of food to eat."

"Twolegs?"

"Housefolk. That's what the Clans call them."

Smudge looked bewildered for a second; then his expression changed to one of complete astonishment. "You mean you're really living with the wildcats?"

"Yes!" Firepaw paused. "You know, you smell . . . different. Unfamiliar."

"Unfamiliar?" Smudge echoed. He sniffed. "I suppose you're used to the smell of those wildcats now."

Firepaw shook his head, as if to clear his mind. "But we were kittens together. I should know your smell like I'd know the smell of my birth mother." Then Firepaw remembered. Smudge had passed six moons. No wonder he looked so soft and fat, and smelled so strange. "You've been to the Cutter!" He gasped. "I mean, the vet!"

Smudge shrugged his plump black shoulders. "So?" he mewed.

Firepaw was speechless. So Bluestar was right.

"Come on, then! What's it like, living wild?" Smudge demanded. "Is it as good as you thought it'd be?"

Firepaw thought for a moment: about last night, sleeping in a damp den. He thought about mouse bile and clearing away Yellowfang's dirt, and trying to please both Lionheart and Tigerclaw at once during training. He remembered the teasing he suffered about his kittypet blood. Then he remembered the thrill of his first catch, of charging through the forest in pursuit of a squirrel, and of warm evenings beneath the stars sharing tongues with his friends.

"I know who I am now," he meowed simply.

Smudge tipped his head to one side and stared at Firepaw, clearly confused. "I should be getting home," he mewed. "Mealtime soon."

"Go carefully, Smudge." Firepaw leaned forward and gave his old friend an affectionate lick between the ears. Smudge nuzzled him in return. "And stay alert. There may be another

cat in the area who is not as fond of kittypets—I mean, house cats—as I am."

Smudge's ears flicked nervously at these words. He looked around cautiously and leaped up onto the trunk of the fallen tree. "Good-bye, Rusty," he mewed. "I'll tell everyone at home that you're okay!"

"'Bye, Smudge," meowed Firepaw. "Enjoy your meal!"

He watched the white tip of Smudge's tail disappear over the edge of the tree. In the distance he could hear the rattle of dried food being shaken, and a Twoleg voice calling.

Firepaw turned, his tail high, and started back toward his own home, sniffing the air as he went. *I'll find a finch or two here*, he decided. *Then I'll catch something else on the way back through the pines.* He felt bursting with energy after meeting Smudge and realizing just how lucky he was to live in the Clan.

He looked up at the branches above him and began to stalk silently across the forest floor, every sense alert. Now he just needed to impress Bluestar and Tigerclaw, and the day would be perfect.

CHAPTER 11

♣

Firepaw returned with a chaffinch gripped firmly between his teeth. He dropped it in front of Tigerclaw, who stood waiting in the hollow.

"You're the first one back," meowed the warrior.

"Yeah, but I've got loads more prey to fetch," Firepaw mewed quickly. "I buried it back—"

"I know exactly what you did," Tigerclaw growled. "I've been watching you."

A swish of bushes announced Graypaw's return. He was carrying a small squirrel in his mouth, which he dropped beside Firepaw's chaffinch. "Yuck!" he spat. "Squirrels are too furry. I'll be picking hairs out of my teeth all evening."

Tigerclaw paid no attention to Graypaw's grumbling. "Ravenpaw's late," he observed. "We'll give him a bit longer and then return to camp."

"But what if he's been bitten by an adder?" Firepaw protested.

"Then it's his own fault," Tigerclaw replied coldly. "There's no room for fools in ThunderClan."

They waited in silence. Graypaw and Firepaw exchanged

glances, worried about Ravenpaw. Tigerclaw sat motionless, apparently lost in his own thoughts.

Firepaw was the first to scent Ravenpaw's arrival. He jumped to his paws as the black cat leaped into the clearing, looking unusually pleased with himself. Dangling from his mouth was the long, diamond-patterned body of an adder.

"Ravenpaw! Are you okay?" Firepaw called.

"Hey!" meowed Graypaw, rushing forward to admire Ravenpaw's catch. "Did that bite you?"

"I was too quick for it!" Ravenpaw purred loudly. Then he caught Tigerclaw's eye and fell silent.

Tigerclaw fixed all three excited apprentices with a cold stare. "Come on," he said shortly. "Let's collect the rest of your prey and get back to camp."

Firepaw, Graypaw, and Ravenpaw entered the camp, strolling behind Tigerclaw. Their impressive day's catch hung from their mouths, although Ravenpaw kept tripping over his dead snake. As they emerged from the gorse into the camp, a group of young kits scrambled out of the nursery to watch them pass.

"Look!" Firepaw heard one of them say. "Apprentices, just back from hunting!" He recognized the little tabby Yellowfang had hissed at the day before. Sitting next to him was a fluffy gray kit, no more than two moons old. A tiny black kit and a small tortoiseshell stood beside them.

"Isn't that the kittypet, Firepaw?" squeaked the gray kit.

"Yeah! Look at his orange fur!" mewed the black one.

"They say he's a good hunter," the tortoiseshell added. "He looks a bit like Lionheart. Do you suppose he's as good as him?"

"I can't wait to start my training," mewed the tabby. "I'm going to be the best warrior ThunderClan has ever seen!"

Firepaw lifted his chin, feeling proud at the kits' admiring comments. He followed his two friends into the center of the clearing.

"An *adder!*" Graypaw mewed again, as the apprentices dropped their catch for the other cats to share.

"What shall I do with it?" asked Ravenpaw, sniffing the snake's long body as it lay beside the heap.

"Can you eat adders?" asked Graypaw.

"Trust you to think of your stomach!" Firepaw joked, butting Graypaw with his head.

"Well, I wouldn't want to eat it," murmured Ravenpaw. "I mean, my mouth tastes pretty foul after carrying it back."

"Let's put it on the tree stump, then," suggested Graypaw, "so that Dustpaw and Sandpaw can see it when they get back."

They each carried a piece of their fresh-kill, and the adder, back to their den. Graypaw carefully placed the adder on the stump, arranging the snake so that it could be seen clearly from all sides. Then they ate. When they had finished they sat close together to groom one another and talk.

"I wonder who Bluestar will choose to go to the Gathering?" Firepaw meowed. "It'll be full moon tomorrow."

"Sandpaw and Dustpaw have been twice already," replied Graypaw.

"Perhaps Bluestar will choose one of us this time," mewed

Firepaw. "After all, we've been training for almost three moons now."

"But Sandpaw and Dustpaw are still the eldest apprentices," Ravenpaw pointed out.

Firepaw nodded. "And this Gathering will be an important one. It'll be the first time the Clans have met since WindClan disappeared. No cat knows what ShadowClan is going to say about it."

Tigerclaw's low meow interrupted them. "You are right, youngster." The warrior had strolled up to them unnoticed. "By the way, Firepaw," he added smoothly, "Bluestar wants to see you."

Firepaw looked up, startled. Why would Bluestar want to see him?

"Now—if you can spare the time," Tigerclaw meowed.

Firepaw jumped up immediately and bounded off across the clearing toward Bluestar's den.

Bluestar was sitting outside, her tail flicking restlessly back and forth. When she saw Firepaw she stood up and looked steadily down at him. "Tigerclaw has told me that he saw you talking with a cat from the Twolegplace today," she meowed quietly.

"But—" Firepaw began.

"He said that you began by fighting with this cat but ended up sharing tongues with it."

"That's true," Firepaw admitted, feeling his fur prickle defensively. "But he was an old friend. We grew up together." He paused and swallowed. "When I was a kittypet."

Bluestar looked at him for a long moment. "Do you miss your old life, Firepaw?" she asked. "Think carefully, now."

"No." *How can Bluestar think that?* Firepaw wondered. His head was spinning. What was Bluestar trying to make him say?

"Do you wish to leave the Clan?"

"Of course not!" Firepaw was shocked by her question.

Bluestar didn't seem to hear the passion in his answer. She shook her head, looking suddenly old and tired. "I won't judge you if you leave us, Firepaw. Perhaps I expected too much of you. Perhaps my judgment has been clouded by the Clan's need for new warriors."

Panic swept through Firepaw at the thought of leaving the Clan forever. "But my place is here! This is my home," he protested.

"I need more than that, Firepaw. I need to be able to trust in your loyalty to ThunderClan, especially now that it looks like ShadowClan is planning an attack. We don't have room for anyone who isn't sure whether their heart lies in the past or the present."

Firepaw took a deep breath and chose his next words carefully. "When I saw Smudge today—that's the house cat Tigerclaw saw me talking with—I saw what life would have been like if I had stayed with the Twolegs. I felt happy that I had not stayed. I was proud I left." He held Bluestar's gaze without flinching. "Meeting Smudge made me certain I made the right decision. I could never have been satisfied with the soft life of a kittypet."

Bluestar looked closely at him for a moment, her eyes

narrow. Then she nodded. "Very well," she said. "I believe you."

Firepaw dipped his head respectfully and let out a silent sigh of relief.

"I spoke to Yellowfang earlier," meowed Bluestar in a lighter tone. "She thinks a lot of you. She's a wise old she-cat, you know. And I suspect she wasn't always bad-tempered. Indeed, I think that I could grow to like her."

Firepaw felt an unexpected glow of pleasure at these words. Maybe, in caring for Yellowfang, his admiration for her had grown into affection, despite the she-cat's ill temper. Whatever the reason, he was glad Bluestar liked her too.

"But there is something about her that I don't trust," Bluestar went on quietly. "She will stay with ThunderClan for now, but remain as a prisoner. The queens will care for her. You must concentrate on your training."

Firepaw nodded and waited to be dismissed, but Bluestar hadn't finished. "Firepaw, although you showed bad judgment today in talking to a house cat, Tigerclaw *was* impressed by your hunting skills. In fact, he reported that you all did well. I am pleased with your progress. You will come to the Gathering—all three of you."

Firepaw could hardly stand still. His body tingled with excitement. The Gathering! "What about Sandpaw and Dustpaw?" he mewed.

"They will remain behind and guard the camp," replied Bluestar. "Now you may go." She flicked her long tail to show he was dismissed, and returned to her grooming.

※　※　※

Graypaw and Ravenpaw looked stunned to see Firepaw bounding happily toward them. They had been waiting nervously for him beside the tree stump. Firepaw sat down and looked at his friends.

"Well?" Graypaw demanded. "What did she say?"

"Tigerclaw told us you'd been sharing tongues with a *kittypet* this morning," burst out Ravenpaw. "Are you in trouble?"

"No. Although Bluestar wasn't pleased," Firepaw admitted ruefully. "She thought I might want to leave ThunderClan."

"You don't, do you?" asked Ravenpaw.

"Of course he doesn't!" mewed Graypaw.

Firepaw gave his gray friend an affectionate swipe. "Yeah, you'd hate that. You need me to catch mice for you! All you can catch these days are hairy old squirrels!"

Graypaw dodged out of the way of Firepaw's blow, and reared up on his back legs to retaliate.

"You'll never guess what else she said!" Firepaw went on. He was too excited to waste time play-fighting.

Graypaw immediately dropped back onto all four paws. "What?" he asked.

"We're going to the Gathering!"

Graypaw let out a yowl of delight and bounded up onto the tree stump. One of his back paws knocked the adder flying. It hit Ravenpaw on the head and wrapped itself around his neck.

Ravenpaw spat with alarm and surprise, and then turned on Graypaw. "Watch it!" he hissed crossly. He shook the adder onto the ground.

"Scared it might try to bite you?" Firepaw teased. He crouched down, hissing, and sidled up to Ravenpaw.

Ravenpaw twitched his whiskers and retorted, "Some snake you'd make!" He leaped onto Firepaw and rolled him easily onto his back.

Graypaw reached down from the tree stump and gave Ravenpaw's tail a tug. As Ravenpaw turned to thump Graypaw with a soft forepaw, Firepaw jumped to his feet and leaped into them both, sending Graypaw flying from the stump. All three cats tumbled into the dirt and tussled on the ground. Finally they fell apart and settled themselves, panting, beside the tree stump.

"Are Sandpaw and Dustpaw coming too?" puffed Graypaw.

"Nope!" Firepaw replied, unable to disguise the note of triumph in his voice. "They have to stay behind and guard the camp."

"Oh, let me tell them!" begged Graypaw. "I can't wait to see the looks on their faces!"

"Me neither!" Firepaw agreed. "I can't believe *we're* going instead of *them*! Especially after Tigerclaw saw me with Smudge today!"

"That was just bad luck," answered Graypaw. "We all caught a load of prey in the assessment. That must be what decided it."

"I wonder what the Gathering will be like," mewed Ravenpaw.

"It'll be fantastic," Graypaw replied confidently. "I bet all the great warriors will be there. Clawface, Stonefur . . ."

But Firepaw wasn't listening anymore. Instead, he found himself thinking about Tigerclaw and Smudge. Graypaw was right—it *was* bad luck that the great warrior had been observing him when he had met his old friend. Why couldn't he have been watching Graypaw or Ravenpaw instead? In fact, it was bad luck that Tigerclaw had sent him so near the Twolegplace at all.

Suddenly a dark thought entered Firepaw's mind: Why *had* Tigerclaw sent him so near his old haunts? Had he wanted to test him? Could it be the great dark warrior didn't trust his loyalty to ThunderClan?

CHAPTER 12

❧

Firepaw peered over the brow of a bush-covered slope. Graypaw and Ravenpaw crouched beside him. Next to them a group of ThunderClan elders, queens, and warriors waited in the undergrowth for Bluestar to give the signal.

Firepaw had not been to this place since his first journey with Lionheart and Tigerclaw. The steep-sided glade looked different now. The rich greenness of the woods had been bleached away by the cold light of the full moon, and the leaves on the trees glowed silver. At the bottom stood the large oaks that marked where the corner of each Clan's territory touched the other three.

The air was thick with the warm scents of cats from the other Clans. Firepaw could see them quite clearly in the moonlight, moving about below in the grassy clearing that lay between the four oaks. In the center of the clearing, a large, jagged rock rose from the forest floor like a broken tooth.

"Look at all those cats down there!" hissed Ravenpaw under his breath.

"There's Crookedstar!" Graypaw hissed back. "RiverClan's leader."

"Where?" Firepaw mewed, nudging Graypaw impatiently.

"That light-colored tabby, beside the Great Rock."

Firepaw followed Graypaw's nod and saw a huge tom, even bigger than Lionheart, sitting at the center of the clearing. His striped coat shone pale in the moonlight. Even from this distance, his old face showed the signs of a harsh life, and his mouth looked twisted, as if it had once been broken and had healed badly.

"Hey!" mewed Graypaw. "Did you see Sandpaw spit when I told her I hoped she had a nice evening at home?"

"You bet!" Firepaw purred.

Ravenpaw interrupted them with a muffled growl. "Look! There's Brokenstar—ShadowClan's leader," he hissed.

Firepaw looked down at the dark brown tabby. His fur was unusually long and his face was broad and flattened. There was a stillness in the way he sat and stared around him that made Firepaw's fur prickle uncomfortably.

"He looks pretty nasty," Firepaw muttered.

"Yeah," agreed Graypaw. "He's certainly got a reputation among all the Clans for not suffering fools gladly. And he's not been leader that long—four moons, ever since his father, Raggedstar, died."

"What does the leader of WindClan look like?" Firepaw asked.

"Tallstar? I've never seen him, but I know he's black and white with a very long tail," answered Graypaw.

"Can you see him now?" asked Ravenpaw.

Graypaw peered down, searching the crowd of cats below. "Nope!"

"Can you scent *any* WindClan cats?" Firepaw asked.

Graypaw shook his head. "No."

Lionheart's meow sounded softly beside them. "The WindClan cats may just be late."

"But what if they don't turn up at all?" mewed Graypaw.

"Hush! We must all be patient. These are difficult times. Now keep quiet. Bluestar will give the signal to move soon," Lionheart meowed quietly.

As he spoke, Bluestar stood, and, holding her tail high, flicked it from one side to the other. Firepaw's heart missed a beat as the ThunderClan cats rose as one and bounded through the bushes, down toward the meeting place. He raced alongside them, feeling the wind rush in his ears and his paws tingle with anticipation.

The ThunderClan cats paused instinctively on the edge of the clearing, outside the boundary of the oaks. Bluestar sniffed the air. Then she nodded and the troop moved forward into the clearing.

Firepaw felt thrilled. The other cats looked even more impressive close up, milling about the Great Rock. A large white warrior strode past. Firepaw and Ravenpaw looked at him in awe.

"Look at his paws!" Ravenpaw murmured.

Firepaw looked down and realized the huge paws of this great tom were jet black.

"It must be Blackfoot," mewed Grewpaw. "ShadowClan's new deputy."

Blackfoot stalked over to Brokenstar and sat down beside

him. The ShadowClan leader acknowledged him with a twitch of one ear, but said nothing.

"When does the meeting begin?" Ravenpaw asked Whitestorm.

"Be patient, Ravenpaw," he answered. "The sky is clear tonight, so we have plenty of time."

Lionheart leaned over and added, "We warriors like to spend a little time boasting about our victories, while the elders swap tales about the ancient days before the Twolegs came here." All three apprentices looked up at him and saw his whiskers twitch mischievously.

Dappletail, One-eye, and Smallear headed straight off toward a group of elderly cats who were settling themselves below one of the oak trees. Whitestorm and Lionheart strolled over to another pair of warriors whom Firepaw did not know. He sniffed the air and recognized their scent as RiverClan.

Bluestar's voice sounded behind the three apprentices. "Don't waste any of your time tonight," she warned. "This is a good opportunity to meet your enemies. Listen to them; remember what they look like and how they behave. There is a great deal to be learned from these meetings."

"And say little," warned Tigerclaw. "Don't give anything away that might be used against us once the moon has waned."

"Don't worry; we won't!" Firepaw promised hastily, looking into Tigerclaw's eyes. The feeling that Tigerclaw didn't trust his loyalty lingered with him still.

The two warriors nodded and moved on, and the apprentices were left alone. They looked at each other.

"What do we do now?" Firepaw asked.

"What they said," replied Ravenpaw. "Listen."

"And don't say too much," Graypaw added.

Firepaw nodded gravely. "I'm going to see where Tigerclaw went," he mewed.

"Well, I'm going to find Lionheart," mewed Graypaw. "You coming, Ravenpaw?"

"No, thanks," Ravenpaw replied. "I'm going to find some of the other apprentices."

"Okay, we'll meet up later," mewed Firepaw, and he trotted in the direction Tigerclaw had taken.

He scented Tigerclaw easily and found him sitting at the center of a group of huge warriors, behind the Great Rock. Tigerclaw was speaking.

It was a tale Firepaw had heard many times at camp. Tigerclaw was describing his recent battle against the RiverClan hunting party. "I wrestled like a LionClan cat. Three warriors tried to hold me but I threw them off. I fought them until two lay knocked out and the other had run off into the forest like a kit crying for its mother."

This time Tigerclaw didn't mention killing Oakheart in vengeance for Redtail's death. *Perhaps it's so he doesn't offend the RiverClan warriors,* Firepaw decided.

Firepaw listened politely to the end of the story, but a familiar scent was distracting him. As soon as Tigerclaw had finished speaking, Firepaw turned and crept away toward the sweet smell, which was coming from a group of cats nearby.

He found Graypaw sitting among these cats, but that was not the scent he had been following. Sitting opposite Graypaw, between two RiverClan toms, was Spottedleaf. Firepaw glanced at her shyly and settled himself beside his friend.

"Still no scent of WindClan," he mewed to Graypaw.

"The meeting hasn't begun yet; they may still come," replied his friend. "Look, there's Runningnose. He's the new ShadowClan medicine cat, apparently." He nodded toward a small gray-and-white cat at the center of the group.

"I can see why they call him Runningnose," Firepaw remarked. The medicine cat's nose was wet at the tip and encrusted around the edges.

"Yep," replied Graypaw with a scornful growl. "I can't see why they appointed him when he can't even cure his own cold!"

Runningnose was telling the cats about a herb that medicine cats had used in the old days to cure kitten-cough. "Since the Twolegs came and filled the place with hard earth and strange flowers," he complained in a high-pitched yowl, "the herb has disappeared, and kittens die needlessly in cold weather."

The cats gathered around him yowled their disapproval.

"It never would have happened in the time of the great Clan cats," growled a black RiverClan queen.

"Indeed," mewled a silver tabby. "The great cats would

have killed any Twolegs that dared enter their territory. If TigerClan roamed this forest still, Twolegs would not have built this far into our land."

Then Firepaw heard Spottedleaf's quiet mew. "If TigerClan still roamed these forests, *we* would hardly have made our territory here, either."

"What's TigerClan?" mewed a small voice beside them. Firepaw noticed a little tabby apprentice from one of the other Clans sitting beside him.

"TigerClan is one of the great cat Clans that used to roam the forest," Graypaw explained quietly. "TigerClan is cats of the night, big as horses, with jet-black stripes. Then there is LionClan. They're . . ." Graypaw hesitated, frowning as he tried to remember.

"Oh! I've heard of them," mewed the tabby. "They were as big as TigerClan cats, with yellow fur and golden manes like rays of the sun."

Graypaw nodded. "And then there is the other one, SpottyClan or something like that. . . ."

"I suspect you're thinking of LeopardClan, young Graypaw," meowed a voice from behind them.

"Lionheart!" Graypaw greeted his mentor with an affectionate touch of his nose.

Lionheart shook his head in mock despair. "Don't you youngsters know your history? LeopardClan are the swiftest cats, huge and golden, spotted with black pawprints. You can thank LeopardClan for the speed and hunting skills you now possess."

"Thank them? Why?" asked the tabby.

Lionheart gazed down at the little apprentice and answered, "There is a trace of all the great cats in every cat today. We would not be night hunters without our TigerClan ancestors, and our love of the sun's warmth comes from LionClan." He paused. "You are a ShadowClan apprentice, aren't you? How many moons are you?"

The tabby stared awkwardly down at the ground. "S-six moons," he stammered, not meeting Lionheart's eye.

"Rather small for six moons," Lionheart murmured. His tone was gentle, but his gaze was searching and serious.

"My mother was small too," answered the tabby nervously. He bowed his head and backed away, disappearing into the crowd of cats with a twitch of his light brown tail.

Lionheart turned to Firepaw and Graypaw. "Well, he might be small, but at least he was curious. If only you two showed as much interest in the stories your elders tell!"

"Sorry, Lionheart," Firepaw and Graypaw mewed, exchanging doubtful glances.

Lionheart grunted good-naturedly. "Oh, go away, the pair of you! Next time I hope Bluestar decides to bring apprentices who appreciate what they hear." And with a half-hearted growl he chased them away from the group.

"Come on," purred Graypaw as they leaped away. "Let's see where Ravenpaw's gotten to."

Ravenpaw was in the middle of a group of apprentices who were clamoring for him to tell them about the battle with RiverClan.

"Go on, Ravenpaw; tell us what happened!" called a pretty black-and-white she-cat.

Ravenpaw shyly shuffled his paws and shook his head.

"Come on, Ravenpaw!" insisted another.

Ravenpaw looked around and saw Firepaw and Graypaw at the edge of the crowd. Firepaw nodded encouragingly. Ravenpaw flicked his tail in acknowledgment and began his story.

He stumbled a bit at first, but as he continued, the tremor disappeared from his voice and his audience leaned in, their eyes growing wider.

"Fur was flying everywhere. Blood spattered the leaves of the bramble bushes, bright red against green. I'd just fought off a huge warrior and sent him squealing into the bushes when the ground shook, and I heard a warrior scream. It was Oakheart! Redtail raced past me, his mouth dripping blood and his fur torn. 'Oakheart is dead!' he howled. Then he rushed off to help Tigerclaw as he fought another warrior."

"Who would have thought Ravenpaw was such a good story-teller," Graypaw murmured to Firepaw, sounding impressed.

But Firepaw was thinking of something else. What was it Ravenpaw had said? That *Redtail* had killed Oakheart? But according to Tigerclaw, Oakheart had killed Redtail and he, Tigerclaw, had killed Oakheart in revenge.

"If Redtail killed Oakheart, who killed Redtail?" Firepaw hissed to Graypaw.

"If who did what?" Graypaw echoed absentmindedly. He was only half listening to Firepaw.

Firepaw shook his head to clear it. *Ravenpaw must have been mistaken*, he thought. *He must have meant Tigerclaw.*

Ravenpaw was coming to the end of his story. "Finally, Redtail dragged the wailing cat off Tigerclaw by his tail and, with the strength of the whole of TigerClan, flung him into the bushes."

A moving shadow caught Firepaw's eye. He glanced around and saw Tigerclaw standing a short distance away. The warrior was watching Ravenpaw with an iron stare. Unaware of his mentor's presence, Ravenpaw continued to answer question after question from his enthusiastic audience.

"What were Oakheart's dying words?"

"Is it true that Oakheart had never lost a battle before?"

Ravenpaw replied promptly, with his voice high and clear and his eyes shining. But when Firepaw glanced back at Tigerclaw, he saw a look of horror and then fury creep over the warrior's face. Clearly Tigerclaw wasn't enjoying Ravenpaw's story at all.

Firepaw was just about to say something to Graypaw when a loud yowl signaled to all the cats for quiet. Firepaw couldn't help feeling relieved as Ravenpaw fell silent at last, and Tigerclaw turned away.

Firepaw looked up to see where the yowl had come from. Three cats sat silhouetted against the moonlit sky on top of the Great Rock. They were Bluestar, Brokenstar, and Crookedstar.

The Clan leaders were about to begin the meeting. But where was the WindClan leader?

"Surely they won't start the meeting without Tallstar?"

Firepaw hissed under his breath.

"I don't know," Graypaw muttered back.

"Haven't you noticed? There isn't a single WindClan cat here," whispered a RiverClan apprentice on the other side of Firepaw.

Firepaw guessed that similar conversations were going on all around him. As the other cats were gathering beneath the Great Rock, an unsettled murmuring rumbled in their throats.

"We can't start yet," yowled one voice above the noise. "Where are the WindClan representatives? We must wait until all the Clans are present."

On top of the rock, Bluestar stepped forward. Her gray fur glowed almost white in the moonlight. "Cats of all Clans, welcome," she meowed in a clear voice. "It is true that WindClan is not present, but Brokenstar wishes to speak anyway."

Brokenstar padded noiselessly up to stand beside Bluestar. He surveyed the crowd for a few moments, his orange eyes burning. Then he took a deep breath and began. "Friends, I come to speak to you tonight about the needs of ShadowClan—"

But he was interrupted by raised, impatient voices from below.

"Where is Tallstar?" cried one.

"Where are the WindClan warriors?" yowled another.

Brokenstar stretched up to his full height and lashed his tail from side to side. "As the leader of ShadowClan, it is my right to address you here!" he growled in a voice full of menace. The crowd fell into an uneasy silence. All around him, Firepaw could smell the acrid tang of fear.

Brokenstar yowled again. "We all know that the hard time of leaf-bare, and late newleaf, have left us with little prey in our hunting grounds. But we also know that WindClan, RiverClan, and ThunderClan lost many kits in the freezing weather that came so late this season. ShadowClan did not lose kits. We are hardened to the cold north wind. Our kits are stronger than yours from the moment they are born. And so we find ourselves with many mouths to feed, and too little prey to feed them."

The crowd, still silent, listened anxiously.

"The needs of ShadowClan are simple. In order to survive, we must increase our hunting territory. That is why I insist that you allow ShadowClan warriors to hunt in your territories."

A shocked but muted growl rippled through the crowd.

"Share our hunting grounds?" called the outraged voice of Tigerclaw.

"It is unprecedented!" cried a tortoiseshell queen from RiverClan. "The Clans have never shared hunting rights!"

"Should ShadowClan be punished because our kits thrive?" yowled Brokenstar from the Great Rock. "Do you want us to watch our young starve? You *must* share what you have with us."

"*Must!*" spat Smallear furiously from the back of the crowd.

"Must," repeated Brokenstar. "WindClan failed to understand this. In the end, we were forced to drive them out of their territory."

Snarls of outrage burst from the crowd, but Brokenstar's caterwaul rang loud above them: "And, if we have to, we will drive you all from your hunting grounds in order to feed our hungry kits."

There was instant silence. On the other side of the clearing, Firepaw heard a RiverClan apprentice start to mutter something, but he was quickly hushed by an elder.

Satisfied that he had every cat's attention, Brokenstar continued. "Each year, the Twolegs spoil more of our territory. At least one Clan must remain strong, if all the Clans are to survive. ShadowClan thrives while you all struggle. And there may come a time when you will need us to protect you."

"You doubt our strength?" hissed Tigerclaw. His pale eyes glared threateningly at the ShadowClan leader, and his powerful shoulders rippled with tension.

"I do not ask for your answer now." Brokenstar ignored the warrior's challenge. "You must each go away and consider my words. But bear this in mind: Would you prefer to share your prey, or be driven out and left homeless and starving?"

Warriors, elders, and apprentices looked at one another in disbelief. In the anxious pause that followed, Crookedstar stepped forward. "I have already agreed to allow ShadowClan some hunting rights in the river that runs through our territory," he meowed quietly, gazing down on his Clan.

Horror and humiliation rippled through the RiverClan cats at their leader's words.

"We were not consulted!" cried a grizzled silver tabby.

"I feel that this is best for our Clan. For all the Clans," Crookedstar explained, his voice heavy with resignation. "There are plenty of fish in the river. It is better to share our prey than to spill blood fighting over it."

"And what of ThunderClan?" Smallear croaked. "Bluestar? Have you, too, agreed to this outrageous demand?"

Bluestar unwaveringly met the old cat's gaze. "I have made no agreement with Brokenstar except that I shall discuss his proposal with my Clan after the Gathering."

"Well, at least that's something," muttered Graypaw in Firepaw's ear. "We'll show them we're not as soft as that yellow-bellied RiverClan."

Brokenstar spoke up again, his rasping voice sounding arrogant and strong after Crookedstar's surrender. "I also bring news that is important to the safety of your kits. A ShadowClan cat has turned rogue and spurned the warrior code. We chased her out of our camp, but we do not know where she is now. She looks a mangy old creature, but she has a bite like TigerClan."

Firepaw's fur bristled. Could Brokenstar possibly be talking about Yellowfang? He pricked up his ears, curious to hear more.

"She is dangerous. I warn you—do not offer shelter to her. And"—Brokenstar paused dramatically—"until she is caught and killed, I urge you to keep a close eye on your kits."

Firepaw knew from the nervous growl that rumbled in the throats of the ThunderClan cats that they, too, had thought of Yellowfang. The bold she-cat had done nothing to endear herself to her reluctant hosts, and Firepaw guessed it wouldn't take much to drum up hatred against her—even the words of a despised enemy like Brokenstar would be enough.

The ShadowClan warriors began to push their way out of the throng of cats. Brokenstar leaped down from the rock, and his warriors immediately surrounded him and escorted him away from Fourtrees, back into ShadowClan territory. The remaining ShadowClan cats followed quickly behind, including the undersize tabby Lionheart had questioned earlier. But among the other ShadowClan apprentices, the tabby no longer looked unusually small—they all looked tiny and undernourished, more like kits of three or four moons than full-fledged apprentices.

"What do you think of all that?" Graypaw mewed in a low voice.

Ravenpaw bounded over before Firepaw could reply. "What's going to happen now?" he wailed, his fur fluffed up in alarm and his eyes wider than ever.

Firepaw didn't answer. The elders of ThunderClan were gathering nearby, and he was straining to hear what they were saying.

"That must be Yellowfang he was talking about," growled Smallear.

"Well, she did snap at Goldenflower's youngest kit the other day," murmured Speckletail darkly. She was the oldest nursery queen, and fiercely protective of all the kits.

"And we've left her behind, with the camp virtually unguarded!" wailed One-eye, who for once seemed to be having no trouble hearing everything.

"I tried to tell you she was a danger to us," hissed Darkstripe. "Bluestar has to listen to reason now and get rid of her before she harms any of our young!"

Tigerclaw strode up to the group. "We must return to camp at once and deal with this rogue!" he yowled.

Firepaw didn't stop to hear more. His mind was spinning. Loyal as he was to his Clan, he just couldn't believe that Yellowfang would be a danger to kits. Frightened for the old she-cat, burning with questions only she could answer, he raced away from Graypaw and Ravenpaw without a word.

He charged up the hillside and pelted through the forest. Had he been mistaken about Yellowfang? If he warned her about the danger she was in, would he be risking his own position in ThunderClan? Whatever trouble he got himself into, he had to find out the truth from her before the other cats got back to the camp.

CHAPTER 13

❧

Firepaw reached the edge of the ravine and looked down at the camp. He was panting and his paws were slippery with dew. He sniffed the air. He was alone. There was still time to speak to Yellowfang before the others returned from the Gathering. Silently, he jumped down the rocky slope and slipped through the gorse tunnel unnoticed.

The camp was still and quiet, apart from the muted snuffles of sleeping cats. Firepaw quickly crept around the edge of the clearing to Yellowfang's nest. The old medicine cat was curled on top of her mossy bedding.

"Yellowfang," he hissed urgently. "Yellowfang! Wake up; it's important!"

Two orange eyes opened and glinted in the moonlight. "I wasn't sleeping," meowed Yellowfang quietly. She sounded calm and alert. "You came straight from the Gathering to me? That must mean you've heard." She blinked slowly and looked away. "So Brokenstar kept his promise."

"What promise?" Firepaw felt very confused. Yellowfang seemed to know more than he did about what was going on.

"ShadowClan's noble leader promised to drive me from

every Clan territory," Yellowfang replied dryly. "What did he say about me?"

"He warned us that our kits were in danger as long as we sheltered the ShadowClan rogue. He didn't say your name, but ThunderClan guessed who he was talking about. You must leave before the others get back. You are in danger!"

"You mean they believed Brokenstar?" Yellowfang flattened her ears and swished her tail angrily.

"Yes!" Firepaw meowed urgently. "Darkstripe says you're dangerous. The other cats are scared of what you might do. Tigerclaw is planning to come back and . . . I don't know. . . . I think you should go before they get here!"

In the distance Firepaw could hear the yowls of angry cats. Yellowfang struggled stiffly to her paws. Firepaw gave her a nudge to help her up, his mind still spinning with questions. "What did Brokenstar mean when he warned us to keep a close eye on our kits?" he couldn't stop himself from asking. "Would you really do something like that?"

"Would I *what*?"

"Would you harm our kits?"

Yellowfang flared her nostrils and looked steadily at him. "Do *you* think so?"

Firepaw met her gaze without flinching. "No. I don't believe you would ever harm a kit. But why would Brokenstar say such a thing?"

The noise of the cats was coming nearer, and with it, the scents of aggression and anger. Yellowfang looked wildly from side to side.

"Go!" Firepaw urged. Her safety was more important than his curiosity.

But Yellowfang remained where she was and stared at him. A calm look suddenly came into her wide eyes. "Firepaw, you believe I'm innocent, and I'm grateful for that. If *you* believe me, then others might. And I know Bluestar will give me a fair hearing. I can't run forever. I'm too old. I shall stay here and face whatever your Clan decides for me." She sighed and sank down onto her bony haunches.

"But what about Tigerclaw? What if he—"

"He is headstrong, and he knows the power he has over the other Clan cats—they are in awe of him. But even he will obey Bluestar."

Rustling in the undergrowth beyond the camp boundary told Firepaw that the cats were almost at the entrance.

"Go away, Firepaw," hissed Yellowfang, baring her blackened teeth at him. "Don't make trouble for yourself by being seen with me now. There is nothing you can do for me. Have faith in your leader, and let her decide what happens to me."

Firepaw realized Yellowfang had made up her mind. He touched his nose to her patchy fur, then crept silently away into the shadows to watch.

Through the gorse came the cats—Bluestar first, accompanied by Lionheart. Frostfur and Willowpelt were right behind them. Frostfur raced away from the troop immediately and ran toward the nursery, the fur on her tail bristling in alarm. Tigerclaw and Darkstripe strode into the clearing, shoulder to shoulder, looking grim. The others followed behind, with Ravenpaw and Graypaw at the rear. As soon as he saw his friends, Firepaw trotted out to join them.

"You went to warn Yellowfang, didn't you?" whispered Graypaw when Firepaw reached his side.

"Yes, I did," Firepaw admitted. "But she won't leave. She trusts Bluestar to treat her fairly. Did anyone miss me?"

"Only us," replied Ravenpaw.

Around the camp, the cats who had stayed behind began to wake up. They must have scented the aggression and heard the tension in the voices of the returning cats, for they all came running into the clearing, their tails held high.

"What has happened?" called a tabby warrior named Runningwind.

"Brokenstar has demanded hunting rights for ShadowClan in our territory!" replied Longtail loudly enough for all the cats to hear.

"And he warned us about a rogue cat who will harm our kits!" added Willowpelt. "It must be Yellowfang!"

Meows of anger and distress rose from the crowd.

"Silence!" ordered Bluestar, leaping onto the Highrock. Instinctively, the cats settled in front of her.

A loud screech made every cat turn its head toward the fallen tree where the elders slept. Tigerclaw and Darkstripe were dragging Yellowfang roughly from her nest. She shrieked furiously as they hauled her into the clearing and dumped her in front of the Highrock. Firepaw felt every muscle in his body tense. Without thinking, he dropped into a low crouch, ready to spring at Yellowfang's persecutors.

"Wait, Firepaw," growled Graypaw in his ear. "Let Bluestar deal with this."

"What is going on?" demanded Bluestar, jumping down from the Highrock and glaring at her warriors. "I gave no order to attack our prisoner."

Tigerclaw and Darkstripe instantly let go of Yellowfang, who crouched in the dust, hissing and spitting.

Frostfur appeared from the nursery and pushed her way through to the front of the Clan. "We got back in time," she meowed with a gasp. "The kits are safe!"

"Of course they are!" snapped Bluestar.

Frostfur seemed taken aback. "But . . . you *are* going to throw Yellowfang out, aren't you?" she meowed, her blue eyes wide.

"Throw her out?" spat Darkstripe, unleashing his claws. "We should kill her now!"

Bluestar fixed her piercing blue eyes on Darkstripe's angry face. "And what has she done?" she asked with icy calm.

Firepaw held his breath.

"You were at the Gathering! Brokenstar said she—" Darkstripe began.

"Brokenstar said only that there is a rogue somewhere in the woods," meowed Bluestar, her voice menacingly quiet. "He did not mention Yellowfang by name. The kits are safe. For as long as she is in my Clan, Yellowfang will not be harmed in any way."

Bluestar's words were met with silence, and Firepaw heaved a sigh of relief.

Yellowfang looked up at Bluestar and narrowed her eyes respectfully. "I will leave now, if you wish it, Bluestar."

"There is no need," Bluestar replied. "You have done nothing wrong. You will be safe here." The ThunderClan leader lifted her gaze to the crowd of cats that surrounded Yellowfang and meowed, "It is time we discussed the real threat to our Clan: Brokenstar. We have already begun to prepare for an attack by ShadowClan," Bluestar began. "We'll carry on with those preparations, and patrol our borders more frequently. WindClan has gone. RiverClan has given hunting rights to ShadowClan warriors. ThunderClan stands alone against Brokenstar."

A murmur of defiance rippled through the cats, and Firepaw felt his fur prickle with anticipation.

"Then we're not going to agree to Brokenstar's demands?" meowed Tigerclaw.

"Clans have never shared hunting rights before," Bluestar answered. "They have always managed to support themselves in their own territories. There is no reason why this should change." Tigerclaw nodded approvingly.

"But can we defend ourselves against a ShadowClan attack?" asked Smallear's tremulous voice. "WindClan didn't manage it! RiverClan won't even try!"

Bluestar met his old eyes with her steady gaze. "We must try. We will not give up our territory without a fight."

All around the clearing, Firepaw saw the cats nodding in agreement.

"I shall travel to the Moonstone tomorrow," Bluestar

announced. "The warriors of StarClan will give me the strength I need to lead ThunderClan through this dark time. You must all get some rest. We have a lot to do when daylight comes. I wish to talk with Lionheart now." Without another word, she turned and strode toward her den.

Firepaw noticed the look of wonder that had entered the eyes of some of the cats when Bluestar had mentioned the Moonstone. Now the Clan cats hurriedly gathered in groups, meowing in hushed voices full of excitement.

"What's the Moonstone?" Firepaw asked Graypaw.

"It's a rock deep underground that shines in the dark," whispered Graypaw. His voice was hoarse with awe. "All Clan leaders have to spend one night at the Moonstone when they are first chosen. There, the spirits of StarClan share with them."

"Share *what* with them?"

Graypaw frowned. "I don't know," he admitted. "I know only that the new leaders have to sleep near the stone, and as they sleep, they have special dreams. After that, they have the gift of nine lives, and take the name 'star.'"

Firepaw watched Yellowfang limp back to her shadowy nest. It looked like Tigerclaw's rough treatment had aggravated her old injury. As he trotted back to the apprentices' den, Firepaw decided to ask Spottedleaf for more poppy seeds in the morning.

"So what happened?" mewed Dustpaw eagerly, popping his head out of the den. He seemed to have forgotten how much he resented the new apprentice in his eagerness to hear about the Gathering.

"It's like Longtail said. Brokenstar demanded hunting rights. . . ." Graypaw began.

Sandpaw and Dustpaw sat and listened, but Firepaw was watching the camp. He could see the silhouettes of Bluestar and Lionheart sitting close together outside her den, talking urgently.

Then he noticed the small shape of Ravenpaw at the entrance to the warriors' den. Tigerclaw stood beside him. Firepaw saw Ravenpaw's ears flatten as the young cat flinched away from Tigerclaw's fierce words. The dark warrior loomed over him, twice his size, his eyes and teeth flashing in the moonlight. What was he saying to Ravenpaw? Firepaw was just about to creep nearer and listen when Ravenpaw backed away, turned, and ran across the clearing.

Firepaw greeted Ravenpaw as he reached the apprentice's den, but Ravenpaw hardly seemed to notice him. Instead, he pushed his way inside the den without a word.

Firepaw got up to follow him when he saw Lionheart approaching.

"Well," meowed the ThunderClan deputy, striding up to the apprentices. "It seems that Firepaw, Graypaw, and Ravenpaw are about to reach another important stage in their training."

"What's that?" mewed Graypaw, looking excited.

"Bluestar wishes you three to accompany her on her journey to the Moonstone!" Lionheart didn't miss the look of disappointment on the faces of Dustpaw and Sandpaw, because he added, "Don't worry, you two; you'll make the journey soon enough. For now, ThunderClan needs your strength and skill at the camp. I will remain here also."

Firepaw looked past Lionheart to his leader. She was moving from one group of warriors to another, meowing instructions to each. Why had she chosen him for this journey? he wondered.

"She wants you to rest now," Lionheart continued. "But first go to Spottedleaf and collect the herbs you will need on this expedition. It's a long way. You will need something to give you strength and quell your appetite. There will be little time for catching prey."

Graypaw nodded, and Firepaw dragged his gaze away from Bluestar and nodded too.

"Where is Ravenpaw?" asked Lionheart.

"He's in his nest already," replied Firepaw.

"Good. Leave him to sleep. You can fetch herbs for him," meowed Lionheart. "Rest well. You leave at dawn." He flicked his tail and walked back to Bluestar's den.

"Well, then," mewed Sandpaw. "You'd better go and see Spottedleaf."

Firepaw listened for sourness in her voice, but there was none. There was no time for jealousy now. All the cats in the Clan seemed to be united against the threat from ShadowClan.

Firepaw and Graypaw walked quickly toward Spottedleaf's den. The fern tunnel was dark. Not even the full moon penetrated its thick covering.

Spottedleaf seemed to be expecting them as they emerged

into her moonlit clearing. "You have come for some traveling herbs," she meowed.

"Yes, please," Firepaw answered. "And I think Yellowfang needs more poppy seeds. She seemed to be feeling her wounds."

"I will take her some after you have gone. And your traveling herbs are ready."

Spottedleaf indicated a pile of carefully made leaf wraps. "Enough for the three of you. The dark green herb will stop your hunger pangs during the journey. The other will give you strength. Eat them both just before you leave. They're not as good as fresh prey, but the taste won't last long."

"Thanks, Spottedleaf," mewed Firepaw. He leaned down and picked up one of the parcels. As he bent his head, Spottedleaf stretched over and gently rubbed his cheek with her nose. Firepaw breathed in her sweet, warm scent and purred his thanks.

Graypaw picked up the other two and the friends turned and headed back through the tunnel.

"Good luck!" Spottedleaf called after them. "Travel safely."

They arrived at the entrance to their den and dropped the bundles.

"Well, I just hope these herbs don't taste too revolting!" muttered Graypaw.

"It must be a long way to the Moonstone. We've never been given herbs before. Do you know where it is?" Firepaw asked.

"Beyond Clan territory, at a place called HighStones. It lies deep underground, in a cave we call Mothermouth."

"Have you ever been there before?" Firepaw was impressed that Graypaw knew so much about this mysterious place.

"No, but all apprentices have to make the journey there before they become warriors."

The thought of becoming a warrior made Firepaw's eyes gleam with excitement, and he couldn't help standing a little taller.

"Don't get your hopes up. We still have to finish our training!" Graypaw warned, as if reading his thoughts.

Firepaw looked up through the canopy of leaves at the stars glittering in the black sky above. Moonhigh had passed. "We should get some sleep," he mewed. But he couldn't imagine being able to sleep with the thought of tomorrow's adventure spinning through his mind. Attending the Gathering, a journey to the Moonstone—how far away his kittypet life seemed now!

CHAPTER 14

❧

The cold air chilled Firepaw's bones as blackness wrapped itself around him. He could hear nothing, and his nostrils were filled with the musty scent of damp earth.

Out of nowhere, a brilliant ball of light flared in front of him. Firepaw ducked his head, screwing up his eyes against the glare. The light shone, dazzling coldly like a star; then it blinked out, disappearing as quickly as it had come. The darkness fell away, and Firepaw found himself in the forest. He felt comforted by the familiar smells of the woods. He breathed in the moist green scents, and calmness flowed through his body.

Without warning, a dreadful noise burst from the trees. Firepaw's fur bristled. It was the screeching of terrified cats racing out from the bushes up ahead. Firepaw recognized their ThunderClan pelts as they fled past him. He stood rooted to the spot, unable to move. Then came great cats, huge dark warriors, their eyes glittering cruelly. They thundered toward him, pounding the earth with massive paws, their claws unsheathed. And out of the shadows, Firepaw heard a high, desperate cry filled with grief and rage. Graypaw!

Firepaw woke, horrified. His dream vanished, leaving his ears ringing and his fur standing on end. As he opened his eyes, he saw the face of Tigerclaw peering into the den. Firepaw leaped to his feet, instantly alert.

"Something wrong, Firepaw?" asked Tigerclaw.

"Just a dream," Firepaw mumbled.

Tigerclaw gave him a curious look, then growled, "Wake the others. We leave shortly."

Outside the den, the sky glowed with a new dawn, and dew sparkled on the ferns. It would be a warm day once the sun was up, but the early-morning dampness reminded Firepaw that the time of leaf-fall was not far off.

Firepaw, Graypaw, and Ravenpaw quickly gulped down the herbs that Spottedleaf had given them. Tigerclaw and Bluestar sat watching them, ready to leave. The rest of the camp was still asleep.

"Ugh!" complained Graypaw. "I knew they'd be bitter. Why couldn't we eat a fat, juicy mouse instead?"

"These herbs will keep your hunger at bay longer," answered Bluestar. "And they will make you strong. We have a long journey ahead of us."

"Have you eaten yours already?" Firepaw asked.

"I cannot eat if I'm going to share dreams with StarClan at the Moonstone tonight," replied Bluestar.

Firepaw felt his paws tingle when he heard these words. He was itching to begin the journey. With the dawn's light and the familiar voices, the terror of his dream had left him. All that remained was the memory of the brilliant light, and Bluestar's words sent a renewed thrill of excitement through him.

The five cats made their way through the gorse tunnel and out of the camp.

Lionheart was just returning with a patrol. "Safe journey," he meowed.

Bluestar nodded. "I know I can trust you to keep the camp safe," she answered.

Lionheart looked at Graypaw and dipped his head. "Remember," he meowed, "you are almost a warrior. Don't forget what I have taught you."

Graypaw looked back at Lionheart with affection. "I will always remember, Lionheart," he mewed, nudging his head against the tabby's broad golden flank.

They retraced their route to Fourtrees. This was the quickest way to pass into WindClan territory. HighStones lay beyond.

As Firepaw bounded down the side of the glade toward the Great Rock, he could still smell the scents of last night's Gathering. He followed the others through the grassy clearing and up the slope on the other side, into WindClan territory. The bushy slope became steeper as they climbed, and rockier, until the cats had to leap from boulder to boulder up the side of a craggy cliff face.

Firepaw paused when they reached the top. Ahead of them, the ground flattened out into a wide plateau. The wind blew in a steady gust that rippled the grass and bent the trees. The soil was stony, and outcroppings of bare rock dotted the landscape here and there.

The air still carried the scents of WindClan, but they were stale. Much fresher, and more alarming, were the pungent markings of ShadowClan warriors.

"All Clans are entitled to safe passage to the Moonstone, but ShadowClan seems to have no respect for the warrior code anymore, so be alert," warned Bluestar. "We mustn't hunt outside our territory, though. We'll follow the warrior code, even if ShadowClan doesn't."

They set off across the plateau as the sun rose into the sky, following the tracks through the heather. Firepaw had grown used to living under a canopy of trees. Without their shade, his flame-colored pelt felt heavy and hot, and his back seemed to burn. He was thankful for the steady breeze blowing from the forests behind.

Suddenly Tigerclaw stopped dead. "Watch out!" he hissed. "I smell a ShadowClan patrol."

Firepaw and the others lifted their noses, and sure enough, the scent of ShadowClan warriors traveled on the wind.

"They are upwind. They won't know we are here if we keep moving," meowed Bluestar. "But we must hurry. If they move ahead they'll detect us. It's not far to the edge of WindClan territory now."

They moved on quickly, leaping over the rocks, pushing their way through the sweet-smelling heather. Every few steps, Firepaw sniffed the air and glanced over his shoulder, on the lookout for the ShadowClan patrol. But gradually the odor grew fainter and fainter. *They must have turned back*, he thought with relief.

Finally they reached the edge of the uplands. The landscape

changed dramatically, shaped and altered beyond recognition by Twolegs. Wide earth tracks crisscrossed green and golden meadows, small woods dotted the land, and Twoleg nests were scattered here and there among the fields. In the distance Firepaw saw a familiar wide, gray path, and an acid tang that stung his throat drifted on the breeze.

"Is that the Thunderpath?" he asked Graypaw.

"Yes," replied Graypaw. "It runs up from ShadowClan territory. Can you see HighStones behind it?"

Firepaw looked at the distant horizon. The land rose sharply up to a point, jagged and barren. "Do we have to cross the Thunderpath then?"

"Yep," mewed Graypaw. His voice was strong and confident, almost cheerful, as he faced the difficult journey.

"Come on!" Bluestar meowed. She bounded forward. "We can be there by moonrise as long as we keep up the pace."

Firepaw followed her with the others, down the hill, away from the bleak hunting grounds of WindClan and into the lush Twoleg territory.

Keeping near the hedges, the cats walked on. Once or twice Firepaw could smell prey-scent from the bushes, but Spottedleaf's herbs had succeeded in taking the edge off his hunger. The sun was still hot on his back, even in the shadows of the hedgerows.

They skirted a Twoleg nest. It stood on a wide expanse of hard white stone, with smaller nests round the edges. Keeping low, the cats crept past the fence that surrounded the white stone. A sudden barrage of barking and snarling made them spin around.

Dogs! Firepaw's heart missed a beat. He arched his back, fur bristling from nose to tail.

Tigerclaw peered through the fence. "It's all right. They're tied up!" he hissed.

Firepaw looked at the two dogs scrabbling on the stone barely ten tail-lengths away. They were nothing like the pampered pets that lived in the gardens of the Twolegplace. These creatures stared at him with wild, killing eyes. They strained at their ties and reared up on their hind legs. They growled and barked, their lips drawn back to reveal huge teeth, until the shout of an unseen Twoleg silenced them. The cats moved on.

The sun was beginning to sink by the time they reached the Thunderpath. Bluestar signaled to them to stop and wait beneath a hedge. His eyes and throat stinging from the fumes, Firepaw watched as the great monsters flashed to and fro in front of him.

"We'll go one at a time," meowed Tigerclaw. "Ravenpaw, you first."

"No, Tigerclaw," Bluestar interrupted. "I shall go first. Don't forget, this will be the first time of crossing for the apprentices. Let them see how it is done."

Firepaw stared at his leader as she padded to the edge of the Thunderpath and looked up and down. She waited calmly as one monster after another flew past her, ruffling her fur. Then, when the earsplitting roar paused for a moment, she raced across to the other side.

"Off you go, Ravenpaw; now you've seen how it's done," meowed Tigerclaw.

Firepaw saw Ravenpaw's eyes widen with fear. He knew just how his friend felt. He could smell his own fear-scent. The small black cat crept forward to the edge of the road. It was quiet, but Ravenpaw hesitated.

"Go!" hissed Tigerclaw from the hedge. Firepaw saw Ravenpaw's muscles tighten as he prepared to run. Then the ground began to tremble beneath his paws. A monster sped out of the distance and hurtled past. The black cat shrank back for a moment, then pelted over to join Bluestar. A monster coming in the other direction threw dust up where his paws had been just a heartbeat before. Firepaw felt his fur shiver and he took a deep breath to calm himself.

Graypaw was lucky. A long lull let him cross safely. Then it was Firepaw's turn.

"Go on, then," growled Tigerclaw. Firepaw looked from Tigerclaw to the Thunderpath, and then walked out from beneath the hedge. He waited at the edge, as Bluestar had done. A monster was rushing toward him. Firepaw looked at the approaching monster. *After this one*, he thought, and waited for it to pass. Suddenly his heart lurched as he realized the monster had veered off the Thunderpath and was bumping along the grass. It was heading straight for him! A Twoleg was jeering from an opening in its side. Firepaw leaped backward, claws out, battered by the storm of wind from the Twoleg monster as it roared past him only a whisker away. He crouched, trembling, in the dirt and stared as it swerved back onto the path and disappeared into the distance. Through the roaring of blood in his ears, Firepaw realized the Thunderpath was quiet again, and he raced across, running faster than he had ever done in his life.

"I thought you were fresh-kill!" cried Graypaw as Firepaw cannoned into him, almost knocking him over.

"Me too!" Firepaw gasped. He was trying to stop shaking. He turned back to watch Tigerclaw dart over the path toward them.

"Twolegs!" he spat as he arrived at their side.

"Do you want to rest before we go on?" Bluestar asked Firepaw.

Firepaw looked up. The sun was low in the sky. "No," he answered. "I'm okay." But he had leaped so frantically out of the monster's way that his claws felt frayed and tender.

The cats carried on, with Bluestar in the lead. The earth was darker on this side of the Thunderpath and the grass felt coarser underpaw. As they approached the foot of HighStones, the grass gave way to bare, rocky soil, dotted with patches of heather. The land sloped up now, toward the sky. Craggy rocks topped the slope, blazing orange in the sun.

Bluestar stopped once more. She chose a sun-warmed rock to sit upon, flat and wide enough for all five cats to rest side by side.

"Look," she meowed, tilting her nose toward the dark slope before them. "Mothermouth."

Firepaw peered upward. The glare of the setting sun blinded him, and the slope was engulfed in shadow.

The cats waited in silence. Gradually, as the sun dropped down behind HighStones, Firepaw began to make out the cave entrance, a square black hole that yawned darkly beneath a stone archway.

"We'll wait here until the moon is higher," meowed Bluestar. "You should hunt if you are hungry and then get some rest."

Firepaw was pleased to have a chance to find food. He was starving now. Graypaw clearly felt the same and leaped away into a clump of heather, following the prey-scent that was thick in the air. Firepaw and Ravenpaw followed him. Tigerclaw set off in the opposite direction, but Bluestar remained where she was. She sat still and silent, gazing unblinkingly at Mothermouth.

The three apprentices gathered plenty of fresh-kill. With Tigerclaw they crouched on the stony hillside and feasted. But in spite of their easy hunt, no cat said much, and the air still felt thick with tension and anticipation.

Afterward, the cats rested beside their leader until the warmth had seeped out of the rock on which they lay and cold black shadows reached up on all sides. Only then did Bluestar call out, "Come. It is time."

CHAPTER 15

✤

Bluestar stood and began to pad toward Mothermouth. Tigerclaw
walked beside her, matching her strides step for step.

"Come on, Ravenpaw!" called Graypaw. Ravenpaw was
still sitting on the rock, staring up at the rocks. At Graypaw's
mew, he stood and began to follow slowly. Firepaw realized
his friend had hardly said a word the whole journey. *Is he just
worried about ShadowClan, or is there something else troubling him?*
Firepaw wondered.

It took the cats only a few moments to reach Mothermouth.
Firepaw stood on the threshold and peered inside. The blackness beyond the stone archway was darker than the cloudiest
night. Firepaw narrowed his eyes, trying to see where the
tunnel led, but he couldn't see a thing.

Beside him, Graypaw and Ravenpaw craned their heads
nervously around the entrance. Even Tigerclaw seemed
unsettled by the black hole ahead of them. "How will we find
our way in such darkness?" he asked.

"I will know the way," answered Bluestar. "Just follow
my scent. Ravenpaw and Graypaw, you will remain on
guard outside. Firepaw, you will accompany me and

Tigerclaw to the Moonstone."

Firepaw felt a thrill jolt through him. What an honor! Firepaw glanced sideways at Tigerclaw. The warrior sat with his chin boldly raised, but Firepaw could detect a subtle fear-scent coming from him. It grew stronger as Bluestar stepped forward into the blackness.

Tigerclaw shook his mighty head and padded after Bluestar. With a brief nod to the other apprentices, Firepaw followed.

Inside the cave, his eyes still detected nothing. The complete and utter blackness felt strange, but he was surprised to find that he wasn't frightened. His eagerness to discover what lay ahead was stronger.

The cold, damp air reached through his thick fur and into his bones, stiffening his muscles. Even the coldest nights did not hold the same chill as the air here. *This ground has never known the warmth of the sun*, thought Firepaw, feeling the rock smooth like ice beneath his paws. Freezing air filled his lungs with each breath, until he felt light-headed.

He followed Bluestar and Tigerclaw through the darkness, judging his way by scent and feel alone. They were walking along a tunnel that sloped down and down, winding first one way and then the other. Firepaw's whiskers brushed the side of the cave, telling him where to walk and where to turn. His nose told him that Bluestar and Tigerclaw were only a tail-length ahead of him.

On and on they went. *How far have we come?* Firepaw wondered. Then he felt a tingle in his whiskers. The air in his nostrils seemed fresher than before. He sniffed again, relieved to smell the familiar world above. He could smell peat, and prey, and the scent of heather. There must be a hole somewhere in the roof of the tunnel. "Where are we?" he mewed into the darkness.

"We have entered the cavern of the Moonstone," came Bluestar's soft reply. "Wait here. It will be moonhigh soon."

Firepaw folded his hind legs under him on the chilly stone floor and waited. He could hear the steady breathing of Bluestar and the more rapid, fear-scented panting of Tigerclaw.

Suddenly, in a flash more blinding than the setting sun, the cave was lit up. Firepaw's eyes were wide open after the blackness of the tunnel. He closed them quickly against the cold, white light. Then slowly he opened them into tiny slits and peered ahead.

He saw a gleaming rock, which glittered as if it were made from countless dewdrops. *The Moonstone!* Firepaw looked around. In the cold light reflected from the stone, he could make out the shadowy edges of a high-roofed cavern. The Moonstone rose up from the middle of the floor, three tail-lengths high.

Bluestar was staring upward, her fur bleached white in the glow of the Moonstone. Even Tigerclaw's dark pelt shone silver. Firepaw followed Bluestar's gaze. High in the roof was an opening that revealed a narrow triangle of night sky. The moon was casting a beam of light through the hole, down onto the Moonstone, making it sparkle like a star.

Beside him, Firepaw smelled Tigerclaw's fear-scent growing,

until it became overpowering. Firepaw felt startled. Could the warrior see something else here, something dangerous? He saw a flash of movement, felt fur rush past him, and heard the fleeing pawsteps of Tigerclaw racing back to the entrance.

"Firepaw?" Bluestar's voice was quiet and calm.

"I'm still here," he answered nervously. What had frightened Tigerclaw?

"Bluestar?" Firepaw mewed again when she didn't answer. His heart was beating fast, making the blood roar in his ears.

"It is all right, young warrior; don't be afraid," Bluestar murmured. Her calm voice settled him a little. "I think Tigerclaw was surprised by the power of the Moonstone. In the world above, Tigerclaw is a fearless and mighty warrior, but down here, where the spirits of StarClan speak, a cat needs a different kind of strength. What do you feel, Firepaw?"

Firepaw sniffed the air deeply, and forced his body to relax. "Only my own curiosity," he admitted.

"That is good," Bluestar replied.

Firepaw looked back at the Moonstone. His eyes had gotten used to its light and he was no longer dazzled. Instead, it soothed him. With a twitch of his tail, he remembered his dream. This was the brilliant ball of light he had seen!

Spellbound, Firepaw watched as Bluestar padded up to the stone and lay down beside it. She reached her head forward and touched the Moonstone with her nose. Her blue eyes sparkled with its reflection for a moment before she closed them. Now she rested her head on her paws, her eyelids flickering, her paws twitching occasionally. *Was she sleeping?* Then

Firepaw remembered Graypaw's words: "new leaders have to sleep near the stone, and as they sleep, they have special dreams."

He waited. The chill was not so intense here, but still he found himself shivering. He had no idea how much time had passed, but suddenly the rock stopped glowing. The cavern was plunged into darkness once more. Firepaw looked up to the opening in the roof of the cavern. The moon had passed on, out of sight. All that remained were tiny stars shimmering in blackness.

Firepaw could just make out the pale shape of his leader, lying beside the Moonstone. He wanted to call out her name, but did not dare break the silence.

After more endless moments, she spoke to him. "Firepaw? Are you still there?" Her voice sounded remote and agitated.

"Yes, Bluestar." Firepaw heard Bluestar's pawsteps approaching.

"Hurry," she hissed. He felt her fur brush past him. "We must return to camp."

Firepaw raced after her, astonished by the speed with which she rushed through the blackness. He followed her scent blindly, up and up the stone tunnel, until she led him safely back to the outside world.

Tigerclaw was waiting at the opening beside Graypaw and Ravenpaw as Bluestar and Firepaw climbed out of the cave. His expression was cold and his fur was slightly ruffled, but he sat motionless and dignified.

"Tigerclaw." Bluestar greeted him but did not mention the warrior cat's flight from the depths.

Tigerclaw relaxed a little. "What did you learn?"

"We must return to camp immediately," Bluestar meowed briefly.

Firepaw saw a look of desperation in his leader's eyes. Now the horror of his dream forced its way back into his memory: the fleeing cats; the great, dark warriors; the ear-splitting wail of distress. Firepaw tried to ignore the cold fear that gripped his muscles, and followed Bluestar as she and the others raced down the dark slope away from Mothermouth. Was his nightmare vision about to come true?

CHAPTER 16

❧

They headed back the way they had come. The moon had disappeared behind a bank of clouds. It was dark, but at least the Thunderpath was quieter now. The only monster they heard was far off in the distance. The cats crossed the path together and pushed their way through the hedge on the other side.

Firepaw could feel his muscles growing stiff with tiredness as they hurried on. Bluestar kept up a swift pace with her nose thrust forward and her tail high. Tigerclaw loped beside her. Firepaw followed a few paces behind with Graypaw, but Ravenpaw was flagging.

"Keep up, Ravenpaw!" Tigerclaw growled over his shoulder.

Ravenpaw flinched and bounded forward until he caught up with Firepaw and Graypaw.

"Are you okay?" Firepaw asked.

"Yes," Ravenpaw panted, not meeting Firepaw's eyes. "Just a bit tired."

They scrambled down a deep ditch and up the other side.

"What did Tigerclaw say when he came out of the cave?" Firepaw meowed, trying not to sound too curious.

"He wanted to check that we were still guarding the entrance," replied Graypaw. "Why?"

Firepaw hesitated. "Did you scent anything strange about him?" he asked.

"Only that damp old cave," Graypaw mewed, looking surprised.

"He seemed a little edgy," ventured Ravenpaw.

"He wasn't the only one!" Graypaw meowed, looking at the black cat.

"What do you mean?" asked Ravenpaw.

"Just that the fur on your neck stands up whenever you see him these days," whispered Graypaw. "You nearly jumped out of your skin when he came out of the cave."

"He just surprised me, that's all," Ravenpaw protested. "You have to admit, it was a bit creepy by Mothermouth."

"I suppose so," agreed Graypaw.

The cats slipped under a hedge into a cornfield that glowed silver in the moonlight, and followed the ditch that ran around its edge.

"So what was it like inside, Firepaw?" Graypaw demanded. "Did you see the Moonstone?"

"Yes, I did. It was amazing!" Firepaw felt his fur tingle at the memory.

Graypaw shot him an admiring glance. "So it's true! The rock really does shine underground."

Firepaw didn't reply. He closed his eyes for a moment, savoring the image of the Moonstone that dazzled his mind. Then pictures from his dream crowded into his head, and his eyes shot open. Bluestar was right: they had to get back to camp as quickly as they could.

Ahead, Tigerclaw and Bluestar had leaped through a fence, out of the cornfield. The apprentices followed, squeezing under the fence, onto an earth track. It was the path that led past the Twoleg nest and the dogs. Firepaw looked up and saw Bluestar and Tigerclaw trotting tirelessly together, silhouetted against a skyline tinged with red. The sun would be rising soon.

"Look!" he called to Graypaw and Ravenpaw. An unfamiliar cat had jumped out in front of the two warriors.

"It's a loner!" hissed Graypaw. The three apprentices hurried forward.

The stranger was a stout black-and-white tom, shorter than the warriors, but well muscled.

"This is Barley," Bluestar explained to the apprentices as they caught up. "He lives near this Twoleg nest."

"Hi!" meowed the cat. "I haven't seen any of your Clan for some moons. How are you, Bluestar?"

"I'm well, thank you," replied Bluestar. "And you, Barley? How's the prey been running since we last passed this way?"

"Not so bad," replied Barley, with an amiable gleam in his eye. "One good thing about Twolegs—you'll always find plenty of rats nearby." The black-and-white tom went on: "You seem in more of a hurry than usual. Is everything all right?"

Tigerclaw looked at Barley. A growl rumbled deep in his chest. Firepaw could sense that the warrior was suspicious of the loner's curiosity.

"I don't like to be away from my Clan too long," Bluestar answered smoothly.

"As always, Bluestar, you are tied to your Clan like a queen to her kits," observed Barley, not unkindly.

"What is it you want, Barley?" asked Tigerclaw.

Barley flashed him a reproachful look. "I just wanted to warn you that there are two dogs here now. You'd be safer going back into the cornfield instead of past the yard."

"We know about the dogs. We saw them earlier—" Tigerclaw began impatiently.

"We are grateful to you for the warning," interrupted Bluestar. "Thank you, Barley. Until next time . . ."

Barley flicked his tail. "Have a safe journey," he meowed as he bounded away up the track.

"Come," ordered Bluestar, heading off the track. She pushed her way through the long grass between the path and the fence that led back into the cornfield. The three apprentices followed, but Tigerclaw hesitated.

"You trust the word of a loner?" he meowed.

Bluestar stopped and turned to face him. "Would you rather face those dogs?"

"They were tied up when we passed them earlier," Tigerclaw pointed out.

"They may be untied now. We're going this way," meowed Bluestar. She ducked under the fence into the field. Firepaw slipped after her, followed by Graypaw, Ravenpaw, and finally Tigerclaw.

By now, the sun had lifted its head above the horizon. The

hedgerows sparkled with dew, promising another warm day.

The cats padded along the edge of the ditch. Firepaw looked down into the deep gully, steep-sided and filled with nettles. Firepaw could smell prey-scent. There was something familiar about the bitter odor, but it was one he hadn't smelled for a long time.

An earsplitting squeal made Firepaw whip around. Ravenpaw was struggling and clawing at the earth. Something had hold of his leg and was dragging him down into the ditch.

"Rats!" spat Tigerclaw. "Barley has sent us into a trap!"

Before they could react, all five cats were surrounded. Huge brown rats swarmed out of the ditch, squeaking shrilly. Firepaw could see their sharp front teeth glinting in the early dawn light.

Suddenly one leaped onto Firepaw's shoulder. Fiery pain shot through his shoulder as the rat sank its teeth into his flesh. Another grasped his leg between its powerful jaws.

Firepaw flung himself down and writhed madly, trying to shake free. He knew the rats were not as strong as he was, but there were so many of them. Yowls, hisses, and spits told him that the others were also being attacked.

Firepaw slashed fiercely with his claws, slicing out at a rat that held on to his leg. It let go, but another one gripped his tail. Fast as lightning, powered by fear and rage, Firepaw fought and hacked at his attackers. Twisting his head around, he sank his teeth into the rat that had embedded itself into his shoulders. He felt the bones of its neck crunch in his mouth and its body go limp, before it fell away onto the dirt track.

Firepaw gasped with pain as yet another rat leaped onto his back and sank its teeth in. Out of the corner of his eye, he saw a flash of white fur. For a moment he was confused; then he felt the rat being dragged off him. Firepaw spun around to see Barley flinging the rodent into the ditch.

Without hesitating, Barley glanced around and sprinted over to Bluestar. She was writhing on the path, covered in rats. In a flash Barley had the spine of one between his teeth and was plucking it off her with practiced ease. He spat it onto the ground and grabbed another in his mouth as Bluestar thrashed beneath him.

Firepaw rushed over to Graypaw, who was being attacked from both sides by two smaller rats. Firepaw lunged at the nearest one, giving it a bite that left it dead. Graypaw managed to turn and pin down the other with his claws. He grabbed it with his teeth and flung it into the ditch as hard as he could. It did not come back.

"They're running away!" Tigerclaw yowled.

Sure enough, the remaining rats were fleeing down into the safety of the ditch. Firepaw could hear the scrabbling of small paws disappearing into the nettles. The bites in his shoulder and hind leg stung sharply. He licked carefully at his fur, wet and matted with blood, its sharp tang mingling with the stench of the rats.

Firepaw looked around for Ravenpaw. Graypaw was standing at the edge of the nettles, mewing encouragement as Ravenpaw pulled himself out of the ditch, muddy and stung. A young rat was still hanging on to his tail. Firepaw bounded over and finished it off quickly while Graypaw helped to pull Ravenpaw over the top of the ditch.

Now Firepaw looked for Bluestar. He saw Barley first, standing at the top of the ditch, scanning the depths for more rats. Bluestar was lying on the path nearby. Alarmed, Firepaw dashed to his leader's side. The thick gray fur at the back of her neck was drenched with blood. "Bluestar?" he mewed.

Bluestar did not reply.

A furious yowl made Firepaw look up.

Tigerclaw leaped on top of Barley and pinned him to the ground. "You sent us into a trap!" he snarled.

"I didn't know the rats were here!" spat Barley, his paws scrabbling in the dust as he struggled to stand up.

"Why did you send us this way?" hissed Tigerclaw.

"The dogs!"

"The dogs were tied when we passed them earlier!"

"The Twoleg unties them at night. They guard his nest," Barley panted, wheezing under the weight of Tigerclaw's massive paws.

"Tigerclaw! Bluestar is injured!" Firepaw burst out.

Tigerclaw released Barley at once. Barley got up and shook the dust from his coat. The great warrior bounded over to Bluestar's side and sniffed her wounds.

"Is there anything we can do?" Firepaw asked.

"She is in the hands of StarClan now," meowed Tigerclaw solemnly, stepping back.

Firepaw opened his eyes wide with shock. Did Tigerclaw mean that Bluestar was dead? His fur prickled as he looked down at his leader. Is this what the spirits at the Moonstone had warned her about?

Graypaw and Ravenpaw had joined them and stood beside their leader, horror-struck. Barley hung back, craning his neck to see what was happening.

Bluestar's eyes were open but glazed, and her gray body lay motionless. She didn't even appear to be breathing.

"Is she dead?" whispered Ravenpaw.

"I don't know. We must wait and see," replied Tigerclaw.

The five cats waited in silence as the sun began to climb into the sky. Firepaw found himself wordlessly begging StarClan to protect his leader, to send her back to them.

Then Bluestar stirred. The end of her tail twitched and she lifted her head.

"Bluestar?" mewed Firepaw, his voice trembling.

"It's all right," Bluestar rasped. "I am still here. I have lost a life, but it wasn't my ninth."

Joy flooded Firepaw. He looked at Tigerclaw, expecting to see relief on his face, but the dark warrior was expressionless.

"Right," Tigerclaw meowed in a commanding tone. "Ravenpaw, fetch cobwebs for Bluestar's wounds. Graypaw, find marigold or horsetail." The two apprentices dashed away. "Barley, I think you should leave us now."

Firepaw looked over to the loner who had fought so bravely to help them. He wanted to thank him, but under Tigerclaw's fierce gaze, he didn't dare. Instead of speaking, Firepaw gave Barley a tiny nod. Barley seemed to understand, for he nodded in return and left without another word.

Bluestar was still lying on the dirt track. "Is everyone all right?" she asked hoarsely.

Tigerclaw nodded.

Ravenpaw came charging back, his left forepaw wrapped in a thick wad of cobwebs. "Here," he mewed.

"Shall I put them on her wounds?" Firepaw asked Tigerclaw. "Yellowfang showed me how."

"Very well," agreed Tigerclaw. He walked away and scanned the ditch again, his ears pricked for more rats.

Firepaw peeled a clump of cobwebs from Ravenpaw's paw and began to press them firmly onto Bluestar's wounds.

She winced under his touch. "If it had not been for Tigerclaw, those rats would have eaten me alive," she murmured, her voice tight with pain.

"It wasn't Tigerclaw who saved you. It was Barley," Firepaw whispered as he took some more cobwebs from Ravenpaw.

"Barley?" Bluestar sounded surprised. "Is he here?"

"Tigerclaw sent him away," Firepaw answered quietly. "He thinks Barley sent us into a trap."

"And what do you think?" Bluestar rasped.

Firepaw didn't look up, but concentrated on pressing the last bit of cobweb into place. "Barley is a loner. What would he gain by sending us into a trap only to rescue us from it?" he mewed eventually.

Bluestar laid down her head and closed her eyes again.

Graypaw returned with some horsetail. Firepaw chewed the leaves and spat the juice onto Bluestar's wounds. He knew it would help stop infection, but he still wished Spottedleaf were with him, with her knowledge of and confidence in healing.

"We should rest here while Bluestar recovers," announced Tigerclaw, padding up.

"No," Bluestar insisted. "We must return to the camp." Narrowing her eyes in pain, she struggled to her paws. "Let's keep going."

The ThunderClan leader limped along the edge of the field. Tigerclaw walked at her side, his face dark with unknowable thoughts. The apprentices exchanged anxious glances, and then followed.

"It is a long time since I saw you lose a life, Bluestar." Firepaw overheard Tigerclaw's whispered words. "How many have you lost now?"

Firepaw couldn't help feeling surprised at Tigerclaw's open curiosity.

"That was my fifth," replied Bluestar quietly.

Firepaw strained his ears, but Tigerclaw did not reply. He padded on, lost in thought.

CHAPTER 17

Sunhigh came and went as the cats made their way through WindClan's old hunting grounds. Their heavy silence showed that they were still sore after the rat fight. Firepaw felt scratched and bitten all over. He could see Graypaw was limping, occasionally hopping on three legs to protect his injured back leg. But it was Bluestar who worried him most. Her pace was even slower now, but she refused to stop and rest. The grim look on her face, clouded by pain, told Firepaw how much she wanted to reach the ThunderClan camp.

"Don't worry about ShadowClan warriors," she meowed through gritted teeth as Tigerclaw paused to sniff the air. "You won't find any here today."

How could she be so sure? Firepaw wondered.

They picked their way carefully down the steep, rocky hillside that led to Fourtrees and joined the familiar trail that led home. It was late afternoon, and Firepaw began to think longingly of his nest, and a plump helping of fresh-kill.

"I can still smell the stench of ShadowClan," Graypaw muttered to Firepaw as they trekked through ThunderClan's hunting grounds.

"Perhaps the breeze has carried it down from WindClan's territory," Firepaw suggested. He could smell it too, and his whiskers were trembling.

Suddenly Ravenpaw stopped. "Can you hear that?" he mewed in a hushed voice.

Firepaw strained his ears. At first he heard only the familiar sounds of the forest—leaves rustling, a pigeon calling. Then his blood ran cold. In the distance he could hear battle-hungry yowls, and the shrill squeal of terrified kits.

"Quick!" Bluestar howled. "It is as StarClan warned me. Our camp is being attacked!" She tried to leap forward, but stumbled. She pushed herself up and limped onward.

Tigerclaw and Firepaw pelted forward side by side. Graypaw and Ravenpaw followed, their tail fur bristled to twice its usual size. Firepaw forgot his soreness as he charged toward the camp. His only concern was to protect the Clan.

The sounds of battle grew louder and louder as he neared the camp entrance, and the stench of ShadowClan filled his nostrils. He was right behind Tigerclaw as the cats dashed through the tunnel and into the clearing.

They were met by a frenzy of fighting, ThunderClan cats battling furiously with ShadowClan warriors. The kits were out of sight, and Firepaw hoped they were safely hidden in the nursery. He guessed the weakest elders would be sheltering inside the hollow trunk of their fallen tree.

Every corner of the camp seemed alive with warriors. Firepaw could see Frostfur and Goldenflower clawing and biting at a huge gray tom. Even the young tabby queen Brindleface was fighting, though she was very close to kitting. Darkstripe was locked in a fierce tussle with a black warrior. Three of the elders, Smallear, Patchpelt, and One-eye, were nipping bravely at a tortoiseshell that fought with twice their speed and ferocity.

The returning cats hurled themselves into the battle. Firepaw caught hold of a tabby warrior queen, much larger than him, and sank his teeth deep into her leg. She yowled with pain and turned on him, lashing out with sharp claws and lunging at his neck with her teeth bared. He twisted and ducked to avoid her bite. She couldn't match his speed, and he managed to grasp her from behind and pull her down into the dirt. With his strong hind legs he clawed at her back till she squealed and struggled away from him, running headlong into the thick undergrowth that surrounded the camp.

Firepaw glanced around to see that Bluestar had arrived. Despite her injuries, she was fighting another tabby. Firepaw had never seen her fight before, but even wounded, she was a powerful opponent. Her victim struggled to escape but she held him tightly and clawed him so fiercely that Firepaw knew he would bear the scars of this fight for many moons.

Then he saw a white ShadowClan cat with jet-black paws dragging a ThunderClan elder away from the nursery. Firepaw remembered those unusual dark paws from the Gathering. Blackfoot! The ShadowClan deputy made quick work of killing the elder, who had been guarding the kits, and began to reach into the bramble nest with one massive paw. The kits were squealing and mewling, undefended now as their mothers wrestled with other ShadowClan warriors in the clearing.

Firepaw prepared to spring toward the nursery, but a claw sliced painfully down his side and he whipped around to see a scrawny tortoiseshell leap on top of him. As he slammed into the ground, he tried to call out to the other ThunderClan cats that the kits were in danger. Fighting with all his strength to escape the tortoiseshell's grip, he wrenched his head around so he could see the bramble nest.

Blackfoot had scooped two kits from their bedding already and was reaching in for a third.

Firepaw saw no more as the tortoiseshell raked his belly with her hind claws. Firepaw scrabbled onto his feet and crouched low, as if in defeat. The trick had worked before and it worked now. As the tortoiseshell gripped him triumphantly and began to sink her teeth into Firepaw's neck, Firepaw sprang upward as hard as he could and flung the warrior away. He spun around and was on the winded warrior in an instant. This time he showed no mercy, plunging his teeth deep into the cat's shoulder. The bite sent the she-cat howling into the undergrowth.

Firepaw jumped up, dashed over to the nursery, and thrust his head through the nursery entrance. Blackfoot was nowhere to be seen. Inside the nest, crouching over the terrified kits, was Yellowfang. Her gray fur was spattered with blood, and one of her eyes was painfully swollen. She looked up at Firepaw with a ferocious hiss, then, realizing it was him, she yowled, "They're okay. I'll protect them."

Firepaw looked at her as she calmed the helpless kits, and Brokenstar's dire warning about the ShadowClan rogue flashed through his mind. He didn't have time to think about that now. He would have to trust Yellowfang. He nodded quickly and ducked back out of the brambles.

There were now only a few ShadowClan cats left in the camp. Ravenpaw and Graypaw were fighting side by side, lashing out at a black tom until he fled howling into the bushes. Whitestorm and Darkstripe chased the last two intruders out of the camp, sending them off with a few extra scratches and bites.

Firepaw sat down, exhausted, and stared around the camp. It was devastated. Blood spattered the clearing, and tufts of fur drifted in the dust. The surrounding wall of undergrowth was ripped open where the invaders had crashed through.

One by one, the ThunderClan cats gathered beneath the Highrock. Graypaw came to sit by him, his sides heaving and blood trickling from a torn ear. Ravenpaw flopped down and began to lick a wound on his tail. The queens ran to the nursery to check on their kits. Firepaw found himself waiting tensely for their return, his view blocked by the other cats. He relaxed when he heard squeals and purrs of joy coming from the bramble nest.

Frostfur wove her way back through the crowd, followed by Yellowfang. The white queen stepped forward and addressed them. "Our kits are all safe, thanks to Yellowfang. A ShadowClan warrior killed brave Rosetail and was trying to steal them from their nest, but Yellowfang fought him off."

"It was no ordinary ShadowClan warrior either," Firepaw put in. He was determined to let the Clan know how much they owed Yellowfang. "I saw him. It was Blackfoot."

"The ShadowClan deputy!" meowed Brindleface, who had fought so bitterly to protect the unborn kits in her swollen belly.

There was a stir at the edge of the group, as Bluestar limped forward and made her way over to the apprentices. The grave expression on her face was enough to tell Firepaw that something was wrong.

"Spottedleaf is with Lionheart," she murmured. "He was injured in the battle. It looks bad." She turned her head toward the shadow on the far side of the Highrock where the warrior lay, a motionless bundle of dusty golden fur.

A high-pitched wail rose from Graypaw's throat and he raced over to Lionheart. Spottedleaf, who had been leaning over the ThunderClan deputy, stepped back to let the young apprentice share tongues for the last time with his mentor. As Graypaw's howl of grief echoed around the clearing, Firepaw's fur tingled and his blood ran cold. It was the cry he had heard in his dream! For a moment his head swam; then he gave himself a shake. He had to keep calm, for Graypaw's sake.

Firepaw looked at Bluestar, who nodded, and he padded over to join his friend by the Highrock. He stopped for a moment beside Spottedleaf.

She looked exhausted and dull-eyed with grief. "I can't help Lionheart now," she mewed quietly to him. "He is on his way to join StarClan." She pressed her body against Firepaw's side, and he felt comforted by the touch of her warm fur.

The other cats looked on in silence as the sun slowly set

behind the trees. Finally Graypaw sat up and cried out, "He's gone!" He lay down again beside Lionheart's body and rested his head on his front paws. The rest of the Clan walked silently forward to carry out their own grieving rituals for their beloved deputy.

Firepaw joined them. He licked Lionheart's neck and murmured, "Thank you for your wisdom. You taught me so much." Then he sat down beside Graypaw and began gently to groom his friend's ears.

Bluestar waited until the other cats had left before padding quietly up. Graypaw didn't even seem to notice his leader's presence. Firepaw looked away as Bluestar spoke her last words to her old friend.

"Oh, what am I going to do without you, Lionheart?" she whispered. Then she limped back to her den and crouched down outside, staring grief-stricken into the distance. She didn't even try to lick clean her bloody, matted fur. It was the first time Firepaw had seen her look utterly defeated, and he felt a chill run through him.

He sat with Graypaw and Lionheart until the moon rose high. Ravenpaw joined him and together they kept company with their grieving friend. Tigerclaw strode over and briefly shared tongues with Lionheart. Firepaw waited to hear what words he would share with his warrior friend, but Tigerclaw remained silent as he licked the matted fur. To Firepaw's confusion, the dark tabby's eyes seemed to be fixed on Ravenpaw rather than the fallen deputy.

Spottedleaf padded lightly around the camp, tending to

wounds and battered nerves. Firepaw watched her approach Bluestar twice, but each time the leader sent her away to see to the others. Only when Spottedleaf had attended to the wounds of all the other cats did Bluestar allow her to treat her bites and scratches.

When she had finished, Spottedleaf turned and walked back to her den. Bluestar stood and slowly hauled herself up onto the Highrock. The Clan cats seemed to have been waiting for her. As soon as she had settled herself in her usual spot, they began to gather in the clearing below, unusually silent and somber-faced.

Firepaw and Ravenpaw got stiffly to their paws and joined them, leaving Graypaw behind with Lionheart's body. The gray apprentice was still lying with his nose resting against Lionheart's cooling golden pelt. Firepaw guessed Bluestar would excuse Graypaw from the Clan meeting this time.

"It is nearly moonhigh," meowed Bluestar as Firepaw slipped into place next to Ravenpaw. "And it is once more my duty—much, much too soon—to name ThunderClan's new deputy." Her voice was tired and cracked with sadness.

Firepaw looked from warrior to warrior. They were all looking expectantly at Tigerclaw. Even Whitestorm had turned to watch the dark tabby. From the bold expression on his face, and the way his whiskers twitched in anticipation, Tigerclaw seemed to agree with them.

Bluestar took a deep breath and continued. "I say these words before the body of Lionheart, so that his spirit may hear and approve my choice." She hesitated. "I have not forgotten how one cat avenged the death of Redtail and brought his body back to us. ThunderClan needs this fearless loyalty even more now." Bluestar paused again and then meowed the name loud and clear. "Tigerclaw will be the new deputy of ThunderClan."

There was a yowl of approval, with the loudest voices belonging to Darkstripe and Longtail. Whitestorm sat calmly, his eyes closed, his tail wrapped neatly around him. He was nodding slowly and approvingly.

Tigerclaw lifted his chin proudly, his eyes half-closed as he listened to the Clan. Then he stalked through the crowd, accepting tributes with the smallest of nods, and leaped up onto the Highrock beside Bluestar. "ThunderClan," he yowled, "I am honored to accept the position of Clan deputy. I never expected to gain such high rank, but by the spirit of Lionheart, I vow to serve you as best I can." He gravely dipped his head, fixing the crowd with his wide yellow eyes, and jumped down from the Highrock.

Firepaw heard Ravenpaw murmur, "Oh, no!" under his breath beside him. He turned to look curiously at his friend.

Ravenpaw's head was hanging low. "She should never have chosen him!" he muttered.

"Are you talking about Tigerclaw?" Firepaw whispered.

"He's wanted to be deputy ever since he took care of Redtail—" Ravenpaw mewed. He stopped abruptly.

"Took care of Redtail?" Firepaw echoed. His mind suddenly raced with questions. What did Ravenpaw know? At the Gathering, had his account of the battle with RiverClan been true? Was *Tigerclaw* responsible for Redtail's death?

CHAPTER 18

"Are you telling Firepaw how I protected Redtail?"

Firepaw felt a cold shiver ruffle the fur on the back of his neck.

Ravenpaw whipped around, eyes wide with fear. Tigerclaw loomed over them, his lips drawn back in a menacing snarl.

Firepaw jumped up and faced the new deputy. "He was just saying he wished you had been here to take care of Lionheart as well, that's all!" he mewed, thinking quickly.

Tigerclaw looked from one to the other, then stalked away in silence. Ravenpaw's green eyes clouded with terror, and he started to tremble uncontrollably.

"Ravenpaw?" Firepaw meowed in alarm.

But Ravenpaw didn't even look up at him. With his head held low, he slunk back to Graypaw and crouched next to him, pressing his skinny black body next to Graypaw's thick fur as if he was suddenly cold.

Firepaw looked helplessly at his two friends as they huddled beside Lionheart's body. Not knowing what else to do, he padded over and settled himself beside them, ready to sit out the night.

As the moon passed overhead, other cats came to join their vigil. Bluestar arrived last, once the camp was calm and quiet. She said nothing, but sat a little way off, gazing at her dead deputy with an expression of such unbearable grief that Firepaw had to look away.

At dawn, a group of elders came to take Lionheart's body away to the burial place. Graypaw followed to help dig the hole where the great warrior would rest.

Firepaw yawned and stretched. He felt chilled to the bone. Leaf-fall was nearly here now, and the woods were clouded with mist, but above the leaves Firepaw saw a rosy morning sky. He watched Graypaw disappear into the dew-soaked undergrowth with the elders.

Ravenpaw jumped to his paws and hurried back to the apprentices' den. Firepaw followed him slowly. By the time he arrived, the black cat was curled up with his nose tucked under his tail, as if asleep.

Firepaw was too exhausted to speak. He circled around on his mossy bed and then settled down for a long sleep.

"Wake up!"

Firepaw heard Dustpaw's voice calling through the den entrance. He opened his eyes. Ravenpaw was already awake, sitting bolt upright with his ears pricked. Graypaw was stirring beside him. Firepaw was surprised to see the familiar gray shape. He hadn't heard him come back after burying Lionheart.

"Bluestar's called another meeting," Dustpaw hissed at

them, and ducked out of the ferns.

The three apprentices crawled out of the warm den. The sun was already past its height, and the air felt cooler than before. Firepaw shivered, and his belly growled. He couldn't remember the last time he had eaten, and he wondered briefly if he would have a chance to hunt today.

Firepaw, Graypaw, and Ravenpaw hurried to join the crowd gathered below the Highrock.

Tigerclaw was speaking from his position beside Bluestar. "During the battle, our leader lost another life. Now that she has only four of her nine lives left, I am going to appoint a bodyguard to stay at her side constantly. No cat will be allowed to approach her unless the guards are present." His amber eyes flicked to Ravenpaw and then back to the rest of the crowd. "Darkstripe and Longtail," he continued, turning his gaze on the warriors, "you will act as Bluestar's guards."

Darkstripe and Longtail nodded importantly, and sat taller.

Bluestar now spoke. Her voice sounded gentle and calming after her deputy's commanding yowl. "Thank you, Tigerclaw, for your loyalty. But the Clan must understand that I am still here for them. No cat should hesitate to approach me, and I am happy to speak to anyone with or without my bodyguards." Her eyes darted briefly in Tigerclaw's direction. "As the warrior code says, the safety of the Clan is more important than the security of any single member." She paused, and her sky-blue gaze rested briefly on Firepaw. "And now, I wish to invite Yellowfang to join ThunderClan."

Meows of surprise rose from some of the warriors. Bluestar looked at Frostfur, who nodded her agreement. The other queens looked on silently.

Bluestar continued. "Her actions last night proved that she is brave and loyal. If she wishes it, we would welcome her as a full member of this Clan."

From her place at the edge of the crowd, Yellowfang looked up at the Clan leader and murmured, "I am honored, Bluestar, and I accept your offer."

"Good," meowed Bluestar, her voice firm as if the matter was now closed.

Firepaw purred with delight and nudged Graypaw. He was surprised to realize just how much Bluestar's public show of trust in Yellowfang meant to him.

Bluestar began to speak again. "Last night we successfully defended ourselves against ShadowClan, but they are still a great threat. The repair work we began this morning will continue. Our boundaries will be patrolled constantly. We must not assume that the war is over."

Tigerclaw stood up, his tail held high, and glared down at the assembled cats. "ShadowClan attacked while we were away from camp," he growled. "They chose their moment well. How did they know that the camp was so poorly defended? Do they have eyes inside our camp?"

Firepaw froze in horror as Tigerclaw fixed his cold stare on Ravenpaw. Some of the cats followed their new deputy's gaze and stared in puzzlement at the black apprentice. Ravenpaw looked at the ground and shifted his paws nervously.

Tigerclaw went on. "We still have a while before sunset. We must concentrate on rebuilding our camp. Meanwhile, if you suspect anything, or anyone, tell me. Be assured, anything you say will be in confidence." He nodded to dismiss the Clan, then turned and began murmuring to Bluestar.

The cats separated and began to move around the camp, assessing damage and forming work groups.

"Ravenpaw!" Firepaw called, still shocked by Tigerclaw's dark hint that his own apprentice had betrayed the Clan. But Ravenpaw had already bounded away. Firepaw could see him offering to help Halftail and Whitestorm, before rushing off to collect twigs so they could patch the holes in the boundary wall. Ravenpaw clearly didn't want to talk.

"Let's go and help him," suggested Graypaw. His voice was flat and exhausted, and his eyes were dull.

"You go. I'll be there in a moment," Firepaw answered. "First I want to check on Yellowfang, see if she's okay after her fight with Blackfoot."

He looked for Yellowfang in her nest by the fallen tree. She was stretched out in the shadows, her eyes thoughtful.

"Firepaw," she purred when she saw him. "I'm glad you have come."

"I wanted to check that you were all right," Firepaw mewed.

"Old habits stay longer than old scents, eh?" meowed Yellowfang with a flash of her old spirit.

"I suppose so," Firepaw confessed. "How are you feeling?"

"This old leg injury is playing up again, but I'll be fine," Yellowfang told him.

"How did you manage to fight Blackfoot off?" Firepaw asked, unable to keep the admiration out of his voice.

"Blackfoot's strong, but he's not a clever fighter. Fighting you was more of a challenge."

Firepaw looked for the flicker of humor in the old cat's eyes, but there was none.

She continued, "I've known him since he was a kit. He hasn't changed—a bully, but no brains."

Firepaw sat down beside her. "I'm not surprised Bluestar asked you to join the Clan," he purred. "You certainly showed your loyalty last night."

Yellowfang twitched her tail. "Perhaps a truly loyal cat would have fought at the side of the Clan that raised her."

"But then I'd be fighting for my Twolegs!" Firepaw pointed out.

Yellowfang shot him an admiring glance. "Well said, youngster. But then, you have always been a thinker."

Sorrow pierced Firepaw's heart as he remembered these were Lionheart's words too. "Do you miss ShadowClan?" he asked Yellowfang.

Yellowfang blinked slowly. "I miss the old ShadowClan," she meowed at last. "The way it used to be."

"Until Brokenstar became leader?" Firepaw was curious.

"Yes," Yellowfang admitted softly. "He changed the Clan." She gave a wheezy laugh. "He always knew how to give a good speech. He could make you believe a mouse was a rabbit if he set his mind to it. Perhaps that is why I was so blind to his faults." The old she-cat stared into the distance, lost in memories.

"Bet you can't guess who the new ShadowClan medicine cat is?" Firepaw mewed, suddenly remembering what he had learned at the Gathering. It felt like moons ago now.

His words seemed to shake Yellowfang back into the present. "Not Runningnose?" she meowed.

"Yep!"

Yellowfang shook her head. "But he can't even cure his own cold!"

"That's what Graypaw said!" They purred together for a moment, amused. Firepaw got to his paws. "I'll leave you to rest now. Call me if you need anything else today."

Yellowfang lifted her head. "Before you go, Firepaw, I hear you were in a rat fight. Did they draw blood?"

"It's okay, Spottedleaf has treated my wounds with marigold."

"Sometimes marigold is not strong enough for rat bites. Go and find a patch of wild garlic to roll in. I think there's some not far from the camp entrance. That will draw out any poisons the rats may have left. Although," she added dryly, "your den mates might not thank me for my advice!"

"Well, I do. Thanks, Yellowfang!" Firepaw purred.

"Go carefully, young one." Yellowfang held his gaze for a moment, then let her chin rest on her front paws and closed her eyes.

Firepaw slipped under the branches around Yellowfang's nest and headed for the gorse tunnel, in search of the wild garlic. The sun was setting now, and he could hear the queens settling their kits for the night.

"Where do you think you're going?" growled a voice from the shadows. It was Darkstripe.

"Yellowfang told me to go out and—"

"You don't take orders from that rogue!" hissed the warrior. "Go and help with the repairs. No cat is to leave the camp tonight!" He lashed his tail from side to side.

"Yes, Darkstripe," Firepaw mewed, dipping his head submissively. He turned and muttered "Dirtstripe!" under his breath, then headed toward the camp boundary, where he could see Graypaw and Ravenpaw busily patching a large hole in the wall of greenery.

"How's Yellowfang?" asked Graypaw as Firepaw trotted up.

"She's fine. She said wild garlic would be good for my rat bites. I was on my way to find some, but Darkstripe ordered me to stay in camp," Firepaw told him.

"Wild garlic?" mewed Graypaw. "I wouldn't mind trying that. My leg still stings."

"I could sneak out and get some," Firepaw offered. He had resented Darkstripe's offhand treatment and welcomed the chance to outwit him. "No one would notice if I slipped out of this hole here. It'd only take a couple of rabbit hops."

Ravenpaw frowned, but Graypaw nodded. "We'll cover for you," he whispered.

Firepaw nuzzled him gratefully and jumped out through the tear in the boundary wall.

Once outside the camp, he began to make his way to the wild garlic patch, the sharp tang alerting him easily to its location. The moon was rising in the violet sky as the sun sank below the horizon. A cold breeze ruffled Firepaw's fur. Suddenly he caught a cat-scent carried toward him on the wind. He sniffed cautiously. ShadowClan? No, just Tigerclaw, and two other cats. He sniffed the air again. Darkstripe and Longtail! What were they doing here?

Curious, Firepaw dropped into a stalking position. He prowled through the undergrowth paw by paw, keeping downwind so that he was not detected. The warriors were standing in the shadow of a clump of ferns, their heads very close together. Soon Firepaw was near enough to hear them speak.

"StarClan knows, my apprentice has shown little promise from the start, but I never expected him to turn traitor!" growled Tigerclaw.

Firepaw's eyes widened and his fur prickled with shock. It sounded like Tigerclaw intended to do more than just hint that Ravenpaw had betrayed the Clan!

"How long did you say Ravenpaw was missing on the journey to Mothermouth?" asked Darkstripe.

"Long enough to have traveled to ShadowClan's camp and back," came the deputy's menacing answer.

The fur on Firepaw's tail bristled angrily. *That's impossible!* he thought. *He was with us the whole time!*

Longtail's voice sounded now, high-pitched with excitement: "He must have told them that ThunderClan's leader and the strongest warrior had left the camp. Why else would they attack when they did?"

"We are the last Clan to stand against ShadowClan. We

must remain strong," purred Tigerclaw. His tone had become velvety soft now. He waited in silence for a response.

It was Darkstripe who answered, eagerly, as if he were still Tigerclaw's apprentice, giving the correct answer to a question on hunting techniques. His words made Firepaw breathless with fear. "And the Clan would be better off without a traitor like Ravenpaw."

"I have to say I agree with you, Darkstripe," murmured Tigerclaw, his voice heavy with emotion. "Even though he's my own apprentice . . ." He trailed off as if he were too upset to say any more.

Firepaw had heard enough. Forgetting all about the wild garlic, he turned and crept as silently and as quickly as he could back toward the camp.

He decided not to tell Ravenpaw what he had heard. He would be terrified. Firepaw's mind raced. What could he do? Tigerclaw was the Clan deputy, a great warrior, and popular with all of the other cats. No one was going to listen to any accusations made by an apprentice. But Ravenpaw was in terrible danger. Firepaw shook himself, trying to clear his head. There was only one thing to do—he must tell what he had heard to Bluestar, and somehow convince her that he was telling the truth!

CHAPTER 19

Graypaw and Ravenpaw were still patching the hole when Firepaw reached them. They had left a gap just wide enough for him to squeeze back through.

"No luck with the garlic," Firepaw panted as he slipped in. "Darkstripe's prowling around out there."

"Never mind," mewed Graypaw. "We can get some tomorrow."

"I'll go and get you some poppy from Spottedleaf," Firepaw offered. He was worried by the dull look in his friend's eyes, and the way his muscles seemed stiff with pain.

"No, don't worry," mewed Graypaw. "I'll be fine."

"It's no trouble," Firepaw insisted, and before Graypaw could argue, he bounded off toward Spottedleaf's den.

She was pacing her small clearing, her eyes clouded with unhappiness.

"Are you okay?" Firepaw asked.

"The spirits of StarClan are restless. I think they are trying to tell me something," she replied, flicking her tail uneasily. "What can I do for you?"

"I think Graypaw could do with some poppy seeds for his

leg," Firepaw explained. "His rat bites are still hurting him."

"The pain of losing Lionheart will make his injuries feel worse. But he'll mend in time; don't worry. In the meantime, you're right, poppy seeds will help." Spottedleaf went into her den and brought out a dried poppy head. She placed it carefully on the ground. "Just shake out one or two and give them to him," she meowed.

"Thanks," Firepaw mewed. "Are you sure you're okay?"

"Go and see to your friend," answered Spottedleaf, avoiding his gaze.

Firepaw picked up the poppy head between his teeth and began to walk away.

"Wait," Spottedleaf hissed suddenly.

Firepaw spun around expectantly and met her tawny gaze. Her eyes burned back at him.

"Firepaw," she hissed. "StarClan spoke to me moons ago, before you joined the Clan. I sense they want me to tell you this now. They said only fire can save our Clan."

Firepaw stared at Spottedleaf, mystified.

The strange passion faded from her eyes. "Take care, Firepaw," she meowed in her normal voice, and turned away.

"See you," Firepaw replied uncertainly. He padded back through the fern tunnel. Her strange words were echoing in his mind, but he could not make sense of them. Why had she shared them with him? Surely fire was an enemy to all who lived in the forest. He shook his head in frustration, and bounded over to the apprentices' den.

⟡   ⟡   ⟡

"Graypaw!" Firepaw hissed into the ear of his sleeping friend. They'd been allowed to rest all morning, after working on repairs for most of the night. Tigerclaw had ordered them to be ready to begin training at sunhigh. The strong yellow light filtering through to the den told Firepaw it was already near that now.

He'd had a restless night. Dreams swirled through his mind each time he fell asleep, confusing and indistinct, but full of darkness and menace.

"Graypaw!" Firepaw hissed again. But his friend did not stir. He'd eaten two of the poppy seeds before he'd slept, and now he was in a deep slumber.

"Are you awake, Firepaw?" Ravenpaw mewed from his nest.

Firepaw spat silently under his breath. He had wanted to talk to Graypaw before Ravenpaw awoke.

"Yes!" he replied.

Ravenpaw sat up in his bed of moss and heather and began to wash with quick flicks of his tongue. "Are you going to wake him?" he asked, nodding toward Graypaw.

A deep voice growled outside their den. "I hope so! Training is about to start."

Firepaw and Ravenpaw jumped.

"Graypaw, wake up!" Firepaw poked his friend with one paw. "Tigerclaw is waiting!"

Graypaw lifted his head. His eyes were still heavy with sleep.

"Are you ready yet?" called Tigerclaw.

Firepaw and Ravenpaw crept out of the den, blinking as they emerged into the sunlight.

The deputy was sitting beside the tree stump. "Is the other one coming?" he asked.

"Yes," Firepaw replied, feeling defensive on behalf of his friend. "He's only just woken up."

"Training will do him good," growled Tigerclaw. "He's grieved for long enough."

Firepaw held the menacing amber gaze for a few moments. Warrior and apprentice, for a heartbeat their eyes were locked as enemies.

Graypaw scrambled sleepily out of the den.

"Bluestar will be ready for you in a moment, Firepaw," announced Tigerclaw. The words distracted Firepaw from his anger. His first training session with Bluestar! Excitement surged through him. He had expected his wounded mentor to be resting still.

"Graypaw," continued Tigerclaw, "you can join my training session. Do you think you're up to it, Ravenpaw?" He glowered at his apprentice. "After all, you got some pretty nasty nettle stings while the rest of us were fighting those rats."

Ravenpaw looked at the ground. "I'm fine," he mewed.

Graypaw and Ravenpaw followed the deputy out of the camp entrance. Ravenpaw's head hung low as he disappeared through the gorse tunnel.

Firepaw sat and waited for Bluestar. She did not keep him long. The gray queen emerged from her den and padded across the clearing. Her fur was still matted in places where her wounds were fresh, but she betrayed no pain in her confident stride. "Come," she called to him.

Firepaw noticed with surprise that she was alone. Darkstripe and Longtail were nowhere to be seen. A thought occurred to him and suddenly his excitement was tinged with anxiety—here was an opportunity to tell Bluestar what he had overheard last night.

He caught up with her as she headed for the gorse tunnel and fell in step behind her. "Will your guards be joining us?" he asked hesitantly.

Bluestar replied without looking back, "I've ordered Darkstripe and Longtail to help with the camp repairs. Securing ThunderClan's base is our first priority."

Firepaw's heartbeat quickened. He would tell her about Ravenpaw as soon as they left camp.

The two cats followed the trail to the training hollow. The path was strewn with freshly fallen golden leaves that rustled beneath their paws. Firepaw's mind raced as he searched for suitable words. What should he tell his leader? That Tigerclaw was plotting to get rid of his apprentice? And what would he say when Bluestar asked him why? Could he bring himself to say out loud that he suspected Tigerclaw had killed Redtail? Even though he had no evidence beyond Ravenpaw's excited storytelling at the Gathering?

By the time they reached the sandy hollow, Firepaw had still not spoken. The hollow was empty.

"I asked Tigerclaw to hold his training session in another

part of the forest today," Bluestar explained as she padded into the center of the hollow. "I want to concentrate on your fighting skills, and I want *you* to concentrate on them too— which means no distractions."

I must tell her now, thought Firepaw. *She needs to know about the danger Ravenpaw is in.* His paws prickled with anxiety. *I won't have another chance like this.* . . .

Sudden movement flashed in the corner of his eye. A swish of gray whirled past his nose, and Firepaw fell forward as his forepaws were knocked lightly from underneath him. He staggered, regained his balance, and spun around to see Bluestar sitting calmly beside him. "Do I have your attention now?" she growled.

"Yes, Bluestar. Sorry!" he replied hastily, looking into her blue eyes.

"That's better. Firepaw, you have been with us for many moons now. I have watched you fight. With the rats you were quick; with the ShadowClan warriors you were fierce. You outwitted Graypaw on that very first day we met, and you defeated Yellowfang with your cleverness too." She paused, then lowered her voice to an intense hiss. "But one day you will meet an opponent who is all of these things as well— quick and fierce and clever. It's my duty to prepare you for that day."

Firepaw nodded, completely caught up in her words. His senses were fully alert. All thoughts of Ravenpaw and Tigerclaw had disappeared, and the musty odors and tiny noises of the forest rushed in upon him.

"Let's see how you fight," Bluestar ordered. "Attack me."

Firepaw looked at her, sizing her up and wondering the best way to begin. Bluestar was standing less than three rabbit lengths away. She was twice his size, so it would be a waste of effort to begin with the usual paw swipes and wrestling. But if he could leap straight onto her back with a powerful enough jump, he might be able to unbalance her. She hadn't taken her piercing blue eyes off him for an instant. Firepaw stared back and leaped.

He had aimed to land squarely on her shoulders, but Bluestar was ready for him. She dropped swiftly into a crouch. As Firepaw hit her, she rolled onto her back. Instead of landing on her shoulders he found himself crashing down toward her upturned belly. She caught him with all four paws and flung him easily away from her. Firepaw felt he had been bundled away like a bothersome kit. He hit the dusty ground hard and lay winded for a moment before he scrambled to his feet.

"Interesting strategy, but your eyes betrayed where you were aiming," growled Bluestar as she stood up and shook off the dust from her thick coat. "Now, try again."

This time Firepaw looked at her shoulders but aimed for her paws. When Bluestar dropped to the ground he would hit her as she crouched. Firepaw felt a rush of satisfaction as he leaped, but it turned to confusion as Bluestar unexpectedly sprang into the air and let him crash into the ground where she had stood just a heartbeat before. She timed it perfectly—as he landed, she thundered down on top of him, squashing the breath out of him.

"Now try something I don't expect," she hissed into his ear, climbing off him and backing away with a challenging gleam in her eyes.

Firepaw scrambled up, panting, and shook himself crossly. Even Yellowfang had not been so tricky. He hissed and leaped again. This time, as he flew at Bluestar, he stretched out his forepaws. She reared up on her hind legs and used her forepaws to twist him away. As he felt himself slipping, Firepaw scrabbled with his hind paws in the sand, but it was too late and he flopped heavily onto his side.

"Firepaw," Bluestar meowed calmly, as once more he struggled to his paws, "you're strong and quick, but you must learn to keep control of your speed and body weight so that it's not so easy for me to unbalance you. Try again."

Firepaw backed away, hot, dusty, and out of breath. Frustration raged through him. He was determined to get the better of his mentor this time. Slowly he crouched and began to creep toward Bluestar. She mirrored his crouch and hissed into his face as he approached. He raised a paw and swiped at her left ear. She ducked to avoid his strike and reared up, towering over him. Quickly Firepaw rolled onto his back, slithered beneath her body, and in one fast movement kicked both his back legs upward into her belly. Bluestar was flung backward and fell onto the sandy earth with a loud grunt.

Firepaw flipped himself over and leaped to his paws. He felt jubilant. Then he saw Bluestar lying in the dirt, and for the first time remembered her wounds. Had he reopened them? He dashed to her side and stared down at her. To his relief her eyes glinted proudly back at him.

"That was much better," she puffed. She stood and shook herself. "Now it's my turn."

She sprang at him, knocking him to the ground, then retreated and let him pick himself up before leaping again. Firepaw braced himself, but she bowled him over easily again.

"Look at my size, Firepaw! Don't try to stand up against my attack. Use your wits. If you are fast enough to avoid me, then avoid me!"

Firepaw scrabbled to his feet again, preparing for her attack. This time he didn't dig his paws into the soft ground, but stood lightly, keeping his weight on his toes. As Bluestar flew toward him, he hopped neatly out of her path, reared up onto his hind legs, and, with his forepaws, pushed her flying body onward past him.

Bluestar landed gracefully on all four paws and turned. "Excellent! You learn quickly," she purred. "But that was an easy move. Let's see how you deal with this one."

They trained until sunset. Firepaw heaved a sigh of relief when he heard Bluestar meow, "That's enough for today." She seemed a little tired and stiff but she still leaped easily out of the sandy hollow.

Firepaw scrambled after her. His muscles were aching and his head spinning with all he had learned. As they trekked together back through the trees, he couldn't wait to tell Graypaw and Ravenpaw about this training session. And it wasn't until they reached the camp boundary that Firepaw realized he'd forgotten to tell Bluestar about Ravenpaw.

CHAPTER 20

By *the time Firepaw returned,* the camp was starting to look a little better. Parties of cats had clearly been patching and repairing continuously throughout the day. Frostfur and Goldenflower were still busy fortifying the nursery walls, but the outer wall looked solid and secure once more.

Firepaw trotted across the clearing to see if there was any fresh-kill around. He passed Sandpaw and Dustpaw, who were preparing to leave in the next patrol.

"Sorry," mewed Sandpaw, as Firepaw sniffed hopefully around the eating area. "We ate the last two mice."

Firepaw shrugged. He would catch something for himself later. He headed back to the apprentices' den, where Graypaw was sitting with his back resting against the tree stump, licking a forepaw.

"Where's Ravenpaw?" Firepaw asked as he sat down.

"Not back from his task yet," replied Graypaw. "Look at that!" He held out his paw for Firepaw to inspect. The pad was torn and bleeding. "Tigerclaw sent me fishing and I stepped on a sharp stone in the stream."

"That looks pretty deep. You should get Spottedleaf to take

a look at it," Firepaw advised. "Where did Tigerclaw send Ravenpaw, by the way?"

"Dunno, I was up to my belly in cold water," muttered Graypaw. He stood up and limped away toward Spottedleaf's den.

Firepaw settled down, his eyes fixed on the entrance to the camp, and waited for Ravenpaw. After overhearing the warriors' conversation last night, he couldn't shake the feeling that something dreadful was going to happen to his friend. His heart lurched as he saw Tigerclaw enter the camp alone.

He waited longer. The moon was high in the sky. Surely Ravenpaw should be back by now? Firepaw found himself wishing he'd spoken to Bluestar when he'd had the chance. He could see Darkstripe and Longtail guarding her den now, and he certainly didn't want them to overhear his concerns.

Tigerclaw had brought back fresh-kill, which he was sharing with Whitestorm outside the warriors' den. Firepaw realized he was very hungry. Perhaps he should go and hunt—he might come across Ravenpaw outside the camp. As he wondered what to do, Firepaw saw Ravenpaw trotting through the entrance of the camp. A thrill of relief raced through him, and not just because Ravenpaw was holding fresh-kill between his teeth.

The apprentice came straight over to Firepaw and dropped the mouthful of food on the ground. "Enough for all three of us!" he mewed proudly. "And it should taste extra good—it's from ShadowClan territory."

Firepaw gasped. "You hunted in ShadowClan territory?"

"That was my task," Ravenpaw explained.

"Tigerclaw sent you into enemy territory to hunt!" Firepaw could hardly believe it. "We must tell Bluestar. That was too dangerous!"

At the mention of Bluestar's name, Ravenpaw shook his head. His eyes looked hunted and shadowed with fear. "Look, just keep quiet, okay?" he hissed. "I survived. I even caught some prey. That's all there is to it."

"You survived *this time*!" Firepaw spat.

"Shhh! Tigerclaw's looking. Just eat your share and keep quiet!" snapped Ravenpaw. Firepaw shrugged and took a piece of the fresh-kill. Ravenpaw ate quickly, avoiding Firepaw's eye. "Shall we save some for Graypaw?" he asked after a while.

"He went to see Spottedleaf," Firepaw mumbled through a mouthful. "He cut his paw. I don't know when he'll be back."

"Well, save him whatever you want," replied Ravenpaw, suddenly sounding worn out. "I'm tired; I need to sleep." He stood up and pushed his way into the den.

Firepaw stayed outside, watching the rest of the camp prepare for the night. He was going to have to tell Ravenpaw what he'd overheard in the forest last night. He needed to know just how much danger he was in.

Tigerclaw was lying beside Whitestorm, sharing tongues, but with one eye fixed on the apprentices' den. Firepaw yawned to show Tigerclaw how exhausted he was. Then he got to his paws and followed Ravenpaw inside.

Ravenpaw was asleep, but Firepaw could tell from his twitching paws and whiskers that he was dreaming. He knew it wasn't a good dream by the tiny mewls and squeaks that

Ravenpaw was making. Suddenly the black cat leaped to his paws, his eyes stretched wide in terror. His fur was standing on end, and his back was arched.

"Ravenpaw!" Firepaw meowed in alarm. "Calm down. You're in our den. There's only me here!"

Ravenpaw looked around wildly.

"It's just me," Firepaw repeated.

Ravenpaw blinked and seemed to recognize his friend. He collapsed onto his bed.

"Ravenpaw," mewed Firepaw seriously. "There's something you need to know. Something I heard last night when I was out looking for the wild garlic." Ravenpaw looked away, still trembling from his dream, but Firepaw persisted. "Ravenpaw, I heard Tigerclaw telling Darkstripe and Longtail that you betrayed ThunderClan. He told them you slipped away during the trip to Mothermouth and told ShadowClan that the camp was unguarded."

Ravenpaw spun round to face Firepaw. "But I didn't!" he exclaimed, horrified.

"Of course you didn't," Firepaw agreed. "But Darkstripe and Longtail believe you did, and Tigerclaw persuaded them that they should get rid of you."

Ravenpaw was speechless, his breath coming in gasps.

"Why would Tigerclaw want to get rid of you, Ravenpaw?" Firepaw asked gently. "He's one of the Clan's strongest warriors. What threat are you to him?" Firepaw suspected he already knew the answer, but he wanted to hear the truth from Ravenpaw's own mouth. He waited while Ravenpaw fumbled for words.

At last the black apprentice crawled closer to Firepaw and whispered hoarsely into his ear, "Because the RiverClan deputy didn't kill Redtail; Tigerclaw did."

Firepaw nodded silently, and Ravenpaw continued, his whisper cracking with tension. "Redtail killed the RiverClan deputy—"

"So Tigerclaw didn't kill Oakheart." Firepaw couldn't help interrupting.

Ravenpaw shook his head. "No, he didn't! After Redtail had killed Oakheart, Tigerclaw ordered me back to the camp. I wanted to stay, but he yowled at me to go, so I ran into the trees. I should have carried on running, but I couldn't leave while they were still fighting. I turned and crept back to see if Tigerclaw needed help. By the time I got near, all the RiverClan warriors had fled, leaving just Redtail and Tigerclaw. Redtail was watching the last warrior running away and Tigerclaw"—Ravenpaw paused, then gulped—"Tigerclaw j-jumped on him. He sank his teeth into the back of his neck and Redtail fell to the ground, dead. That's when I ran. I don't know if Tigerclaw saw me or not. I just kept running till I got back to the camp."

"Why didn't you tell Bluestar?" Firepaw pressed gently.

"Would she have believed me?" Ravenpaw's eyes rolled wildly. "Do *you* believe me?"

"Of course I do," Firepaw mewed. He licked Ravenpaw between the ears in an effort to calm and comfort his friend. He was going to have to find another opportunity to tell Bluestar about Tigerclaw's treachery. "Don't worry; I'll sort it out," he promised. "Meanwhile, make sure you stick close to me or Graypaw."

"Does Graypaw know? About them wanting to get rid of me?"

"Not yet. But I'll have to tell him."

Ravenpaw settled silently onto his belly and stared ahead.

"It's okay, Ravenpaw," Firepaw purred, touching the skinny black body with his nose. "I'll help you get out of this."

Graypaw padded into the den at dawn. Sandpaw and Dustpaw had returned from their patrol a while ago and were asleep in their nests.

"Hi!" mewed Graypaw, sounding more cheerful than he had for days.

Firepaw woke at once. "You sound better," he purred.

Graypaw licked Firepaw's ear. "Spottedleaf put some gunk on my cut and made me lie still for hours. I must've fallen asleep. By the way, I hope that chaffinch out there was for me; I was starving!"

"It was. Ravenpaw caught it yesterday. Tigerclaw sent him into—"

"Shut up, you two," growled Sandpaw. "Some of us are trying to sleep."

Graypaw rolled his eyes. "Come on, Firepaw," he mewed. "Brindleface has had her kits; let's go and visit them."

Firepaw purred with pleasure. At last, something for ThunderClan to celebrate. He looked down at Ravenpaw, who was still sleeping, and padded out of the den. With

Graypaw, he trotted across the clearing toward the nursery. The rising sun made his pelt glow with warmth, and he stretched appreciatively, reveling in the suppleness of his spine and the strength in his legs.

"Stop showing off!" Graypaw called over his shoulder. Firepaw stopped stretching and bounded after his friend.

Whitestorm was sitting outside the nursery, guarding the entrance. "Have you two come to see the new kits?" he meowed as Firepaw and Graypaw approached.

Firepaw nodded.

"One at a time only, and you'll have to wait; Bluestar's with her now," Whitestorm told them.

"Well, you can go first," Firepaw offered. "I'll go and see Yellowfang while I'm waiting." He dipped his head respectfully to Whitestorm and headed off toward Yellowfang's nest.

The old cat was washing behind her ears, her eyes half-closed with concentration.

"Don't tell me you're expecting rain!" Firepaw teased.

Yellowfang looked up. "You've been listening to too many elders' tales," she meowed. "What would be the point of a cat washing its ears if they're only going to get rained on anyway?"

Firepaw's whiskers twitched with amusement. "Are you going to see Brindleface's new litter?" he asked.

Yellowfang stiffened and she shook her head. "I don't think I'd be very welcome," she growled.

"But they know you saved—" Firepaw began.

"A she-cat is very protective of her newborns. Especially when it's her first litter. I think I'll stay away," Yellowfang replied in a tone that invited no argument.

"As you wish. But I'm going to see them. It must be a good sign, having new kits in the camp."

Yellowfang shrugged. "Sometimes," she muttered darkly.

Firepaw turned and trotted back to the nursery. Clouds had covered the sun, making the air turn fresher. A fierce breeze tugged at his fur and rustled the leaves around the clearing.

Bluestar was sitting outside the nursery. Behind her, Graypaw's tail was just disappearing into the narrow entrance. "Firepaw," she greeted him. "Have you come to see ThunderClan's newest warriors?" The ThunderClan leader sounded tired and sad.

Firepaw was surprised. Surely the kits were good news for ThunderClan?

"Yes, I have," he replied.

"Well, when you've finished, come and see me in my den."

"Yes, Bluestar," Firepaw mewed as she walked slowly away. He felt his fur prickle. Here was another chance to speak to Bluestar alone. Perhaps StarClan was on his side, after all.

Graypaw crawled out of the nursery entrance. "They're really cute," he mewed. "But I'm starving now. I'm off to find some fresh-kill. I'll save some for you if I find any!" He blinked affectionately at Firepaw and bounded away.

Firepaw purred a good-bye and looked up at Whitestorm, who nodded his permission for him to enter the nursery. Firepaw squeezed through the tiny entrance.

Four tiny kits huddled warmly in Brindleface's deeply lined nest. Their fur was pale gray with darker flecks, just like their mother, except for one tiny dark gray tom. They mewled and squirmed beside Brindleface's belly, their eyes shut tight.

"How are you feeling?" Firepaw whispered to her.

"A little tired," answered Brindleface. She looked down proudly at her litter. "But the kits are all strong and healthy."

"ThunderClan is lucky to have them," Firepaw purred. "I was just talking about them to Yellowfang."

Brindleface didn't answer, and Firepaw couldn't miss the look of worry that flashed in her eyes as she nudged a straying kit closer to her.

Firepaw felt a tremor of anxiety in his belly. Bluestar may have accepted Yellowfang into ThunderClan, but it looked like the old cat was still not trusted by all of the Clan. He touched his nose affectionately to Brindleface's flank, then turned and made his way out into the clearing.

The Clan leader was waiting for Firepaw at the entrance to her den. Longtail sat at her side. The pale tabby warrior stared hard at Firepaw as he approached. Firepaw ignored his gaze and looked expectantly at Bluestar.

"Come inside," she meowed, turning to lead the way. Firepaw trotted after her. Longtail immediately stood up as if to follow them.

Bluestar looked back at him over her shoulder. "I think I'll be safe enough with young Firepaw," she meowed. Longtail looked uncertain for a moment, then sat down again outside the entrance.

Firepaw had never been inside Bluestar's den. He padded after her through the lichen that draped its entrance.

"Brindleface's kits are lovely," he purred.

Bluestar looked serious. "Lovely they may be, but they mean more mouths to feed, and the season of leaf-bare will soon be here." Then she glanced at Firepaw, who was unable to hide his surprise at her melancholy tone. "Oh, don't listen to me," meowed Bluestar, shaking her head impatiently. "The first cold wind always worries me. Come; make yourself comfortable." She tipped her head toward the dry, sandy floor.

Firepaw dropped onto his belly and stretched his paws out in front of him.

Bluestar circled slowly on her mossy nest. "I'm still aching from our training session yesterday," she admitted when she had finally settled herself and curled her tail around her paws. "You fought well, young one."

For once, Firepaw didn't stop to bask in her praise. His heart was thumping. This was the perfect moment to tell his leader his fears about Tigerclaw. He lifted his chin, ready to speak.

But it was Bluestar who spoke first, staring past him at the far wall of her den. "I can still smell the stale stench of ShadowClan in the camp," she murmured. "I hoped never to see the day when our enemy broke into the heart of ThunderClan." Firepaw nodded in silent agreement, sensing Bluestar was going to say more.

"And so many deaths." She sighed. "First Redtail, then Lionheart. I thank StarClan at least the warriors we have left are strong and loyal like them. At least with Tigerclaw as deputy, ThunderClan may still be able to defend itself." Firepaw's heart plummeted and an icy chill cut deep into him as Bluestar went on. "There was a time, when Tigerclaw was a young warrior, that I feared for the strength of his passion. Such energy can need careful channeling. But now I am proud to see how much respect the Clan has for him. I know he is ambitious, but his ambition makes him one of the bravest cats I have ever had the honor to fight alongside."

Firepaw knew at once that he could not tell Bluestar his suspicions about Tigerclaw. Not when Bluestar looked to her deputy to protect the whole Clan. He would have to save Ravenpaw himself. He took a deep breath and blinked slowly, so that when Bluestar turned and looked directly into his eyes, no trace of his shock and disappointment remained.

Her next words were quiet and full of concern. "You know Brokenstar will return. He made it clear at the Gathering that he wants hunting rights in all the territories."

"We fought him off once. We can do it again," Firepaw insisted.

"That's true," Bluestar acknowledged with a wry nod. "StarClan will honor your courage, young Firepaw." She paused and licked a healing wound on her side. "I think you ought to know that, in the battle with the rats, it was not my fifth life that I lost, but my seventh."

Firepaw sat bolt upright, shocked.

Bluestar went on. "I have let the Clan believe it was my fifth because I don't want them to fear for my safety. But two more lives, and I will have to leave you to join StarClan."

Firepaw's mind was racing. Why was she telling him this? "Thank you for sharing this with me, Bluestar," he purred respectfully.

Bluestar nodded. "I am tired now," she rasped. "Off you go. And Firepaw, I don't expect you to repeat this conversation to anyone."

"Of course, Bluestar," Firepaw replied as he nosed his way out through the curtain of lichen.

Longtail was still sitting by the entrance. Firepaw stepped past him and made his way toward his den. He didn't know which part of his conversation with Bluestar had been more bewildering.

He was stopped in his tracks by a yowl of horror coming from the nursery. Frostfur came sprinting into the clearing, her tail bristling and her eyes wide with alarm. "My kits! Someone has taken my kits!"

Tigerclaw bounded over to her. He called to the Clan, "Quick, search the camp! Whitestorm, stay where you are. Warriors, patrol the camp boundary. Apprentices, search every den!"

Firepaw rushed to the nearest den, the warriors', and pushed his way inside. It was empty. He scrabbled through the bedding with his paws but there was neither sight nor scent of Frostfur's kits.

He charged outside and headed for his own den. Ravenpaw and Graypaw were already inside, pushing aside their nests, sniffing every corner. Dustpaw and Sandpaw were searching the elders' den. Firepaw left them to it and charged from one clump of grass to another, pushing his muzzle into them, ignoring the nettles that stung his nose. There was no sign of the kits anywhere. He looked around the camp boundary. Warriors paced backward and forward, urgently sniffing the air.

Suddenly Firepaw spotted Yellowfang in the distance. She was pushing her way through an unguarded part of fern wall. She must have found a scent, he thought, and raced toward her as her tail disappeared into the greenery. By the time he arrived at the fern wall, she had gone. He sniffed the air. No kit-scent, just the bitter smell of Yellowfang's fear. What was she afraid of? Firepaw wondered.

Tigerclaw's yowl sounded from the bushes behind the nursery. All the cats raced over to him, headed by Frostfur. They crowded as closely as they could, jostling to see through the dense undergrowth. Firepaw nosed his way forward and saw Tigerclaw standing over a motionless bundle of dappled fur.

Spottedleaf!

Firepaw stared in disbelief at her lifeless body. Fury rose in him like a dark cloud, and he felt the blood roaring in his ears. Who had done this?

Bluestar stepped through the crowd and leaned over the medicine cat. "She has been killed by a warrior blow," she meowed softly.

Firepaw craned his neck and saw a single wound on the back of Spottedleaf's neck. His head swam and suddenly he was unable to see clearly.

Through his grief, Firepaw heard a murmur at the back of the crowd that swelled into a single piercing yowl.

"Yellowfang is gone!"

CHAPTER 21

"Yellowfang has killed Spottedleaf and taken my kits!" screeched Frostfur. The other queens rushed to Frostfur's side and tried to calm her with licks and caresses, but Frostfur pushed them away and wailed her grief to the darkening sky. As if in reply, the sky rumbled ominously and a cold wind ruffled the cats' fur.

"Yellowfang!" hissed Tigerclaw. "I always knew she was a traitor. Now we know how she managed to fight off the ShadowClan deputy. It was a setup to let her trick her way into our Clan!"

Lightning crackled overhead, punctuating Tigerclaw's words with a glaring white flash, and a clap of thunder rolled around the woods.

Firepaw couldn't believe what he was hearing. Dazed with grief, his mind whirled. Could Yellowfang really have killed Spottedleaf?

Above the shocked murmurings, Darkstripe meowed loudly, "Bluestar! What do you say?"

The cats fell silent as they turned to look at their leader.

Bluestar's gaze moved across the crowd of cats, and settled

finally on Spottedleaf's body. The first drops of rain began to fall, sparkling like dewdrops on the medicine cat's still-glossy fur.

Bluestar blinked slowly. Grief clouded her face, and for a moment Firepaw was afraid that this new death would overwhelm her. But when her eyes opened they glittered with a fierceness that showed her determination to seek revenge for this cruel attack. She lifted her head. "If Yellowfang has killed Spottedleaf and stolen Frostfur's kits, she will be hunted down without mercy." The crowd meowed approvingly. "But we must wait," Bluestar went on. "There is a storm coming, and I am not prepared to risk more lives. If ShadowClan has our kits, they will come to no immediate harm. I suspect Brokenstar wants them as recruits for his own Clan, or as hostages—to force us to let him hunt in our territory. As soon as the storm has passed, a patrol will follow Yellowfang and bring back our kits."

"We cannot waste time, or the scent will be lost in the rain!" Tigerclaw protested.

Bluestar flicked her tail impatiently. "If we send out a hunting party now, our efforts will be wasted anyway. In this weather the scent will already be lost by the time we are ready. If we wait until after the storm, we stand a better chance of success."

There were murmurs of agreement among the Clan. Even though it was barely sunhigh, the sky was growing much darker. The cats were unsettled by the lightning and thunder, and seemed willing to listen to their leader's advice.

Bluestar looked at her deputy. "I'd like to discuss our plans with you, please, Tigerclaw." Tigerclaw nodded and stalked away toward Bluestar's den, but the leader hesitated. She glanced at Firepaw, signaling with a flick of her tail and a ripple of her whiskers that she wanted to speak to him alone.

The other cats gathered around Spottedleaf and began to share tongues with her, their wails of grief sounding above the thunder. Bluestar wound her way through them and went toward the fern tunnel that led to Spottedleaf's den.

Firepaw quietly skirted the mourning cats and followed her inside. It was very dark beneath the ferns. The storm had blotted out the morning sun so that it seemed as if night had fallen. Rain was falling more heavily now, spattering noisily against the leaves, but at least it was sheltered in Spottedleaf's clearing.

"Firepaw," Bluestar meowed urgently as he arrived at her side, "where is Yellowfang? Do you know?"

Firepaw hardly heard her. He couldn't help remembering the last time he had come to this clearing. An image of Spottedleaf, trotting out of her den with her coat gleaming in the sunlight, burned in his mind, and he closed his eyes to preserve it.

"Firepaw," snapped Bluestar, "you must save your grieving for later."

Firepaw shook himself. "I . . . I saw Yellowfang go through the camp boundary after the kits went missing. Do you really think she killed Spottedleaf and took the kits?"

Bluestar gazed steadily at him. "I don't know," she admitted.

"I want you to find her and bring her back—alive. I need to know the truth."

"You're not sending Tigerclaw?" Firepaw couldn't help asking.

"Tigerclaw is a great warrior, but in this case his loyalty to the Clan may cloud his judgment," Bluestar explained. "He wants to give the Clan the vengeance it desires. No cat can blame him for that. The Clan believes Yellowfang has betrayed us, and if Tigerclaw thinks he can reassure the Clan by handing them the dead body of Yellowfang, that's what he will do."

Firepaw nodded. She was right—Tigerclaw would kill Yellowfang without question.

Bluestar looked stern for a moment. "If I find that Yellowfang is a traitor, then I will kill her myself. But if she is not . . ." Her blue eyes burned into Firepaw's. "I will not let an innocent cat die."

"But what if Yellowfang won't come back?" Firepaw meowed.

"She will, if *you* ask her."

Firepaw felt stunned by Bluestar's faith in him. The enormity of what she was asking him to do weighed down on him, and he wondered if he had enough courage to carry it through.

"Go at once!" she ordered. "But be careful; you will be on your own and there may be enemy patrols about. This storm will keep our own warriors in camp for a while."

Thunder rolled overhead as Firepaw dashed out into the

clearing. Rain hammered down, pelting against his fur like tiny stones. A bolt of lightning lit up the faces of Darkstripe and Longtail as they watched him cross the clearing.

Firepaw bounded past the nursery. He couldn't leave without sharing tongues with Spottedleaf. The other cats had run for shelter, abandoning the medicine cat's body to the downpour while they huddled beneath the dripping ferns, meowing their fear and loss.

Firepaw buried his nose in Spottedleaf's wet fur and breathed in her scent one last time. "Good-bye, my sweet Spottedleaf," he murmured.

His ears pricked as he overheard the voices of Frostfur and Speckletail talking nearby. He froze, straining to listen.

"Yellowfang must have had help," Speckletail growled.

"Someone from *ThunderClan*?" came the anxious voice of Frostfur.

"You've heard what Tigerclaw's been saying about Ravenpaw. Perhaps he had something to do with it. I've never felt comfortable with him, myself."

The fur on Firepaw's spine prickled. If Tigerclaw had been spreading his malicious rumors as far as the nursery, Ravenpaw wouldn't be safe anywhere in the camp.

Firepaw realized he had to act quickly. He would find Yellowfang first, then deal with Ravenpaw. He raced to the spot where he had last seen Yellowfang. He knew her scent so well that he could even smell it through the rain-soaked leaves. He began to push through the bushes, mouth open, to detect where her trail led.

"Firepaw!"

Firepaw jumped and then relaxed as he realized it was Graypaw's voice.

"I've been looking for you!" mewed his friend as he rushed toward him.

Firepaw gingerly stepped back out of the ferns.

Graypaw squinted as rain dripped down his long fur and into his eyes. "Where are you going?" he mewed.

"To look for Yellowfang," Firepaw replied.

"On your own?" Graypaw's broad gray face showed concern.

Firepaw thought for a moment and decided to tell Graypaw the truth. "Bluestar asked me to bring Yellowfang back," he mewed.

"What?" Graypaw looked shocked. "Why *you*?"

"Maybe she thinks I know Yellowfang best, and that I'd find her more easily."

"Wouldn't a party of warriors stand more of a chance?" Graypaw pointed out. "Tigerclaw's the best tracker in the Clan, and if anyone could bring her back, *he* could."

"Maybe Tigerclaw wouldn't bring her back," Firepaw murmured.

"What do you mean?"

"Tigerclaw's out for revenge. He would just kill her."

"But if she killed Spottedleaf and took the kits . . ."

"Do you really believe that?" Firepaw asked.

Graypaw looked at his friend, shaking his head in confusion. "Do you think she's innocent?" he mewed.

"I don't know," Firepaw admitted. "And neither does Bluestar. She wants to find out the truth. That's why she's sending me instead of Tigerclaw."

"But if she *ordered* Tigerclaw to bring her back alive . . ." Graypaw's words were drowned by a deafening crack of thunder, and a flash of lightning lit up the trees around them.

In the dazzling light, Firepaw glimpsed Frostfur chasing Ravenpaw away from the nursery. The white queen's face was twisted with fury as she hissed at the young black cat and lunged forward to give him a warning nip on the hind leg.

Graypaw turned to Firepaw. "What's *that* all about?" he mewed.

Firepaw stared back at his friend, his mind leaping ahead to a new idea. It looked like Ravenpaw's time had run out, and Firepaw needed Graypaw's help. But would his friend believe him? The wind was beginning to roar through the trees above them, and Firepaw had to raise his voice. "Ravenpaw's in great danger," he meowed.

"What?"

"I have to get him away from ThunderClan. Right now, before anything happens to him."

Graypaw looked puzzled. "Why? What about Yellowfang?"

"There's no time to explain," Firepaw mewed urgently. "You'll just have to trust me. There must be a way we can get Ravenpaw away. Bluestar's going to keep the warriors in camp till the storm is over, but that doesn't leave us much time." He tried to picture the hidden corners of the woods, beyond ThunderClan territory. "We'll have to take him somewhere Tigerclaw won't find him, somewhere he can survive without the Clan."

Graypaw stared at him for a moment. "What about Barley?"

"Barley!" Firepaw echoed. "You mean, take Ravenpaw to the Twolegplace?" His ears twitched with excitement. "Yes, that might be the best idea."

"Come on, then!" meowed Graypaw. "What are we waiting for?"

Relief washed over Firepaw. He should have known his old friend would help. He shook the rain from his head, then touched Graypaw's fur with his nose. "Thank you," he purred. "Now, let's get Ravenpaw."

They found their friend huddled miserably inside their den. Sandpaw and Dustpaw were in their nests, too, looking tense and scared as the storm crashed overhead.

"Ravenpaw," Firepaw hissed through the entrance.

Ravenpaw looked up. Firepaw flicked his ears and the black cat followed him out into the storm.

"Come on," Firepaw whispered. "We're taking you to Barley."

"Barley?" Ravenpaw mewed in bewilderment, narrowing his eyes against the driving rain. "Why?"

"Because you'll be safe there," Firepaw answered, looking the black cat straight in the eye.

"Did you see what Frostfur did?" mewed Ravenpaw, his voice quavering. "I was only going to check on the kits. . . ."

"Come on," Firepaw interrupted him. "We must hurry!"

Ravenpaw met his friend's gaze. "Thanks, Firepaw," he murmured. Then he turned into the wind and bounded across the clearing.

The three apprentices rushed toward the camp entrance, their fur flattened by the howling wind. As they entered the gorse tunnel, a voice called them back.

"You three! Where are you going?"

It was Tigerclaw.

Firepaw whirled around, feeling his heart sink. He wondered desperately what he could say, when he spotted Bluestar striding toward them. She frowned for a moment; then her face cleared.

"Well done, Firepaw," she meowed. "I see you've persuaded your two friends to go with you. ThunderClan has brave apprentices, Tigerclaw, if they are willing to run an errand in weather like this."

"Surely this is not a time for errands?" objected Tigerclaw.

"One of Brindleface's kits has a cough." Bluestar's voice was icily calm. "Firepaw has offered to fetch some coltsfoot for her."

"Does he really need his friends to go too?" asked Tigerclaw.

"In this storm, I think he's lucky to have the company!" answered Bluestar. She looked deep into Firepaw's eyes, and he was suddenly aware of the trust she was placing in him. "Off you go, you three," she meowed.

Firepaw returned her gaze gratefully. "Thank you," he purred, dipping his head. With a swift glance at his

companions, he led the way along the familiar paths toward Fourtrees. The wind roared through the branches above them and the trees swayed, their trunks creaking and cracking as though they might fall at any moment. The rain poured down through the leaves, soaking the cats to their hides.

They reached the stream, but the stepping-stones they usually leaped across had completely disappeared. The cats stopped on the bank and looked down in dismay at the wide, brown, swirling river.

"This way," Firepaw meowed. "There's a fallen tree up here. We can use it to cross." He led Graypaw and Ravenpaw upstream to a log that rested only a kittenstep above the rushing water. "Be careful, it'll be slippery!" Firepaw warned, leaping carefully up onto it. The log's bark had been stripped away, leaving only smooth, wet wood to balance on. Carefully the three cats walked along the trunk. Firepaw jumped down on the other side and watched his friends until they, too, had landed safely.

The trees were bigger on the other side, offering some shelter from the storm as they hurried on, side by side.

"Are you going to tell me exactly why we need to get Ravenpaw away?" panted Graypaw.

"Because he knows that Tigerclaw killed Redtail," Firepaw answered.

"Tigerclaw killed Redtail!" Graypaw echoed in disbelief, stopping dead and staring first at Firepaw and then at Ravenpaw.

"At the battle with RiverClan," puffed Ravenpaw. "I saw him."

"But why would he do that?" Graypaw protested, setting off again. They started down the slope that led into the clearing at Fourtrees.

"I don't know. Maybe he thought Bluestar would make him deputy," Firepaw suggested, raising his voice against the wind.

Graypaw didn't reply, but his face darkened.

The cats began to climb the steep slope that led up to WindClan territory. As Firepaw leaped upward from rock to rock, he called down to Graypaw behind him. He wanted his friend to understand just how dangerous it was for Ravenpaw in the ThunderClan camp. "I overheard Tigerclaw talking to Darkstripe and Longtail on the night Lionheart was killed," he yowled. "He wants to get rid of Ravenpaw."

"Get *rid* of him? You mean *kill* him?" Graypaw sat heavily on a rock.

Firepaw stopped too. He looked down at his friends. Ravenpaw had halted farther down the slope, his sides heaving as he caught his breath. He looked smaller than ever with his sodden fur clinging to his scrawny body.

"You saw the way Frostfur went for Ravenpaw today?" Firepaw meowed to Graypaw. "Tigerclaw's been hinting to everyone that Ravenpaw is a traitor. But he'll be safe with Barley. Now come on; we must hurry!"

It was impossible to talk in the open expanse of WindClan territory. The wind howled around them while the thunder and lightning rolled and flashed overhead. The three cats lowered their heads and pushed onward into the heart of the storm.

Eventually they reached the edge of the plateau that marked the end of WindClan's territory.

"We can't take you any farther, Ravenpaw," meowed Firepaw through the gale. "We have to get back and find Yellowfang before the storm has passed."

Ravenpaw looked up through the battering rain, alarmed. Then he nodded.

"Will you be able to find Barley alone?" yowled Firepaw.

"Yes, I remember the way," answered Ravenpaw.

"Watch out for those dogs," warned Graypaw.

Ravenpaw nodded. "I will!" Suddenly he frowned, "How can you be sure Barley will welcome me?"

"Just tell him you caught an adder once!" answered Graypaw, affectionately nudging his friend's rain-soaked shoulder.

"Go," Firepaw urged, aware that time was short. He licked Ravenpaw's skinny chest. "And don't worry; I'll make sure everyone knows you didn't betray ThunderClan."

"What if Tigerclaw comes looking for me?" Ravenpaw's voice was small against the rumbling storm.

Firepaw met his gaze steadily. "He won't. I shall tell him you are dead."

CHAPTER 22

Firepaw and Graypaw retraced their steps to ThunderClan territory. Both cats were bone-weary and wet through, but Firepaw kept up the pace. The storm was beginning to move away. A ThunderClan patrol would be out soon and on Yellowfang's trail. They had to find her first.

The sky was still dark, even though the black thunderclouds were beginning to roll away toward the horizon. Firepaw guessed that it must be nearly sunset.

"Why don't we head straight into ShadowClan territory?" suggested Graypaw as they ran down the steep hillside into Fourtrees.

"We need to pick up Yellowfang's scent first," Firepaw explained. "I just hope it won't lead to the ShadowClan camp."

Graypaw glanced sideways at his friend, but didn't reply.

They headed back over the stream, into ThunderClan territory. There was no scent of Yellowfang until they crossed into the oak woods close to the camp.

Now that the rain had finally stopped, the scents around them were beginning to return. Firepaw hoped that the rain had not washed away Yellowfang's trail completely. He stopped and brushed at a fern with the tip of his nose, and recognized the familiar smell. Yellowfang's fear-scent prickled in his nostrils. "She came this way!" he meowed.

He pushed his way through the wet undergrowth. Graypaw followed. The rain was easing, and the thunder was fading into the distance. Time was running out. Firepaw pushed on faster.

To his dismay, he realized Yellowfang's scent was indeed leading them straight to ShadowClan territory. His heart sank. Did this mean Tigerclaw's accusations were true? Firepaw began to hope that each new smell would take them in a different direction, but the trail was unfaltering.

They arrived at the Thunderpath and halted. Several monsters roared by, throwing up fountains of dirty water. The two cats hung back from the edge of the wide, gray track until there was a gap. Then they raced across the path and into ShadowClan territory.

The scent markers that lined the border made Firepaw's paws tingle.

Graypaw halted and looked around nervously. "I always thought I'd have a few more warriors with me when I finally entered ShadowClan territory," he confessed.

"Not afraid, are you?" Firepaw murmured.

"Aren't *you*? My mother warned me about the stench of ShadowClan many times."

"My mother never taught me such things," Firepaw replied. But for the first time he was relieved that his fur was so wet that it clung to his body—Graypaw might not notice the way it was bristling fearfully along his spine.

The two cats prowled onward, alert to every sight and sound. Graypaw was on the lookout for ShadowClan patrols, and Firepaw for the ThunderClan party he knew must come soon.

Yellowfang's scent-trail led them steadily into the heart of ShadowClan's hunting grounds. The woods here were gloomy, the undergrowth crowded with nettles and brambles.

"I can't smell her," complained Graypaw. "It's too wet."

"It's there," Firepaw assured him.

"I can smell *that* though," Graypaw spat suddenly.

"What?" Firepaw hissed. He stopped, alarmed.

"Kitscent. There's kit blood here!"

Firepaw sniffed again, seeking out the smell of ThunderClan offspring. "I smell it too," he agreed. "And something else!" He flicked his tail down sharply, warning Graypaw to keep quiet. Then, silently, he signaled with his whiskers toward a blackened ash tree up ahead.

Graypaw twitched his ears questioningly. Firepaw gave him a tiny nod. Yellowfang was sheltering behind the wide, split trunk.

Instinctively the two cats separated, each moving toward the tree, one on either side. They crept over the soft forest floor, using all the tricks of basic training, stepping lightly, keeping their bodies low.

Then they leaped.

Yellowfang yowled with surprise as the two cats landed beside her and pinned her to the ground. She struggled free, spitting, and backed into a sheltered hollow at the base of the trunk. Firepaw and Graypaw moved forward, blocking her way out.

"I knew ThunderClan would blame me!" she hissed, her eyes flashing with all her old hostility.

"Where are the kits?" Firepaw demanded.

"We can smell their blood!" spat Graypaw. "Have you harmed them?"

"I don't have them," snarled Yellowfang angrily. "I've come to find them and take them back. I stopped because I smelled blood too. But they're not here."

Firepaw and Graypaw looked at one another.

"I don't have them!" insisted Yellowfang.

"Why did you run away, then? Why did you kill Spottedleaf?" Graypaw asked the questions Firepaw couldn't bring himself to say out loud.

"Spottedleaf is *dead*?" There was no mistaking the shock in Yellowfang's voice.

Relief washed over Firepaw. "You didn't know?" he croaked.

"How could I? I left the camp as soon as I heard the kits were missing."

Graypaw looked suspicious, but Firepaw could hear the truth in her voice.

"I know who has taken the kits," she continued. "I smelled his scent near the nursery."

"Who was it?" Firepaw asked.

"Clawface—one of Brokenstar's warriors. And as long as

the kits are with ShadowClan, they're in great danger."

"But surely even ShadowClan wouldn't harm kits!" Firepaw protested.

"Don't be so sure," spat Yellowfang. "Brokenstar intends to use them as warriors."

"But they are only three moons old!" Graypaw gasped.

"That hasn't stopped him before. He has been training kits as young as three moons since he became leader. At five moons he sends them out as warriors!"

"Surely they'd be too small to fight!" Firepaw protested. But in his mind's eye he pictured the undersize ShadowClan apprentices he had seen at the Gathering. They weren't just small; they were kits!

Yellowfang hissed scornfully, "Brokenstar doesn't care about that. He has plenty more kits to spare, and if they run out, he can steal them from other Clans!" Her voice was filled with rage. "After all, we're talking about a cat who killed kits from his own Clan!"

Firepaw and Graypaw were stunned.

"If he killed ShadowClan's kits, why wasn't he punished?" Firepaw asked at last.

"Because he lied," growled Yellowfang. Bitterness made her voice hard. "He accused me of their murder, and ShadowClan believed him!"

Firepaw suddenly understood. "Is that why you were driven out of ShadowClan?" he asked. "You have to come back with us and tell all this to Bluestar."

"Not before I have rescued your kits!" Yellowfang spat.

Firepaw lifted his head and sniffed the air. The rain had stopped, and the wind was dying down. The ThunderClan patrol would be well on its way. They were not safe here.

Graypaw still seemed shocked by Yellowfang's accusation. "How could a leader kill kits from his own Clan?" he demanded.

"Brokenstar insisted on training them too hard and too young. He took two of the kits away for battle practice." Yellowfang took a deep, wheezing breath. "They were only four moons old. They were already dead when he brought them back to me. They bore the scratches and bites of a full warrior, not of apprentices. He must have fought them himself. There was nothing I could do. When their mother came to see them, Brokenstar was with me. He said that he had found me standing over their dead bodies." Her voice cracked and she looked away.

"Why didn't you tell her it was Brokenstar?" Firepaw asked in disbelief.

Yellowfang shook her head. "I couldn't."

"Why not?"

The old she-cat hesitated. When she spoke, her voice was heavy with regret. "Brokenstar is ShadowClan's leader. Noble Raggedstar was his father. His word is law."

Firepaw looked away and the three cats sat in silence for a moment. Then Firepaw meowed, "We'll rescue the kits together. Tonight. But we can't stay here. I can smell the ThunderClan patrol coming." He paused. "If Tigerclaw is with them, Yellowfang doesn't stand a chance. He'll kill her before we can explain."

Yellowfang looked at him, alert and determined again. "There's peat this way; it'll be wet after the rain," she told him. "Our scents will be disguised there."

She leaped into a clump of ferns and Firepaw and Graypaw quickly followed her. They could hear the rustling of undergrowth in the distance now. It was no longer the wind that disturbed the bushes, but an approaching patrol, no doubt hungry for revenge and fired up by Tigerclaw's lies.

An eerie stillness settled over the woods, and a thin fog was beginning to gather between the tree trunks. Firepaw shook the droplets off his coat and impatiently pulled a burr off his chest.

Yellowfang led them onward. The ground grew soggier, and their paws began to sink into the soft peat. The musty smell choked Firepaw's nostrils, but at least it would mask their own trail. Behind them, the noise of cats grew louder.

"Quick, under here," Yellowfang urged, ducking under a broad-leaved bush. The three cats crouched beneath it, drawing in their tails. Firepaw kept as still as he could, trying to ignore the rank wetness of the ground seeping into his belly fur, and listening to the rustling of the ThunderClan patrol as it came nearer and nearer.

CHAPTER 23

❧

Firepaw could tell there were several cats in the patrol, traveling fast. He couldn't recognize the individual scents of the cats through the earthy bog odors, but he knew it was ThunderClan. He held his breath as the pawsteps raced past and away.

"Are we really going to try to rescue the kits from ShadowClan alone?" whispered Graypaw.

Yellowfang answered him first. "I might be able to find us some help from inside ShadowClan. Not all the cats support Brokenstar."

Firepaw pricked up his ears and Graypaw flicked his tail in surprise.

"When he became leader," Yellowfang explained, "Brokenstar forced the elders to leave the security of the inner camp. They had to live on the boundary and hunt for themselves. These are cats who have grown up with the warrior code. Some of them might help us."

Firepaw stared into her old eyes, thinking quickly. "And I might be able to persuade the ThunderClan hunting party to help us too," he meowed. "If I can speak to them before they see Yellowfang, I might be able to make them believe her story. Graypaw, you wait at the dead ash, where we smelled the kit blood, till one of us returns."

Graypaw looked worried. "But do you really trust Yellowfang to bring back help?" he murmured to Firepaw.

"You *must* trust me," growled Yellowfang. "I will return."

Graypaw looked at Firepaw, who nodded.

Without another word Yellowfang sprang past the two apprentices and disappeared into the bushes.

"Have we done the right thing?" asked Graypaw.

"I don't know," Firepaw admitted. "If we have, we are heroes and the kits are safe. If we are wrong, then we are as good as dead."

Firepaw sprinted after the patrol, around brambles, past gorse, and through nettles. The trail was easy to follow. The angry ThunderClan cats weren't trying to disguise their presence in ShadowClan's territory.

Overhead, the thick layer of cloud had finally rolled away. Beyond the treetops, Silverpelt glittered across the night sky. The moon was just rising, but its cold light couldn't pierce the mist that clung to the shadowy undergrowth.

Firepaw concentrated on the scent from up ahead. He could smell Whitestorm. He sniffed again. Tigerclaw wasn't with them. He raced to catch up and skidded to a halt behind the band of ThunderClan cats.

The warriors turned and glared at him, fur bristling, ears flattened aggressively. Darkstripe was with them and the young she-cat Mousefur, as well as the tabby warrior

Runningwind. Mousefur wasn't the only she-cat in the patrol—Willowpelt was there too.

"Firepaw!" growled Whitestorm. "What are you doing here?"

Firepaw gasped for breath. "Bluestar sent me!" he panted. "She wanted me to find Yellowfang before—"

Whitestorm interrupted him. "Ah!" he meowed. "Bluestar told me I might find a friend out here. Now I understand what she meant." He looked thoughtfully at Firepaw.

"Is Tigerclaw nearby?" Firepaw asked, feeling a tingle of pride at their shared gaze.

Whitestorm looked at him curiously. "Bluestar insisted she needed him to remain at camp, to protect the remaining kits."

Firepaw nodded quickly, relieved. He meowed urgently, "Whitestorm, I need your help. I can lead you to the kits. Graypaw is waiting for me. We plan to rescue them tonight. Will you come?"

"Of course we'll come!" The warriors flicked their tails with excitement.

"It will mean raiding the ShadowClan camp," Firepaw warned.

"Can you lead us there?" asked Runningwind eagerly.

"No, but Yellowfang can. And she has promised to bring help from her old allies in the camp."

Mousefur glared at him and thrashed her tail angrily. "You have found Yellowfang?" she hissed.

"I don't understand," meowed Whitestorm, puzzled. "The traitor is going to help rescue the kits she stole?"

Firepaw took a deep breath to calm himself, then looked steadily into Whitestorm's eyes. "Yellowfang didn't take them," he meowed. "Nor did she murder Spottedleaf. She wants to help us rescue our kits."

Whitestorm stared back at him, then blinked slowly. "Lead the way, Firepaw," he ordered.

Graypaw was waiting by the ash tree, pacing restlessly around its rotten trunk. He stopped as soon as he saw the patrol emerge from the mist and twitched his whiskers in greeting.

"Any sign of Yellowfang?" Firepaw asked.

"Not yet," answered Graypaw.

"We don't know how far it is to the ShadowClan camp," Firepaw pointed out quickly, feeling Whitestorm stiffen beside him. "She may be on her way back right now."

"Or she might be happily sharing tongues with her ShadowClan comrades while we sit here like fools waiting to be ambushed!" meowed Graypaw.

Whitestorm watched the two apprentices. His ears flicked uneasily. "Firepaw?" he prompted.

"She will come back," Firepaw promised.

"Well said, young Firepaw." Yellowfang stalked out from behind the ash tree and sat down. "You're not the only one who can sneak up on someone," she meowed at Firepaw. "Remember the day we met? You were looking in the wrong direction that time too."

Three other ShadowClan cats appeared from behind the

tree and settled themselves calmly on either side of Yellowfang. The ThunderClan cats bristled, alert and suspicious.

Both Clans stared silently at each other. Firepaw fidgeted uncomfortably, unsure what to do now. Eventually one of the ShadowClan cats, a gray tom, spoke. His long body was skinny, and his fur looked dull. "We have come to help you, not to harm you. You have come for your kits; we will help you rescue them."

"What's in it for you?" asked Whitestorm warily.

"We want your help to get rid of Brokenstar. He has broken the warrior code, and ShadowClan is suffering."

"So it's that simple, is it?" growled Runningwind. "We just drop into your camp, snatch the kits, kill your leader, and go home."

"You will not meet as much resistance as you think," murmured the gray tom.

Yellowfang stood up. "Let me introduce my old friends," she meowed, weaving her way around the ShadowClan cats. She brushed past the gray tom. "This is Ashfur; he is one of the Clan elders.

"And this is Nightpelt, a senior warrior before Raggedstar was killed." She circled a battered black tom, who nodded at them.

"And this is one of our elder queens, Dawncloud. Two of her kits died driving out WindClan."

Dawncloud, a small tabby, meowed in greeting. "I do not wish to lose any more of my kits," she told them.

Whitestorm gave his chest a quick lick to smooth down his

fur. "You are clearly skilled warriors if you managed to creep up on us like that. But are there enough of you? We need to know what we'll face when we raid the ShadowClan camp."

"The old and sick of ShadowClan are slowly starving," meowed Ashfur. "The casualties among our kits are more than we can cope with."

"But if ShadowClan is a mess," burst out Darkstripe, "how come you have shown so much strength lately? And why is Brokenstar still your leader?"

"Brokenstar is surrounded by a small group of elite warriors," answered Ashfur. "They are the ones to fear, because they would die for him without question. The other warriors obey his orders only because they are frightened. They will fight by his side as long as they think Brokenstar is going to win. If they thought he would lose . . ."

"They would fight against him, not *for* him!" Darkstripe finished the elder's words in disgust. "What sort of loyalty is that?"

The hackles of the ShadowClan cats began to rise.

"Our Clan was not always like this," Yellowfang interrupted. "When Raggedstar led ShadowClan, we were feared for our strength. But in those days our strength came from the warrior code and Clan loyalty, not from fear and bloodlust." The old medicine cat sighed. "If only Raggedstar had lived longer."

"How did Raggedstar die?" asked Whitestorm curiously. "There were so many rumors at the Gatherings, but no one seemed to know for sure."

Yellowfang's eyes clouded with sorrow. "He was ambushed by a warrior patrol from another Clan."

Whitestorm nodded thoughtfully. "Yes, that is what most cats seemed to think. These are bad times indeed, when leaders are picked off in the dark, instead of open and honorable battle."

Firepaw frowned, his mind racing over different battle plans. "Is there any way of taking the kits without alerting the whole Clan?" he asked.

Dawncloud answered him. "They are very closely guarded. Brokenstar will be expecting ThunderClan to try to take them. You won't be able to steal them in secret. Open attack is your only hope."

"Then we must concentrate our attack on Brokenstar and his inner guard," meowed Whitestorm.

Yellowfang had a suggestion. "The ShadowClan warriors should lead me into the ShadowClan camp. They could say they had captured me. We have to make sure Brokenstar and his warriors are out of their dens. News of my capture will bring them into the clearing. Once they're all out in the open, I'll give the signal for you to attack."

Whitestorm was silent for a moment. Then he nodded, his face grave as he committed his warriors to the attack. "Very well, Yellowfang," he meowed. "Please lead the way to the ShadowClan camp."

CHAPTER 24

❧

Yellowfang turned and pushed her way into the bracken. Whitestorm and the others followed her.

Firepaw was tingling with excitement. He didn't feel the damp chill in the air, and his weariness was long forgotten.

Yellowfang guided them to a small hollow surrounded by thick undergrowth and pointed out the entrance to the ShadowClan camp. The tangled mass of brambles looked very different from the neat gorse tunnel that led into the ThunderClan camp. The camp boundary was full of holes and gaps and the stench of rotting meat wafted toward them.

"You eat *crow food?*" whispered Graypaw, curling his lip.

"Our warriors are used for attacking, not hunting," replied Ashfur. "We eat whatever we can find."

"ThunderClan, hide in that clump of bracken over there," hissed Yellowfang. "It's full of toadstools that will disguise your scent. Wait here till you hear me call."

She stepped back to let the other ShadowClan cats lead the way, tucking herself into the center of their group as though she were their prisoner. They headed silently into the camp.

The ThunderClan cats settled themselves among the

toadstools, tense and alert. Firepaw could feel his coat prickling. He looked at Graypaw beside him. The thick fur on the back of his friend's neck was standing on end, and Firepaw could hear him panting with suppressed excitement.

Suddenly yowling erupted from the ShadowClan camp. Without hesitating, the ThunderClan cats sprang from their hiding places and raced through the entrance.

Yellowfang, Ashfur, Dawncloud, and Nightpelt were in a well-trodden, muddy clearing, wrestling with six vicious-looking warriors. Firepaw recognized Brokenstar and his deputy, Blackfoot, among them. The warriors looked hungry and battle-scarred, but Firepaw could see the hard muscles pounding beneath their patchy fur.

Around the edge of the clearing, groups of scrawny cats stared uncertainly at the mayhem. Their skinny bodies seemed to recoil at the violence, while their dull eyes looked on, shocked and confused. Out of the corner of his eye, Firepaw saw Runningnose back away and hide beneath a bush.

At Whitestorm's nodded signal, the ThunderClan cats leaped into the battle.

Firepaw grasped a silver tabby with his claws, but was shaken loose. He tumbled over and the ShadowClan warrior turned on him and gripped him with claws as sharp as blackthorns. Firepaw managed to twist and sink his teeth deep into the cat's flesh. The warrior's yowl told him he had found a tender spot, and he bit harder. The warrior screeched again, ripping himself free, and ran off into the bushes.

Firepaw stood up. A young ShadowClan apprentice leaped

at him from the edge of the camp, its soft kitten fur fluffed up with fear.

Firepaw sheathed his claws and batted him away easily. "This is not your battle," he hissed.

Whitestorm already had Blackfoot pinned to the ground. He gave him a vicious bite and the injured deputy raced away toward the camp entrance and out into the safety of the forest.

"Firepaw!" Firepaw heard Dawncloud screech his name. "Watch out! Clawface is—" He didn't hear the rest. A heavily built brown cat crashed into him. *Clawface!* Firepaw dug his claws into the ground and whirled around to fight. The warrior that killed Spottedleaf! Rage surged through him and he flung himself onto the brown tom.

Firepaw pushed the warrior to the ground and pressed his head into the dirt. Blinded by fury, he prepared to sink his teeth into Clawface's neck. But before he could deal his death blow, Whitestorm knocked him aside and grasped the ShadowClan warrior.

"ThunderClan warriors do not kill unless they have to," he growled in Firepaw's ear. "We just need to let them know not to show their faces here again!" He gave Clawface a fierce bite that sent him screaming out of the camp.

Still raging, Firepaw looked around wildly. Brokenstar's warriors had gone.

An angry screech sounded from behind Graypaw. Graypaw leaped out of the way and Firepaw saw Yellowfang gripping Brokenstar with muddy, bloodstained paws. His body bled from several wounds. His ears were flattened against his head, and his whiskers were drawn back as he crouched, flattened beneath Yellowfang's powerful grasp.

"I never thought you would be harder to kill than my father!" he snarled up at her.

Yellowfang recoiled as if she had been stung by a bee, her face twisted suddenly by shock and grief. She loosened her grip on Brokenstar, and instantly he threw her aside with a twist of his powerful body.

"*You* killed Raggedstar?" Yellowfang wailed, her eyes wide with disbelief.

Brokenstar eyed her coldly. "You found his body. Didn't you recognize my fur between his claws?" Yellowfang stared in horror as he continued. "He was a soft and foolish leader. He deserved to die."

"No!" hissed Yellowfang, her head dropping. Then she gave herself a shake. She looked up at Brokenstar, arching her back. "And Brightflower's kits? Did they deserve to die too?" she rasped.

Brokenstar growled and hurled himself at Yellowfang, forcing her onto her belly. Yellowfang didn't even attempt to struggle against his thorn-sharp claws. Firepaw saw with alarm that her eyes were glazed with sadness.

"Those kits were weak," Brokenstar hissed, bending his face toward Yellowfang's ear. "They would have been no use to ShadowClan. If I hadn't killed them, some other warrior would have."

A wail of grief went up from a black-and-white ShadowClan queen. Brokenstar ignored her. "I should have killed *you* when I had the chance," he spat at Yellowfang. "It seems I must have some of my father's softness. I was a fool to let you leave ShadowClan alive!" He lunged, teeth bared, ready to sink them into her neck.

Firepaw was quicker. He jumped onto Brokenstar's back before he could clamp his jaws shut. Firepaw dug his claws into the matted tabby fur and pulled him off the exhausted queen, flinging him to the edge of the clearing.

Brokenstar twisted around in midair to land on his feet and looked into Firepaw's eyes, spitting viciously. "Don't waste your time, apprentice! I've shared dreams with StarClan. You will have to kill me nine times over before I join them. Do you really think you're strong enough for that?" His eyes glowed with confidence and defiance.

Firepaw stared back at him. His belly tightened. Brokenstar was a Clan leader! How on earth could he expect to defeat him? But the watching ShadowClan cats had begun to pad slowly toward their defeated leader, snarling and hissing with hatred. They were battered and half-starved, but Brokenstar was outnumbered, and he seemed to realize this with a nervous flick of his tail. He crouched and backed away through the bushes. His eyes glittered menacingly from the shadows, his gaze finding Firepaw through the crowd.

"This isn't over, apprentice," he hissed before he turned and vanished into the forest after his broken warriors.

Firepaw looked to Whitestorm. "Should we go after them?" he meowed.

The warrior shook his head. "I think they got the message that they are not welcome here."

Nightpelt, the ShadowClan warrior, nodded in agreement. "Leave them. If they dare to show their faces here again, ShadowClan will be strong enough by then to tackle them alone."

The rest of ShadowClan was huddled together in the ruins of their camp, as if numbed by the realization that their leader had gone. *It will take time to rebuild this Clan,* Firepaw thought.

"The kits!"

Firepaw heard Graypaw's meow from a far corner of the clearing. He rushed over to his friend, Mousefur and Whitestorm bounding at his heels. As they approached, they could hear the pitiful mewling of kits coming from beneath a pile of leaves and twigs. Quickly Graypaw and Mousefur dug down through the foliage until they had uncovered the missing ThunderClan kits at the bottom of a small pit.

"Are they okay?" demanded Whitestorm, his tail twitching with anxiety.

"They're fine," replied Graypaw. "Most have only a few scratches. But that little tabby has a pretty nasty wound on his ear. Can you take a look, Yellowfang?"

The old she-cat was licking her own wounds, but at Graypaw's call she raced to the side of the pit, where Graypaw had carefully deposited the tabby kit.

Firepaw helped Graypaw to lift out the rest of the kits. The last one was gray, like the embers of an old fire. She mewled and squirmed as Firepaw placed her on the ground. Mousefur gathered all the kits to her and comforted them with licks and caresses.

Yellowfang looked closely at the torn ear. "We need to stop this bleeding," she meowed.

Runningnose stepped out of the shadows. His forepaw was

coated in a layer of cobwebs, which he silently passed to Yellowfang. She nodded her thanks and began to treat the kit's wound.

Nightpelt approached the group of ThunderClan cats. "You helped ShadowClan rid itself of a brutal and dangerous leader, and we are grateful. But it is time you left our camp and returned to your own. I promise your hunting grounds will be free of ShadowClan warriors as long as we can find enough food in our own territory."

Whitestorm nodded. "Hunt in peace for one moon, Nightpelt. ThunderClan knows you need time to rebuild your Clan." He turned to Yellowfang. "And you, Yellowfang?" he asked. "Do you wish to return with us, or stay here with your old comrades?"

Yellowfang looked up at him. "I will make the journey back with you." She glanced at a deep gash on Whitestorm's hind leg. "You will need a medicine cat, for yourself as well as your kits."

"Thank you," purred Whitestorm. He signaled to the ThunderClan cats with a sweep of his tail and led them out of the clearing. Mousefur and Willowpelt helped the kits, who stumbled along, exhausted and bewildered. Yellowfang walked close to the wounded tabby kit, lifting him by the scruff of his neck every time he slipped. Firepaw and Graypaw followed them through the brambles, past the camp scent-line and out into the forest.

The moon was still rising in the quiet sky as the ThunderClan party began the long trudge home, while around them showers of brown leaves fluttered to the forest floor.

CHAPTER 25

Buoyed up with relief at being home again, Firepaw and Graypaw sprinted ahead of the patrol into the ThunderClan camp. Frostfur was lying in the middle of the clearing, her head resting sadly on her paws. As the two apprentices bounded in she lifted her nose and sniffed the air. "My kits!" she cried. She leaped up and raced past Firepaw and Graypaw to meet the rest of the party as they emerged from the tunnel.

The kits rushed over to Frostfur and nuzzled into her side. She curled her soft body around them and licked them each in turn, purring loudly.

Yellowfang hung back at the camp entrance and looked on silently.

Bluestar strode up to the returning patrol. She glanced fondly at Frostfur and her kits and then turned her eyes to Whitestorm. "Are they all right?" she asked.

"They're fine," meowed Whitestorm.

"Well done, Whitestorm. ThunderClan honors you."

Whitestorm bent his head to accept her praise, and added, "But it was thanks to this apprentice that we found them."

Firepaw lifted his head and tail proudly, about to speak,

but Tigerclaw's accusing snarl sounded from across the clearing.

"Why did you bring back the traitor?" The dark warrior stalked up to the patrol and stood beside his leader.

"She is no traitor," Firepaw insisted. He looked around the camp. The rest of the cats had quickly gathered in the clearing to see the kits and congratulate the hunting party. Some of them had spotted Yellowfang and were eyeing her with looks of pure hatred.

"She killed Spottedleaf," spat Longtail.

"Look between Spottedleaf's claws," Graypaw suggested. "You will find the brown fur of Clawface, not Yellowfang's gray fur!"

Bluestar nodded at Mousefur, who darted away from the crowd, toward the spot where Spottedleaf's body lay, waiting for its dawn burial. The Clan waited in tense silence till she returned.

"Graypaw is right," Mousefur panted, rushing back to the clearing. "Spottedleaf was not attacked by a gray cat."

A murmur of surprise rippled through the crowd.

"But that doesn't mean she didn't help to take the kits!" hissed Tigerclaw.

"Without Yellowfang we never would have recovered the kits!" Firepaw spat, his exhaustion making him impatient. "She knew that a ShadowClan warrior had taken them. She was hunting for them when I found her. She risked her life returning to the ShadowClan camp. It was Yellowfang who thought up the battle plan that got us into the ShadowClan camp and gave us a chance to defeat Brokenstar!"

The cats listened to Firepaw's words, astonished.

"He's right," Whitestorm meowed. "Yellowfang is a friend."

"I'm glad to hear it," murmured Bluestar, catching Firepaw's eye.

Frostfur's anxious meow sounded from the crowd. "Is Brokenstar dead?" she asked.

"No, he escaped," Whitestorm told her. "But he will never lead ShadowClan again."

Frostfur sighed in relief and returned to nuzzling her kits.

Whitestorm looked at Bluestar. "I promised ShadowClan we would leave them in peace until next fullmoon," he explained. "Brokenstar's leadership has left their Clan in chaos."

Bluestar nodded. "That was a wise and generous offer," she meowed approvingly. The ThunderClan leader walked past Whitestorm and the rest of the patrol and approached Yellowfang. Yellowfang lowered her eyes as Bluestar touched the gray cat's rough coat with her nose.

"Yellowfang, I wish you to replace Spottedleaf as medicine cat to ThunderClan," Bluestar meowed. "I'm sure you'll find all her supplies as she left them."

The other cats began to murmur to each other, tails flicking with excitement. Yellowfang looked around at them anxiously and said nothing.

Frostfur glanced at the other queens before she met Yellowfang's gaze and slowly nodded her approval.

Yellowfang bent her head respectfully to the white cat before addressing her new leader. "Thank you, Bluestar. ShadowClan is not the Clan I once knew. ThunderClan is my Clan now."

Firepaw felt a surge of satisfaction that the old she-cat he had come to love would be his Clan's medicine cat from now on. Then his tail dropped as he realized that he would never again find Spottedleaf in her clearing, the sunlight gleaming on her soft fur, her amber eyes shining in welcome.

"Where's Ravenpaw?" meowed Bluestar suddenly, jolting Firepaw out of his bittersweet remembrances.

"Yes," Tigerclaw chimed in, "where is my apprentice? Strange that he should disappear along with Brokenstar." He looked meaningfully around the Clan.

"If you think he might have been helping Brokenstar," Firepaw meowed boldly, "then you are wrong!"

Tigerclaw stiffened, a menacing gleam in his yellow eyes.

"Ravenpaw is dead," Firepaw went on, dropping his head as if weighed down with grief. "We found his body in ShadowClan territory. From the scents around him, he must have been slain by a ShadowClan patrol." He looked at Bluestar. "I will tell you everything later," he promised.

Yellowfang shot Firepaw a questioning look. Firepaw returned her gaze with a silent plea for her to hold her tongue. She twitched her ears briefly in understanding and looked away.

"I never said that Ravenpaw was a traitor," hissed Tigerclaw. He paused and allowed an expression of sorrow to cloud his eyes before he turned to address the rest of the Clan. "Ravenpaw might have made a fine warrior. His death has come too soon, and his loss will be felt by many of us for a long time."

Empty words! thought Firepaw bitterly. What would Tigerclaw say if he knew that Ravenpaw was safe, far beyond the forest, catching rats with Barley?

Bluestar broke the silence. "We will miss Ravenpaw, but we shall mourn him tomorrow. First there is another ritual that must be performed—one, I know, that Ravenpaw would have taken pleasure in." She turned to Firepaw and Graypaw. "You have shown great courage tonight. Did they fight well, Whitestorm?" she asked.

"Like warriors," Whitestorm replied solemnly.

Bluestar met his yellow-eyed gaze and gave a slight nod. Then she lifted her chin and fixed her eyes on Silverpelt's swath of stars. Her voice rang out, clear and measured in the hushed woods. "I, Bluestar, leader of ThunderClan, call upon my warrior ancestors to look down on these two apprentices. They have trained hard to understand the ways of your noble code, and I commend them to you as warriors in their turn." She looked down at Firepaw and Graypaw, narrowing her eyes. "Firepaw, Graypaw, do you promise to uphold the warrior code and to protect and defend this Clan, even at the cost of your lives?"

Firepaw felt something stir within him, a fire that burned in his belly and rang in his ears. He suddenly felt that everything he had done for the Clan so far—all the prey he had stalked, all the enemy warriors he had fought—had been for the sake of this single moment. "I do," he replied steadily.

"I do," echoed Graypaw, his fur bristling with excitement.

"Then by the powers of StarClan I give you your warrior names: Graypaw, from this moment you will be known as Graystripe. StarClan honors your bravery and your strength, and we welcome you as a full warrior of ThunderClan." Bluestar stepped forward and rested her muzzle on top of Graystripe's bowed head. He bent lower to give her shoulder a respectful lick, then straightened up and walked over to join the other warriors.

Bluestar stood and studied Firepaw for a long moment before speaking. "Firepaw, from this moment you will be known as Fireheart. StarClan honors your bravery and your strength, and we welcome you as a full warrior of ThunderClan." She touched her muzzle to his head and murmured, "Fireheart, I am proud to have you as my warrior. Serve your Clan well, young one."

Fireheart's muscles were trembling so much that he could hardly stoop to lick Bluestar's shoulder. He purred hoarsely to show his thanks, then slipped away to stand beside Graystripe.

Meows of tribute sounded from the crowd, and the voices of the Clan rose in the still night air to chant the new warrior names. "Fireheart! Graystripe! Fireheart! Graystripe!"

Fireheart looked around the Clan, seeing faces that had grown so familiar over the last few moons. He listened to them as they called his new name and felt overwhelmed by the kindness and respect he saw shining in their eyes.

"It is almost moonhigh," meowed Bluestar. "In the tradition of our ancestors, Fireheart and Graystripe must sit in silent vigil until dawn, and guard the camp alone while we sleep."

Fireheart and Graystripe nodded solemnly.

As the rest of the Clan began to melt away back to their dens, Tigerclaw pushed past Fireheart. The ThunderClan deputy slowed as he passed and hissed quietly into his ear, "Don't think you can outwit me, kittypet. Be careful what you tell Bluestar."

A cold shiver ran down Fireheart's spine. Bluestar had to know about Tigerclaw's treachery!

As Tigerclaw headed back to the warriors' den, Fireheart left Graystripe sitting alone in the clearing and bounded after Bluestar. He caught up with her outside her den. "Bluestar, I know I'm breaking the vow of silence, but I must speak with you before I begin my vigil."

Bluestar looked at Fireheart and shook her head. "This is an important ritual, Fireheart. You can speak to me in the morning."

Fireheart dipped his head in acceptance. Tigerclaw was not a problem that could be solved overnight anyway. He returned to Graystripe's side in the middle of the clearing. The two friends exchanged glances, but said nothing.

Fireheart looked at the moon above his head. His orange coat glowed silver in the cold light. Around him, the bushes and trees were draped in mist that brushed damply against his fur. Fireheart closed his eyes and recalled the dreams of his kittenhood. The cool forest scents in his nostrils were real now, and the life of a warrior stretched ahead of him. He felt unrestrained joy flood up from his paws and surge through his body. Then he opened his eyes with a jolt. Another pair of eyes was shining back at him from the warriors' den.

Tigerclaw!

Fireheart stared back without blinking. He was a warrior now. He had made an enemy of the Clan's deputy, but Tigerclaw had made an enemy of him. Fireheart was not the same naive young cat who had joined the Clan all those moons ago. He was bigger, stronger, faster, and wiser. If he was destined to oppose Tigerclaw, then so be it. Fireheart was ready for the challenge.

KEEP WATCH FOR

WARRIORS

BOOK 2:

FIRE AND ICE

Fireheart is a warrior now—so why does he find himself strangely drawn to a mysterious and familiar house cat? As tensions escalate between the Clans, loyalties are tested and Fireheart must decide who can be trusted . . . and who will betray him.